THE
CRIMSON
CIPHER

THE
CRIMSON
CIPHER

SUSAN PAGE DAVIS

summerside
PRESS™

Summerside Press™
Minneapolis 55438
www.summersidepress.com
The Crimson Cipher
© 2010 by Susan Page Davis

ISBN 978-1-60936-012-2

Scripture references are from the following source:
The Holy Bible, King James Version (KJV).

All characters are fictional. Any resemblances to
actual people are purely coincidental.

Cover design by Chris Gilbert | www.studiogearbox.com.

Interior design by Müllerhaus Publishing Group |
www.mullerhaus.net.

*Summerside Press™ is an inspirational publisher offering fresh,
irresistible books to uplift the heart and engage the mind.*

Printed in USA.

Dear Reader,

Many people will read this book and wonder how much of it really happened. During my research, I learned that the sabotage and espionage going on in North America in 1915 reached a massive scale. The bombing of the bridge at Vanceboro, Maine, is a true incident. The bombing of the Peabody plant and many other factories happened, as did the attempted bombing of the occupied armory at Windsor, Ontario. The sinking of the ships *William P. Frye* and the *Gulflight,* as well as the sabotage of the *Minnehaha* and the *Nebraskan,* really happened. These, along with the *Lusitania,* are only a few of the Allied ships attacked or bombed that year. However, the *Larkin* is a fictional ship.

While several German diplomats in America were arrested in connection with espionage, passport fraud, and other crimes, most of them were apprehended later than this story's timeframe. Otto van Wersten ("Kobold") is a fictional character.

Erich Muenter's (alias Frank Holt's) bombing of the U.S. Senate reception room and subsequent shooting of J. P. Morgan were real, tragic events occurring in July 1915. The gathering of cryptographers by the U.S. government actually began a little later than this story. Room 20 at Trafton House is loosely modeled after Great Britain's famous Room 40 at Bletchley Park in England. While Alfred Shuster and his cipher machine were slightly ahead of their time, such devices were already appearing in Europe, and it is not unreasonable that a clever mathematician would come up with such a machine at this time.

For more on the pre–World War I espionage in the country, you may want to read French Strother's book, *Fighting Germany's Spies*. If you have a deep interest in cryptography, I recommend David Kahn's *The Codebreakers* and Fletcher Pratt's *Secret and Urgent* as starting places.

For those readers who wish to try their hand at cracking a cipher, be sure you enter the drawing explained at the back of this book.

I love to hear from my readers. You can reach me in care of Summerside Press or at my Web site: www.susanpagedavis.com.

Susan

CHAPTER ONE

Wednesday, January 27, 1915

Emma Shuster hurried across campus against the cold wind coming off Casco Bay. Most of the walkways had been shoveled, but a few students employed by the college worked to clear the last few stretches. Six inches of powdery snow draped the brick buildings in glittery icing, and Emma's heart sang.

A man in a blue wool coat with epaulets on the shoulders and a peaked hat of the same hue approached the Searles Science Building from the opposite direction. Navy, Emma concluded—a fine-looking officer. She looked away before he could catch her eye.

He reached the door of the brick building just as Emma did. "Hello." He smiled brightly and opened the door for her.

"Thank you." As she entered, she tucked the large envelope she carried under her arm. She pulled off her knit gloves and headed for the stairs.

"Excuse me," the man said.

She paused and turned toward him. "Yes?"

He unbuttoned his overcoat, revealing a uniform beneath. "I wonder if you could direct me to Professor Shuster's office."

Emma relaxed and smiled. "I'm just on my way up to see him, sir.

If you'd like to follow me, I'll take you there." Her father was a navy veteran. She wondered what the young man wanted with him.

He followed her to the second floor, where they turned and took the next flight. Classes were in session, and they met no one in the halls. He walked beside her to the third floor landing. The handsome stranger towered nearly a foot over her.

She supposed she should break the silence if she didn't wish to be thought rude. "Several of the mathematics and science professors have their offices up here."

"Indeed. I expect the climb keeps them fit." The young man smiled. "I'm John Patterson."

"And you're with the navy, Mr. Patterson?"

"Yes. Lieutenant, actually."

They'd reached the door of her father's office. Emma gave a quick knock and turned the knob. "Father, I've brought someone to—" With the door halfway open, she broke off with a gasp.

Her father's slender form lay sprawled on the floor. Blood seeped onto the varnished oak boards and the papers strewn near him.

"Father!" She dropped her envelope on the floor and knelt beside him. Bending close, she touched his arm. The awful stillness of his body sent chills through her. A dry, fierce ache filled her throat. Pushing his shoulder slightly, she tried to speak again, but a sob wrenched her chest.

Patterson knelt on the other side and put a hand to the fallen man's throat. After a moment, he reached across and gently touched Emma's sleeve. "I'm sorry, ma'am."

"No, no! He's my father! We need to call a doctor."

"I'm afraid there's nothing a doctor could do for him."

She wept then—great, hot tears splashing down her cheeks.

"Miss Shuster." His quiet voice held authority she couldn't ignore. "Come and sit down."

Emma raised her hand to her mouth, staring at the blood. Her father had received a fatal wound—but how? She struggled to stand, but her knees buckled, and she grabbed the lieutenant's outstretched arm.

He caught her as she wilted. "There, now. Let me help you." He turned a wooden chair to face the door, holding her upright with his steel-like right arm. "Sit down, miss."

Emma sank onto the chair and held her hands over her face.

"Can I get you anything?"

"No," she managed. "Thank you. Just…please, see to Father. Make certain…"

"Only if you assure me you won't topple out of that chair."

"I—yes, thank you." She pulled in a deep breath to prove it.

He left her side, and she shivered, even in her thick woolen coat. She wanted to look over her shoulder and see what Patterson did—to assure herself that she'd been mistaken and only imagined the ghastly scene.

She didn't move.

The lieutenant came back, his jaw tense. "I'm sorry, Miss Shuster. I'm afraid it's too late."

A new sob worked its way up her throat.

He touched her shoulder, and the weight of his hand through her coat was oddly comforting. "We ought to call the police. Is there a telephone box nearby?"

She jerked her chin up and stared at him. His solemn brown eyes reassured her. "There's a phone in the front office of this building, to the right of where we came in."

"I'll run down there and call for an officer. Will you be all right?"

She studied his face, wondering how he expected her to answer that. "I...don't think so."

"No, of course not." He squeezed her shoulder lightly. "I'm so sorry, Miss Shuster. Would there be people in the other offices on this level?"

"Yes, probably." She bit her lip. "Professor Fairleigh is across the hall, and Dr. Shaw is next door."

"All right, I'll be right back."

He was at the door before she forced out a word. "Lieutenant—"

His broad shoulders swung around, and the rest of his lanky form followed. "Yes, ma'am?"

She wanted to say, "Take me with you," but she didn't. Even if she couldn't make herself look at Father again, she couldn't leave him unattended. She shook her head and clenched her hands in her lap.

"I promise I won't be long."

She nodded.

His knocking on another door echoed in the hallway. The murmur of voices was followed by quick, heavy footsteps.

Short, sturdy Dr. Shaw appeared in the doorway. His gaze pinned Emma to her chair then shot past her. He gasped. "Good heavens! Whatever happened?"

"We don't know, sir," Patterson said. "If you would be so good as to go down and ask someone to phone the police..."

"Of course." Dr. Shaw's thick shoes clumped on the oak stairs.

Far away a bell chimed, and the hubbub of students exiting their classes wafted up the stairwell.

Emma raised her chin and blinked back tears.

Patterson stood ramrod straight, just inside the door, as though on guard duty.

"Thank you," she said. *Thank you for sending Dr. Shaw, and for not going yourself*—but she couldn't say that. She would much rather stay in the room with the grave young man than with the overbearing Dr. Shaw. Father had never gotten along with him, and their disagreement over number theory was legendary on campus.

"You're welcome. And if there's anything else…"

"If you are a man of faith, Lieutenant, I'd appreciate any prayers you could spare this morning."

"You have them already. Miss Shuster, I sincerely regret what has happened. I'll help you in any way I can."

Her heart ached, and a fresh stream of tears bathed her face.

Patterson reached into a pocket and produced a spotless cotton handkerchief, folded and ironed into a perfect square. He placed it in her hand and pressed her fingers around it.

For a moment, the warmth of his hand spread to hers. "I don't know what I'd have done if I'd walked in alone." She unfolded the fabric and wiped her cheeks.

* * * * *

An hour later, John entered the small, first-floor chamber where Miss Shuster sat with the dean's secretary, Mrs. Whitson.

Emma huddled in a padded chair near the window with a full cup of tea cooling on the small table beside her. She'd removed her coat, hat, and scarf, and she looked small and vulnerable in her dark green dress.

She turned wide blue eyes up to him. Her face looked too puffy for her fine cheekbones. Dried tears mottled the creamy complexion he'd admired when he'd walked up the stairs with her—ages ago, it seemed.

He nodded to Mrs. Whitson and crossed to Emma's chair. Her lips trembled. He couldn't remain standing, looming over her. He went to one knee on the rug beside her.

"Miss Shuster, I've spoken to the police chief."

"What can you tell me?" Her damp lashes lowered, hiding her reddened eyes.

"Chief Weaver will come and speak to you soon, but I've learned a few things about your father's death."

She shuddered, and he wished he'd cushioned his words.

Mrs. Whitson cleared her throat and rose. "Lieutenant, I shall give you and Miss Shuster some privacy." She pulled over another chair, indicating that he should use it, not kneel before the bereaved young woman like an awkward suitor.

John rose and pulled the chair closer. "Thank you, ma'am. I'll stay with her until Chief Weaver comes."

Mrs. Whitson left the room.

He turned his attention back to Emma, who had made good use of his handkerchief and held it wadded in one hand.

"Did they discover how he…died?"

"The coroner is there now. I'm not sure he's come to a conclusion about that. But the police are treating this as a crime."

She winced, and it hurt him to know he'd made her difficult day a little harder, though she'd have learned that fact soon anyway. He'd leave it to Weaver to give her the details of the investigation.

"Is there anyone you'd like notified? Your mother…?"

"She's been gone since I was seven."

"I'm so sorry."

She sniffed. "There are relatives.... Father's sister...but I'll let them know later—after I've spoken to the chief and had a chance to think."

"Of course." He held out a large envelope. "I retrieved this from your father's office. The police chief said it was all right when I told him you'd carried it in with you this morning."

"Thank you." She tucked it between herself and the side of the armchair. "I've been helping Father with a private project he was working on."

John inhaled and studied her face. "If I may address that topic, would that have been his banking project?"

"I beg your pardon."

If nothing else, his comment had distracted her from the grisly scene upstairs.

"I'm speaking to you confidentially, of course. I'm assigned to the navy's Signal Corps. My supervisor, Captain Waller, is an old friend of your father's."

"Captain Waller?" Emma blinked and nodded slowly. "I've heard Father speak of him. They served together in the Philippines, back in the war."

"Yes, so I understand." John looked toward the door to be sure it was securely shut. "The captain sent me here to speak to your father about a matter they'd discussed before—the possibility of Professor Shuster going back to work for the navy—"

"Father joining the navy again?"

"Not necessarily. The captain wanted to offer him a position with the Signal Corps. We have several civilians working there, and your father could have served in that capacity if he wished."

She pushed back a strand of her light brown hair. "I don't understand. What is it they wanted him to do?"

"To work in cryptography."

She nodded, the light of comprehension in her eyes. "I see. But Father was happy here at Bowdoin College."

"Captain Waller hoped the prospect of adventure would entice him away from his academic nest. Your father told him in confidence about the work he was doing for a banking corporation. Designing a system of encryption to help the bank make long-distance transactions securely, by telegraph transmissions."

Her eyes widened. "I'm surprised Father would disclose even the nature of his work to anyone."

"He and Waller were apparently close friends, and the captain has a deep interest in this type of work. In fact, during their military service together, they had reason to discuss it often. I telephoned the captain, and he has authorized me to discuss it with you."

Again she nodded. She must know that during the war her father's military assignment had included putting messages in code so the Spanish could not decipher them.

"Captain Waller would have come to Maine himself, but his duties prevented that, so he sent me with a private message for Mr. Shuster and instructions to persuade him to come to Washington if at all possible. Waller wanted him badly."

"Are code makers needed so urgently then?"

"Ah, Miss Shuster, if only it were that easy. But you say you assisted your father on this assignment?"

"Yes, I've worked on the project with him since the beginning. It challenged him to his limits, but by God's grace, he was able to find the solution needed by his employers. He was nearly finished."

John nodded, thinking quickly over his instructions and how much he could reveal. "It's not code makers we need just now, but code breakers."

A rap at the door drew their attention. The oak panel swung open, and the chief of police entered. "Miss Shuster?"

"Yes." Emma wobbled slightly as she stood, and John stepped nearer, in case she collapsed again.

"I'm Chief Weaver." He closed the door and walked toward her. Emma extended her hand, and he shook it gravely. "I'm sorry about your father."

"Thank you. Can you please tell me what happened?"

"As near as we can tell—and it's early days yet, ma'am—someone surprised him when he came into the office this morning. The gunman may have been inside when he arrived, and—well, shot him."

Emma caught her breath. "Surely someone would have heard the sound."

"Not if the killer used something to muffle the report. Besides, I understand the professor came to his office early this morning, before there were many others in the building."

"That's true. He left the house about six thirty. Classes don't begin until seven forty-five. He may very well have been the first one here."

The chief took a small pad from his pocket and made a note. "The coroner says your father suffered a gunshot wound to his chest. That's what killed him."

Emma's face paled, and John prayed silently as he watched her, ready to help.

"When you entered, you two were together?" the chief asked.

"Yes," John said. "I met Miss Shuster when I came in and asked directions to the professor's office. I had no idea she was his daughter at that time."

Weaver scribbled in his notebook. "And who entered the room first?"

"I did," Emma said. "I opened the door, and when I saw Father lying there, I ran inside. This gentleman was right behind me."

"That's right. As soon as I saw Professor Shuster, I hurried in and felt for a pulse. There was none. I got Miss Shuster into a chair and went for help. One of the other professors called your department for us."

Weaver nodded. "Now, we've looked all around the room—under his desk and everything. We didn't find a weapon."

Emma said nothing but waited, her lips parted and her brow furrowed.

Weaver coughed. "That is to say, at this point, we don't think it was a suicide."

"Suicide! I should think not. That is the last thing Father would do."

The chief held up his hand. "As I say, miss, we found no weapon. But we had to check, you understand."

"Yes, I suppose so."

"We've reached the conclusion that this was murder."

John raised his arm, ready to catch her, but Emma didn't waver this time. She drew a deep breath and squared her shoulders. "All right, sir. What do you intend to do about it?"

CHAPTER TWO

"I'd be honored to drive you home, Miss Shuster," John said two hours later, when the police had at last persuaded Emma to leave the science building. He didn't like the thought of her walking home alone after her ordeal.

"Thank you, but it isn't necessary. It's less than half a mile, and I walk it frequently."

"I'm sure you'd be fine, but you've had a severe shock and a tiring morning. I have a car just around the corner. Allow me this privilege."

She gave in gracefully, and he offered his arm. She took it, letting her hand rest gently in the crook of his elbow as they walked along the snowy path to the car. He hoped they could get away quickly. The hearse would arrive any minute. She ought not to be present when they carried out her father's body.

The air had warmed, and clumps of melting snow fell from the tree branches. The eaves of the college buildings wept as the sun warmed the roofs.

At the corner, they met several young men walking toward their classes. One of them detached himself from the group and hurried toward them. "Emma! How nice to see you this morning."

He wore a fur hat and stood only a couple of inches taller than Emma. John could tell from the way the newcomer's pupils expanded while gazing at her that he considered meeting her more than simply "nice."

Emma slowed her steps. "Mr. Hibbert." She swallowed hard.

The young man looked up at John and frowned. John schooled his features to remain neutral, but the other fellow's mouth tightened.

"This is Lieutenant Patterson." Emma turned to John. "May I present Mr. Clark Hibbert? He is assisting my father on his private project."

"Pleased to meet you," Hibbert said without offering his hand.

"I must get home," Emma said.

Hibbert leaned toward her, as though his words were only for her ears. "I was hoping I'd see you at your father's office."

"Oh…no. Father…" She looked helplessly up at John.

Reading the signal from her eyes as clearly as he could a semaphore, he pulled his elbow, and her hand, a little tighter against his side. "I'm afraid there's been a tragedy, Mr. Hibbert. Professor Shuster met with misfortune this morning."

"What?" Hibbert stared at him blankly for a moment then at Emma. "What is he talking about? Emma, what's happened?"

John said quietly, "If you please, sir, keep your voice down. The professor is dead. It will be all over Brunswick before the day is out, but we don't wish to draw attention to Miss Shuster just now, do we?"

"I—no, certainly not." Hibbert's dark eyes searched Emma's face frantically. "It can't be true!"

"It is true." Emma's eyes glistened, and she gently tugged on John's arm. "If you would please see me home now, Lieutenant."

"Of course."

"No, wait!" Hibbert seized Emma's arm. "What about the project? What will happen now?"

"I don't know. That's a decision to be made by someone other than me. Now, please, let me go."

John edged Emma past the stunned young man, toward the Model T he'd rented at the local garage. He opened the passenger door for her and helped her up. After she arranged her long skirt, he closed the door and hurried to crank the engine. He glanced up the sidewalk. Hibbert had regained his mobility and strode down the path toward them. The engine caught, and John jumped into the driver's seat. Without his customary period of warming up the motor, he eased the car away from the curb and drove down the street.

"Which way?"

Emma raised her chin and looked at him. "Oh, I'm sorry. Turn left down there."

After performing the turn, he asked softly, "You lived with your father?"

"Yes. Father's had the house since he came here to teach six years ago."

He wondered what she would do now, but he didn't raise the question. It was too soon. "Will you be all right tonight?"

"I expect so. I'll call my aunt and uncle. They'll probably drive over from Woolwich."

"I'm staying at the inn in town tonight. If you don't mind, I'll check on you in the morning and see how you are doing."

"I don't mind." Her eyes flickered toward him. "It doesn't seem real yet."

"No, I suppose not. The offer of my services was sincere. Please contact me if I can help with anything. I have room 14 at the inn."

"Thank you. You've been most kind. Father went out the door this morning optimistic and contented." She gave a little sigh that twisted his heart. "Turn right at the next corner."

He swung the car into the cross street. "It's been just you and the professor at the house then?"

"Yes. My mother died a long time ago—while Father was away to war."

"How dreadful for you."

She nodded. "I went to stay for a while with Aunt Althea and Uncle Gregory."

"Are they the ones you said will come when you call them?"

"Yes. Their children are grown now. I'm sure Aunt Thea will want to come immediately."

"She'll help you with the arrangements?"

Emma pressed her lips together and nodded. After a moment she said, "There. The small brick house on the left."

He pulled up in front of the house she indicated and went around to help her down from the car. As they walked toward the front entrance, she took a key from her pocket.

"I hate to leave you alone," he confessed.

"I'll be all right. Mrs. Whitson said the dean will call on me this evening, and I expect others will come around, too, as the word spreads."

"Could you tell me a little more about the gentleman who spoke to us on the walkway?" John asked.

"Clark Hibbert?"

"Yes. You said he was helping your father."

She inserted the key in the lock. "He's an advanced student in engineering. I believe he graduated last year and is continuing his studies and tutoring new students. He's been building the machine Father designed for the bankers."

John's pulse quickened. "What sort of machine?"

"Well, I..." She bit her lip. "Father was very secretive about it."

"Of course. Forgive me."

"No, it's all right. You know about his work."

"How long have you been working with your father?"

"A year and a half now—since I finished my degree at Smith and came home to live."

"So, you know all about the ciphers he developed," John said.

"Yes. This machine is for secure encryption of financial information—any message, really. But Father didn't have the mechanical know-how to construct it, so he looked around for a student with the ability, and he found Clark."

"And how has that worked out?"

"Fine, I suppose. Father drew some rudimentary sketches, showing how he envisioned it working, and Clark seemed able to translate that into a physical apparatus. You heard him say he's nearly done with the project." She sighed. "I suppose I'll have to contact the bankers tomorrow. I ought to have brought home Father's files."

"The police will keep the office locked up until they're done investigating. I doubt you'll be able to go inside for a few days."

"Oh. Then I'll just have to wait."

"Yes. You need to rest and take care of the arrangements. And if I may be of service...I could perhaps drive you to any appointments you find necessary tomorrow morning."

"Thank you. I'll know more after I speak to my aunt. You've been a great deal of help."

She extended her hand, and he held it for a moment, gazing down at her.

Even in her grief-stricken state, she held an appealing air of grace. Her face was well-formed, though not beautiful. A single woman living on the campus of an all-male college. Why wasn't she married yet? Of course, she'd gone away to further her own education, and she'd chosen an exclusively female school. Now that she'd returned, most of the students might consider her too old for them and perhaps too intellectual—though Clark Hibbert had practically salivated in her presence. Probably many more like him haunted the halls of Bowdoin.

He realized he'd been staring. "Good day, Miss Shuster. It's been a delight to meet you, though I regret the circumstances."

"Thank you." She went inside and closed the door.

John walked briskly back to his car. Emma Shuster had backbone. Within the last year, he'd gone to England, France, and Belgium as an observer for the navy's Signal Corps. In his travels, he'd met many smart young women, but he hadn't met a girl he admired quite so much. Yes, Emma had wavered at the first shock, but since then, she'd held up, insisting that the police tell her what they knew. He'd stood by her and championed her right to know, yet tried to shield her from the harshest details.

She was the first woman he'd met who knew how complex ciphers worked. That brought a smile to his face. He'd planned to head back to Washington early in the morning. Instead, he would check in with Captain Waller by telephone this afternoon and offer his services to Emma in the morning. Until he knew more about Shuster's work—and his daughter's expertise—he would go nowhere.

* * * * *

For a long time Emma sat on the parlor sofa, weeping silently and soaking up her tears with a stack of fresh handkerchiefs. At last, she stirred and fixed a pot of tea. She opened the icebox, knowing she ought to eat something. After a moment, she closed the door and went to the breadbox. A cornmeal muffin would do.

After her meager repast, she steeled herself to call Aunt Thea. It was now past three o'clock, and the house was chilly. She used that as an excuse to put off the telephone call for another ten minutes while she descended to the cellar and stoked the coal furnace.

She couldn't delay any longer. Already her relatives would wonder why she'd waited so long to notify them. She went to the dining room, where the telephone was mounted between two windows, and lifted the earpiece.

Less than a minute later, her aunt greeted her. Althea Meyer had married a man who emigrated from Germany as a boy and still spoke the language. Unlike the Shusters, the professor's sister and her family sometimes spoke German in their home.

"Aunt Thea, it's Emma."

"Emma, *leibchen*, how are you?"

"I'm—not so well, Auntie."

"What is wrong, child?"

The fist-sized lump had reclaimed its place in her throat. She gulped and fished in her pocket for the latest handkerchief. "It's Father. He…"

"What now?"

"I—he…" Emma sucked in a whoosh of air. "He's dead, Auntie."

Stark silence hovered for a good five seconds. She almost spoke again, when her aunt at last responded.

"Did you say dead? My brother is dead?"

"Yes."

A muffled chattering reached Emma through the instrument she held to her ear. She supposed Aunt Thea had covered the mouthpiece with her hand and was telling Uncle Gregory.

"Emma?" His deep, stern tone came over the wire.

"Hello, Uncle Gregory."

"What is this? Your father has met with an accident?"

"No accident, I fear. Someone has killed him."

"What?" Uncle Gregory went off into a string of rapid German.

"No, no, not here at home," Emma said, trying to follow his words. "He was at his office. Yes, the police are looking into it."

Her aunt came back on the line. "I'm sorry, Emma. This is such a shock. What is being done, child? Did you speak to the undertaker?"

Emma sobbed and wiped her face again. "Yes. Father's being taken to a mortuary here in town. I'm going there tomorrow to settle the arrangements."

"We must come right away."

"I don't want to trouble you…"

"Nonsense! Of course we'll come. Will you be all right tonight? We can come tomorrow."

"Yes, that's fine. I'll expect you."

"Good. I shall pack tonight. And we must get someone to keep the dogs—unless you think we could—"

"I think that would be best," Emma said quickly. The two huge Alsatians would crowd her out of her snug little parlor and leave dog hair all about to be swept away daily. "Isn't Herman home? Surely he could keep the dogs."

"No, he's gone to Boston with a friend. Don't worry—I'll speak to your uncle about it. He'll find a place for them."

By the time they'd settled a few more details of the visit, Emma felt a bit claustrophobic. She loved her kin and was grateful for all they'd done for her in her childhood, but Uncle Gregory's hearty presence and Aunt Thea's fretting always made her feel she was being stifled in an airless box. At least their youngest son, Herman, was away and wouldn't arrive with them tomorrow.

"Aunt Thea," she ventured, "if it's too much trouble for you to get away tomorrow, come the next day. I'm leaning toward putting the services off until Monday, and—"

"No, no! You mustn't be there alone. We will come tomorrow and stay until the service is over. Look for us by noon."

"All right."

"Such a shock!" Aunt Thea went off into a wail of despair, and Emma gritted her teeth.

A metallic rapping sounded, and she turned toward the front entrance. "I must go. Someone is calling on me. I expect the dean of the college this evening, but perhaps he came early."

Glad for an excuse to end the conversation, she replaced the earpiece and hurried to the door.

The college president and the dean stood on the steps in their long wool overcoats and fur hats.

"Miss Shuster," the dean said in appropriately somber tones, "may we come in?"

"Of course." She stepped aside, slightly intimidated by their formal demeanor.

"I hope you're not alone this evening," President Mason said, looking about the dim entry.

Emma hadn't had time to light the lamps, and the rooms lay in shadows. "Thank you for coming. Won't you come into the parlor?" She hurried to draw the curtains and light the kerosene lamp.

"Do you have a chaperone?" the dean asked.

She paused with a safety match in her hand. "Why, no, not at this moment, but my aunt and uncle will arrive before noon tomorrow. They'll stay out the week with me."

"Then we shan't stay but a moment," the dean said.

"My dear Miss Shuster," Mason began, eyeing her paternally, "we wanted you to know how much the college has appreciated your father's service."

"Thank you." She adjusted the flame and turned to face them.

Neither made a move to remove his coat.

"Shocking affair," said the dean. "We've never had such a thing happen on the grounds before."

President Mason nodded. "Shameful. Of course, we invite you to stay here until after the funeral services."

Emma blinked at him. "Here?"

"In the house."

"Oh." Her heart plummeted. She hadn't considered that aspect of her newfound situation. Of course the house belonged to the college.

The dean coughed. "We'll get someone to cover your father's classes for the next few weeks, but we'll need to hire another mathematics professor as soon as possible."

"Yes, and when we do, regrettably…" Mason couldn't quite meet her gaze. "We'll need to have your father's office and living quarters available."

"Of course."

"I'm so sorry," the dean said. "Please don't feel pressured about it. We'll let you know when we have a prospect and will need the accommodations."

Emma's lips trembled. "Thank you."

"Indeed." Mason shifted from one foot to the other. "Well, we should get along. Be assured of our sympathy, Miss Shuster. If you need anything, please contact my office."

She showed them out and resisted the urge to collapse on the sofa. With the Meyers arriving tomorrow, she had much to do. She went upstairs and took clean linens from the hall closet. For a moment she stood in the doorway to her father's chamber, storing the image of his most personal space in her memory. This room would never be the same.

Quickly she stripped the bed and made it up again with clean linens, then carried the dirty sheets out and dropped the heap on the landing. She went back to the bedroom and shuffled Father's clothing to one side of the closet rod, leaving space for her aunt and uncle to hang their things. She would have time later to think about what to do with Father's clothes. Perhaps Aunt Thea would help her with that. She started to shut the closet door, but paused and reached for the sleeve of his gray wool jacket. Tears sprang into her eyes. She would not give in to them now.

Hurrying out into the hallway, she decided to take a quick inventory in the small room her father had used as a den. Before the confusion of the funeral arrangements and visitors began, she wanted to know where all of Father's notes on the cipher project lay.

She paused at his desk and picked up the small, framed photograph of them together at Old Orchard Beach. The memory of that pleasant summer day was one she treasured. She wiped away a tear, set the picture aside, and opened a drawer.

A few minutes' work rewarded her. She found two notebooks and a folder of papers pertaining to the project and carried them to her own room. Careful perusal told her that she had the most important papers in her hands. Were these the only ones that had remained here in the house? Were there more at his campus office? The ones she'd just found held the most vital part of his research and the plan for the bank's cipher.

Emma held the notebooks to her chest for a moment. Was this her father's most important work? And was this the reason he'd been killed? She'd felt relief that her aunt and uncle would leave her alone this one night, while she came to terms with Father's untimely death, but now a shadow of fear darkened her spirit. If someone wanted Father's research badly enough to kill him for it, might he not also come here looking for it? Was she in danger, here in the snug little house she loved so much? She shivered and bundled the papers into a hat box, which she shoved to the back of her wardrobe.

As she went downstairs to check all the locks, her thoughts flitted to the tall lieutenant who'd arrived on campus this morning. Was it a coincidence that he'd come in time to share with her the worst moment of her life?

Her cheeks flushed as she reviewed the scene. Patterson had seen her in her weakest, most vulnerable moment. Sharing such a personal time of crisis with a strange man had added to her distress. If she'd had a choice, she would have hidden all emotion from those around her, but he'd seen her shock, her helplessness, and her grief. So many men had surrounded her—policemen, college officials. She wasn't used to being the center of activity like that. And yet, Patterson had acted the perfect gentleman. Without his presence, her grim discovery would have been much harder. She accepted his arrival today as a gift from God.

The reminder of God's care put her more at ease as she prepared for bed. Her heavenly Father would never leave her. He would watch over her during this difficult night alone.

CHAPTER THREE

Thursday, January 28, 1915

John called Captain Waller again from a telephone box in the hotel lobby the next morning. "Nothing new since last night, sir."

"Be sure to express my deepest regrets to Miss Shuster," Waller said.

"I will, sir. I'm heading over to her house now."

"I regret we didn't bring her father here sooner. The man was a cryptographic genius." Waller sighed. "I'll miss my friend."

"I'm sorry I didn't get to meet him," John said.

"I don't know where we'll find another man as knowledgeable on the topic. Well, find out all you can, Patterson, especially about that machine he designed. And bring with you any papers you can get his daughter to release."

Waller had envisioned Professor Shuster bringing a fresh approach to the Navy Signal Corps. Radio had made it possible for combatants to intercept their opponents' messages, and a more secure system of communication was needed.

Losing Shuster's abilities was tragic, but the greater part of John's sadness was for Emma. She had loved her father deeply, and he'd been brutally torn from her.

"Might I stay here in Brunswick until after the funeral, sir?"

"When is it?"

"I'm not certain yet."

"I'd hoped you could catch a train to Boston today. They've found another of those cargo bombs on a ship there. Thank God it was discovered before the ship sailed."

John did some quick thinking. "If I help Miss Shuster this morning, perhaps I could get to Boston by evening."

"Do it if you can. Of course I want you to assist her. And if you settle things quickly in Boston, maybe you can get back up there in time for the service. Wish I could be there myself. I'll send flowers."

When John got to the house, Emma opened the door with a tremulous smile. "Lieutenant Patterson, it's kind of you to come again. I rose late this morning and am just finishing my breakfast. May I offer you a cup of tea?"

"That would be terrific." He followed her to the kitchen. She had dressed in a gray suit and white blouse, not quite mourning attire but probably the closest she owned. She'd looked much prettier yesterday in the green dress. Her complexion was made for vibrant colors. "Were you able to contact your aunt and uncle?"

"Yes. They'll be here by noon. And the police chief has promised to come by after lunch to keep me abreast of his department's investigation."

John took the chair she indicated. "I hope they find out soon who did this."

"So do I." She lifted the brown teapot from the table and poured out a strong cup of tea for him. "Sugar or cream?"

"Both, thank you."

As John doctored his tea, she sat down and resumed eating. Her delicate hands moved without wasted motion, and she had soon eaten the last few bites on her plate. She sipped her tea. "I plan to go to the mortuary this morning."

"Allow me to take you."

Her cheeks colored. Had she hoped he would renew his offer?

"I'd like that."

John leaned toward her across the table. "I spoke with Captain Waller yesterday, and again this morning. He was most saddened by the news of your father's death. He asked me to express his condolences."

"Thank you. That's kind of you both."

"I'm sorry to intrude on your life at such a distressful time."

"I'm glad you were with me, as I said yesterday. You were very supportive."

He almost smiled at that, recalling how he'd held her up when she'd threatened to crumple.

A few minutes later, Emma donned her coat, gloves, and a dark red woolen hood that added the color she needed. He doubted she realized how it complemented her features.

They went out to his car. Sunlight sparkled on the crusty snow. The thick layer had shrunk and settled but still blanketed the ground.

"I don't know what you're planning for services," he said as he drove toward the funeral home, "but the captain authorized me to arrange a naval detail if you would like it."

"I'd like that very much."

"Four men can come to stand in their dress uniforms—two at the door of the hall and one at either side of the casket. The men can fold the flag and present it to you before the casket is removed from the church."

She nodded. "Perhaps I should wait for my aunt to come before finalizing the details, but the undertaker was most anxious to meet with me, and I think I'd really rather make these decisions myself. Father did not like ostentation. I'm afraid his sister, if given free rein, would turn the occasion into something he would find distasteful."

"Then you should plan it now."

She turned her deep blue eyes on him. "I'm glad you and Captain Waller suggested giving him military honors. Father's service in the navy meant a lot to him, and this will be much nicer than anything Aunt Thea would come up with."

"The captain spoke of Mr. Shuster's loyalty and patriotism. He also said your father was a genius."

"I've always thought so."

John pulled up before the funeral home. "Are you ready to go in, or would you like a minute?"

She inhaled deeply. "Let's go in."

An hour later, he drove back to her street. Emma had retained her poise during the interview, and John felt she'd made wise decisions—economical, but befitting her father's position. On the ride home she looked out the side window, hardly speaking, and he was reluctant to break her reverie.

As they approached her house, he spotted a black car parked before it. The driver's door opened, and a large man climbed out.

"It appears that Chief Weaver is here early," he said.

When he'd parked, Emma got out and greeted the chief.

"Hello," Weaver said. "Your neighbor called. She saw a man poking about your back door and peering in windows, so I drove over."

"What?" Emma stared at him for a moment then hurried up the steps. As she unlocked the door, John and the chief joined her on the porch.

"By the time I got here, no one was about," Weaver said, "but I found footprints in the snow around the side and back of the house."

Emma hurried inside, her face flushed. She strode through the rooms on the lower level and came back to where the men stood in the entry. "Nothing seems disturbed."

"Would you like me to check upstairs and in the cellar, to be sure?" Weaver asked.

"That's probably a good idea," she said.

John unbuttoned his coat. "I can check the cellar if you wish, and I'll build up the fire in the furnace for you."

"Thank you." Emma turned to Weaver. "My aunt and uncle will be here momentarily."

"That's good. You shouldn't be alone right now. I'll take a look, and then I'll tell you how things are going in our investigation." He mounted the stairs.

"I'm sure everything will be all right," John said.

Emma nodded, but her brow remained wrinkled. She showed him the light switch, and he went down into the shadowy basement.

A thorough look around assured him no one hid in the coal bin or behind the furnace. He set about loading the firebox.

When he emerged a few minutes later, he could hear Weaver's voice from in the parlor. He paused in the kitchen and built up the fire in the cook stove. Once the blaze was going well, he walked toward the parlor.

Emma looked up as he reached the doorway. "Please come in, Lieutenant. The chief has just given me some more distressing news."

* * * * *

Emma found John Patterson's presence unexpectedly comforting. On her invitation, he entered the parlor and sat down opposite the police chief.

"I was just telling Miss Shuster that some of her father's files seem to be missing," Weaver said.

"Oh? I didn't see any disarray in his office yesterday—other than where he had fallen, of course."

"My men have turned out the entire room today. They found it very curious that one drawer of his files was empty. I've described its location to Miss Shuster, and she tells me it was where the professor kept his notes and correspondence concerning a private contract he was working on for a banking firm."

Emma glanced at John. Once before, she'd felt that he'd read her thoughts by studying her eyes. Could he do it again?

He nodded almost imperceptibly and turned to the chief. "I'm aware of the project."

"Ah. Then it wasn't confidential?"

"Why would a mathematics professor's work be confidential?"

The chief eyed him thoughtfully. "You said you arrived yesterday from Washington to visit Professor Shuster."

"Actually, I was on my way to the shipyard in Bath, and my supervisor asked me to stop in and greet his old friend. He and Mr. Shuster served together in the Spanish-American War."

"Aha."

The chief didn't seem entirely convinced that Patterson had told him the whole story, but Emma was glad the lieutenant hadn't mentioned that her father's project involved cryptography. Perhaps she should have told Weaver herself, but she felt that would be a betrayal. Her father had guarded the information zealously.

She wondered if the empty drawer in his office was where the papers she'd hidden last night were stored when he took them to the campus. How could she ever know if something else was missing? An in-depth study of the papers she had in hand—those in the hat box and the ones she'd had in the envelope when she discovered her father's body—might help. She could recall several parts of the project she had worked on, but she wasn't certain she'd seen all of it.

The hope had grown in her over the past twenty-four hours that she could gather all his notes, finish his project, and deliver it as planned to the bankers. If it became known what type of work her father had been doing, that might lengthen the police investigation and keep her from being able to close out the project. Of course, that was assuming his notes were intact. Were more missing that she would never recover?

The police chief turned his attention back to the matter at hand. "Well, the professor's files on this banking project appear to have been stolen. At least, they were not in his office when my men arrived on the scene yesterday."

"I'm sorry to hear that." John didn't look at Emma but said smoothly, "And do you have any leads in the investigation, sir?"

"Unfortunately, not yet. Too many people had access to the building. But we've got several crackerjack men on the case." Weaver nodded firmly in Emma's direction. "Don't you worry, miss. We'll find the killer."

Emma tried not to let her doubt show on her face. If some of her father's files on the cipher project had indeed been stolen and he was murdered for them, then the killer had probably long since crossed the Maine border.

Still, the police chief's probing about the time of John's arrival brought back her own vague doubts. Could John's appearance possibly be connected to her father's murder? And was she entirely too trusting? Somehow she couldn't look too closely at those questions. John had helped her so much, she wanted to believe in him without reservation.

When Weaver left, she looked at the clock. Perhaps she had a few minutes left with Lieutenant Patterson before Aunt Thea and Uncle Gregory arrived. "I'm sorry, but I need to put on some potatoes for lunch. You are welcome to join me in the kitchen while I do it."

"I'd like that, if you're sure I'm not intruding. And don't apologize."

She felt her cheeks flush as she turned toward the kitchen. The stove ticked, and her teakettle steamed cheerfully. "You built the cook fire too. How can I thank you?"

"It was nothing."

She smiled as she tied on her apron. Surely her faith in him was not misplaced. She went to her vegetable bin to choose half a dozen potatoes—more than they'd need, but she liked to have plenty when Uncle Gregory was a guest. Did she dare ask the lieutenant to join them?

She searched through her utensil drawer for a paring knife. "Will you stay to eat with us?" Her pulse thrummed when she'd said it, and she felt an uncertain guilt. Ought she to be thinking of how handsome a man was when her father lay dead at the mortuary? Disgraceful, her aunt would call it.

"I mustn't. I'm already later starting out than I'd planned, but thank you for the invitation. I'm glad I was able to speak to the police chief again."

"Yes." She found the knife and turned to face him. "Thank you for not telling him about Father's ciphers. I was of two minds—whether to explain, which could help the police find Father's killer, or to keep quiet, which might prolong the life of the project."

"But if your father's files were taken…"

She frowned. "Yes. I want to thoroughly search the house. Father usually kept the project files here, not at the office, though he sometimes took papers over there to work on between classes. I doubt he'd have left them there overnight. He was a stickler at keeping them secret and safe. I've gathered up some from his study, but I'm not certain I have everything."

"The envelope you had with you yesterday—"

"I was working on a portion of it for him after he went to work. I needed to ask him a question, so I put the papers in an envelope and walked over to his office."

John nodded. "I thought that might be part of the cipher project."

"Yes. And last night I removed some papers from his den upstairs."

"Then you don't think anything of significance was stolen from his office?"

She sighed. "There could be more I didn't know were there."

"Where did he keep the blueprints for the machine?"

Emma paused with a potato in one hand and the knife in the other. "I'm not sure there were any blueprints. He made sketches. Clark must have them. He's been constructing the machine to Father's specifications."

John nodded with a faraway look in his eyes.

What was he thinking? The project was for the bankers, not for the navy.

An imperious knocking reverberated through the house.

She arched her eyebrows at Patterson. "That's Uncle Gregory, to be sure. You must meet him and Aunt Althea."

"I'd like to. And then I should be off. I need to return the car and catch a train."

They went to the entry, and Emma opened the door. She tried to see her family through his eyes. Large, blustery Uncle Gregory shook Patterson's hand vigorously while his eyes roved the young man's face. Trying to size him up, no doubt. Emma could see that she'd have to assure them later that John was not a suitor.

Aunt Thea, short and plump, swooped on the lieutenant. "Are you a friend of Emma's?"

"Yes, ma'am, albeit a new friend," Patterson said. "I was with her yesterday when she learned of her father's death."

Again he showed diplomacy, and Emma was glad. She hadn't told them she'd discovered the body, and she wasn't sure she wanted to.

"I'm sorry you've lost your brother, ma'am," Patterson said gravely.

"Thank you." Aunt Thea squinted up at him. "Are you from this area?"

"No, ma'am. I was here on business, and I must leave you almost at once. I have a long trip ahead of me."

"That's your car out front?" Uncle Gregory asked.

"Rented, sir."

"*Ach.*" Uncle Gregory eyed him for another long moment.

Patterson turned and extended his hand to Emma. "Good day, Miss Shuster. I'll be back on Saturday if at all possible, for the funeral."

"What?" Aunt Thea screeched. "I thought the funeral was Monday. You said Monday, leibchen."

"I know, but Saturday turned out to be more convenient."

"I told all the children. They will come too late."

"Then we'll call them all again, and I shall set them straight." Emma took her aunt's arm. "Come now. Let me take your wraps. I've got lunch cooking."

John threw her a tight smile and edged toward the door. "Good day, ma'am. Sir. Miss Shuster."

Emma took her aunt's coat and hung it in the closet. "Uncle Gregory, don't you want to take your coat off?"

"Not until I get the dogs from the car."

Emma stared at him and counted silently to ten.

CHAPTER FOUR

Friday, January 29, 1915

At nine the next morning, John phoned Emma from the lobby of his hotel in Boston. He'd told himself repeatedly that she would be fine, but he couldn't help worrying a little. He'd seen the huge Alsatians in her uncle's car when he left the house.

"Thank you so much for calling." Her voice sounded a little remote and official. Either he'd misconstrued her warmth yesterday, or her aunt hovered nearby.

"I wondered how you're doing. Are things working out with your aunt and uncle being there?"

"They've been very helpful. I trust you had a safe journey?"

"Yes, thank you. Any word from Chief Weaver about the investigation?"

"He called about thirty minutes ago."

John waited as Emma inhaled. He regretted asking her; the awfulness of her father's murder must have settled on her by now. "I'm sorry. I wish I could be there with you." His words surprised him, but he meant them.

She responded with more confidence in her tone. "I appreciate everything you've done. The chief says every available man is working on it, but to be truthful, I don't think they have any suspects yet."

"I shall be back for the service if at all possible." He held his breath, waiting for her response.

"I do hope you are able."

It was enough. John signed off and put through another call to Waller. "Captain, I questioned the prisoner that the harbormaster's men captured. The city police have him in custody."

"And?"

"There's no doubt he was acting under orders. This bomb is no homemade job. It was manufactured, and unless I'm mistaken, it's not the only one."

Waller sighed. "Any clues to where they're being made?"

"No, but I'm banking on a similar device as the cause of the cargo ship sinking in December. One of these things could blow a substantial hole in a ship's hull. Even if it didn't do that, it would set a massive fire in the cargo hold."

"The other ship sailed from Philadelphia," Waller said.

"Yes, sir. If they're recruiting men in different areas to do their sabotage for them..."

"There's one man giving the orders, I'm sure. Is the Department of Justice there yet?"

"Yes, sir. Their investigators took over the case shortly after I arrived."

"We've received news that an American ship, the *William P. Frye*, was sunk by the Germans yesterday."

"Whereabouts?"

"In the South Atlantic. They're hitting us from without and within." Waller let out a sigh. "All right, Patterson. What about Miss Shuster?"

"I'd like to go back to Brunswick in the morning, sir, but I'll spend today here. Maybe the harbormaster's men and I can turn up something."

* * * * *

"What do you mean, you can't get into the house? Now is the perfect time."

"No, sir. There are two huge dogs in there. I approached in the night, and they started a racket. This morning the people have put the dogs in the backyard, but the house is full of women."

"Women? What are you talking about?" Couldn't the man perform a simple search while the family was off attending the funeral?

"They're setting up food for a wake or something. All the guests from the funeral service go to the dead guy's house afterward and tell his relatives how sorry they are."

"And these women are already there?"

"That's right. I can't get near the place. There must be a dozen of them inside, and those vicious dogs are out back, where the cellar door is."

"You can't sneak past the women and take a look at the old man's papers? How about if you looked like a delivery man?"

"I…don't think so."

The leader swore. Though his secret underlings knew him as "Poppy," he'd heard that his enemies had begun to call him "*Kobold*"—German for "goblin"—because he slithered into places they thought were secure and fouled their best-laid plans. But in truth, he was nearly always hundreds of miles from the scene, as he was today.

His underlings did the tricky maneuvers, but this man didn't seem up to the standard he liked. Already he'd failed once to sneak into the Shuster house because a neighbor saw him and called the police.

"Get some flowers and pretend there was a mix-up at the shop. Someone sent them to the house instead of the church."

"I think it's too late for that, sir. Even if they let me in the door, I couldn't just—"

"Stupid! You will not be paid." Kobold hung up the telephone and paced the floor, wondering how to find a smarter man—one who could get the job done on short notice. This one had bungled a simple burglary at the professor's office and ended up shooting the man. Now he found it impossible to get into the man's house and look for the secret material Shuster had been working on. The idiot! It would serve him right if the police caught him and pinned the murder on him. Of course, then he might spill everything about his contacts.

Kobold sat down and went through the man's file. At last he sat back, calmer. This agent had never received enough information to implicate Kobold. All he knew was that the things he did were for the Fatherland. Maybe all was not lost.

He picked up the telephone earpiece and asked for a number in a Boston suburb. Best to keep one step removed from this operative. He'd been foolish to call him directly one time. That mistake would not be repeated. "Hello. I have new instructions for you."

* * * * *

Saturday, January 30, 1915

Emma arrived at the church with her aunt and uncle an hour and a half in advance of the funeral. Already, an army of church women were at her home, preparing for the gathering that would follow.

She and Aunt Thea had presided at viewing hours the evening before, in the funeral parlor, and Emma had tossed and turned all night.

The undertaker took her arm and guided her to the front of the auditorium, where her father was laid out in the casket. Aunt Thea and Uncle Gregory followed. Their son, Herman, had arrived the night before, and he clomped up the aisle behind them. Masses of flowers surrounded the casket, and a flag was draped over the closed half of the cover.

Emma wished she could have a last moment alone with Father, but her relatives wouldn't understand if she asked for it. She stood looking down at the body and gulping in deep breaths. Father looked so natural, she half expected him to open his eyes and ask for a cup of tea. Her knees began to tremble.

"Ma," Herman called, "Gretchen and Karl just got here."

Emma steadied herself. She could deal with the cousins and the college community if she put her mind to it. As she went to greet Gretchen and Karl, Herman's older siblings, she caught sight of crisp navy uniforms. The honor guard had arrived. Pride surged in her breast. Though he was a quiet man who disliked attention, Father would love this. And John had arranged it. She would have to get an address where she could write him a proper thank you—and one to Captain Waller as well.

The church filled quickly, and the buzz of low conversation muted the organ music. About fifteen minutes before the service would begin, Aunt Thea nudged her. "Your young man just arrived."

Emma couldn't resist a quick look over her shoulder. John Patterson walked swiftly up the aisle. Her heart tripped and she rose to go and greet him. Let Aunt Thea think what she wanted to.

He took her hands in his gently. "Miss Shuster, how are you?"

"I'm well, thank you. It must have inconvenienced you to come back for the service."

"Quite the contrary. I've arranged to spend a couple of days here in Brunswick. I won't intrude on your time with your family, but if there's anything I can do to help you, please let me know."

"How kind of you. I hope you can come over to the house after the service. We've arranged a visiting time."

"I most certainly shall."

She smiled. Having him there would make the reception much easier. "Will you sit with me during the service?"

"Thank you, but I think your family might resent that."

"Of course n—" She swung around and looked toward the front. Perhaps he was right. They would certainly make assumptions. "All right then. I shall see you afterward. And now I must get back to Aunt Thea."

After the service, Emma's head throbbed from her silent weeping, and her hand ached from gripping those of all the people offering condolence. She wished she could go home and lie down, but the house would be full of funeral guests. Not all would go over for the reception, but many would.

Several women from the church had offered to serve refreshments, and they'd admitted at least fifty people from the funeral by the time Emma and her relatives arrived. Emma could put names to most of them, but some she thought were students who might have come out of curiosity or for the refreshments.

The guests sat or stood about the parlor and the dining room, eating small sandwiches and cookies and talking with less restraint than they had at the church. One of the ladies served punch and coffee in cups borrowed from the vestry.

Emma and her aunt and uncle had barely hung their coats in the closet when the college president approached with a cup of coffee in his hand. "Miss Shuster, that was a fine service."

"Yes, it was. Thank you."

As she walked slowly into the parlor and viewed the crowded room, Mason kept pace. "Your father was such a fine man. So intelligent, but so humble. And dedicated—I've never known a professor as hardworking as he was."

"Thank you, sir," Emma murmured, scanning the parlor. Had John arrived yet?

"He's irreplaceable, of course, but—er—we have found someone to take on his course load for the spring semester."

That got Emma's attention, and she turned to gauge his mood. "Indeed?"

"Yes. His credentials are not quite what your father's were, but he has impressive references. We—er—expect him to arrive next week."

"Good. The students in Father's classes won't lose credit."

"That's right. We have an upperclassman filling in to keep the classes going in the meantime. Your father left clear plans—he always created detailed syllabi for his classes."

Emma smiled. "Yes. I used to type them for him."

"Oh. Well, uh, Miss Shuster, I hate to have to ask this of you, but..." Mason licked his lips and looked down at his cooling coffee. "Well, we'll need to have your father's office cleaned out by the end of next week, if at all possible."

Emma swallowed back a protest. "I'll speak to the police chief about it. I'm not sure they'll let me in there yet."

"Fine," said Mason. "As soon as you can, then. Oh, and there's one other thing. I hate to mention it…"

Emma thought she knew what was coming. "Yes, sir?"

"Er—this house. Have you made plans for your removal yet?"

"I'm discussing that with my aunt and uncle. I'll let you know when I'm certain what I shall do."

"To be sure. I suppose we can put Professor Ralston up for a couple of weeks at the inn. Well, keep me informed." He bowed clumsily and turned away. A moment later, Emma saw him buttoning his coat. So, his duty was done.

She moved slowly about the room, greeting people. Aunt Thea sat surrounded by relatives in one corner. Uncle Gregory was no longer in evidence. Emma hoped he had taken the dogs outside. She hadn't seen them since she'd arrived home, for which she was thankful. She caught a glimpse of Herman through the dining room doorway, loading his plate.

Emma's back ached, and her feet throbbed, but she couldn't escape to lie down. She wouldn't have it said that Alfred Shuster's daughter was rude to her guests after the funeral.

As she circulated, she came face to face with Police Chief Weaver. His presence surprised her, but she nodded up at him. "Thank you for coming."

"The professor was a decent man. I wanted to pay my respects."

"How kind of you. I wonder if I could speak to you for just a moment." She drew him aside and lowered her voice. "The college has asked me to clean out my father's office as quickly as possible for the incoming professor who will take his position. Will I be able to do that on Monday?"

"I don't see why not. We've finished collecting evidence there. I'll send a man over first thing Monday morning to open it for you."

"Thank you so much."

As she turned away, she found John standing behind her, obviously waiting for her to finish her conversation.

"Lieutenant, so good to see you again."

"How are you?"

She could tell he was evaluating her condition. Her fatigue must be obvious, though he didn't mention it. "I feel a bit tired, but I'm all right. Thank you again for arranging the honor guard. Several people have remarked on how touching they found it."

"I'm glad. Is there any other way I can help you?"

She hesitated. "You said you are staying over Sunday?"

"Yes. In fact, I hoped you might allow me to attend church with you, if you are going."

"Why, yes, I plan to. I'd like that very much."

He smiled. "What time is the service? I'll call for you in the morning, if I may."

"It's at eleven."

"That will be my pleasure, but what can I do to help you? I can be available Monday even."

"I shall have to move out of this house soon, I fear. And Monday morning I'll be going to Father's office to pack up his books and papers."

"Could I help with that?"

She realized she'd held a faint hope that he might offer but hadn't let herself latch hold of the thought. "I'd hate to ask such a favor."

"It would be an honor. I might even be able to round up some cartons from the inn's staff."

"That would be a big help."

"Have you had any refreshment yet?"

"No, I've been so busy…"

"Come." He took her elbow and guided her toward the dining room. "You should eat something."

She found that she was hungry, and John soon had her seated in a corner of the dining room with a plate of food. He sat down nearby and held a cup of punch for her.

"I'm sorry you have to move so soon," he said. "That will add to your stress."

"Yes, but it will also keep me busy." Emma paused with a carrot stick in her hand. "This house belongs to the college, you see. They maintain it for the department head, so I must give it up."

"I should think they'd give you at least a month to do so."

She shook her head. "The new man arrives in a week. I need to clean out the office first. It sounds as though they'll give me a couple of weeks to empty this house if I need it. My aunt will stay and help if I ask her to, but I hope it won't take that long."

"You can count on me Monday." John held out the punch cup, and she took it. "I can run errands, move boxes—anything you need."

"That would be wonderful. Shall we meet at Father's office at nine?"

"That's perfect."

Emma sipped her punch and handed the cup back to him. His smile melted her tension, and her aches seemed insignificant now.

"Emma?" Clark Hibbert stood beside them, carrying a plate of sweets.

"Yes, Mr. Hibbert?"

"I wanted to ask you about your father's machine. I'm sorry I didn't have it finished before he…passed on."

"It's not your fault," Emma said.

John stood, and she felt the awkwardness of the moment. "You met Lieutenant Patterson a few days ago, I believe."

Clark eyed John from beneath lowered lashes. "I believe so… briefly."

His tone bordered on rudeness, and Emma felt her face heat. "The lieutenant arranged the navy honor guard for my father."

Clark nodded grudgingly. "Very kind. Now, Emma, I need to know what you want me to do with the machine."

"How near finished is it?"

"Very nearly."

"Well, I shall have to leave here soon. Perhaps you should give it to me as it is now, and I'll see if the company that commissioned it wants it."

"I could bring it here tomorrow." Clark's dark eyes shone with eagerness.

Emma glanced at John. "I'll be at church in the morning. Why don't you bring it to my father's office on Monday? I'll be packing Father's things."

"All right." Clark's mouth went a little pouty. "Shall I bring the sketches too?"

"Yes. All the documents that you were working from."

As he walked away a moment later, John gazed after him. Emma wondered what he was thinking. Clark had invited her to attend campus events with him more than once, and had sought a personal relationship with her, but she had gently discouraged him each time. Perhaps too gently.

"Who is that man talking to your cousin?" John asked.

Emma spotted Karl standing near the parlor fireplace, talking to Professor Fairleigh. "With Karl? He's one of my father's colleagues."

"No, not him. I meant your cousin Herman." John gestured slightly with his cup.

Emma swung around. Herman stood near the hall door, talking to a dark-haired man of about thirty. "I don't know. But there are lots of people here whom I've never met before—many from the college."

"Yes." John shrugged and lifted his cup to his lips, but his gaze flicked back to Herman and the stranger.

"I don't recall seeing him at the funeral," Emma said, "but not everyone spoke to us afterward. I suppose he could be a connection of the Meyers'. If you think it's important, I could introduce myself and thank him for coming."

"It looks as though he's taking his leave." John handed her his cup. "Excuse me for a moment, won't you?"

Herman walked out of the parlor with the man, who was still talking. John followed with quicker steps, leaving Emma to stare after him.

CHAPTER FIVE

Cousin Gretchen, her husband Henry, and her brother Karl lingered until after six o'clock. Most of the guests had cleared out gradually. When it got down to just family, John bid Emma good evening and left for the inn. Uncle Gregory let the dogs in. Bergen and Bold sniffed about the lower rooms and at last settled on the parlor rug. Aunt Thea toddled about the kitchen, constantly wiping surfaces and putting things away.

When Henry hinted that they should head home, Gretchen walked with Emma to the front entry. "You must come and spend a few days with me after you move out of here," Gretchen said as she pulled on her overcoat. "We haven't had a cozy visit in years."

"I'm not certain what I'll do yet," Emma said.

"Oh, but Mama said you are going to stay with them, at least for a while."

"I probably will, but I haven't had time to look into my options. I have a dear friend in Connecticut I'd like to visit. I only wrote to her last night to tell her of Father's passing."

"Well, I insist that you spend some time with Henry and me."

"Perhaps I could come directly to you when I'm ready to leave this house."

"That would be nice. I'm sure Mama would understand."

Aunt Thea came from the kitchen with a pasteboard box of

sandwiches and pastries. "Here, Gretchen. Take this with you. We'll never eat all the food that's left here."

Emma waved off Gretchen, Henry, and Karl and closed the door.

"There, my dear, would you like some tea?" Aunt Thea asked.

"I couldn't, Auntie, but thank you. I'm exhausted."

"Of course you are. Off to bed, then. A sound sleep will do you good."

Emma plodded up the stairs. In her room, she kicked off her shoes and let her hair down. Her reflection in the mirror startled her—dull eyes, sunken cheeks. Did John really find her attractive? How was that possible when she looked so gaunt? Perhaps he only cared about her knowledge of ciphers. And what had he done this afternoon when he followed the stranger out the door? He'd never mentioned it again, and she hadn't had a chance to ask him. Enough of these dark thoughts. Surely if the man's presence were important, John would have told her.

She snatched her toothbrush and powder from the dressing table and hurried into the hallway, heading toward the lavatory. A bulky form sliding into her father's den stopped her.

Herman was staying the night. She'd offered him the parlor sofa after some hesitation. Perhaps she ought to have put him in Father's den—it would be more private than the parlor. But she hadn't wanted anyone else in there until she'd sorted through things. Was he moving upstairs without her permission? Or was he planning to search through her father's desk and papers?

She walked quietly to the doorway. Herman stood near the mantel. He picked up an old inkwell that her father had kept on display there and looked inside then turned it over.

"What are you doing?" she asked.

He turned to look at her without so much as blinking. "Is this silver?"

"No, I believe it's pewter."

"Oh. Are you going to pack up everything and move it over to our house?"

Emma eyed him coolly for a moment before answering. "I'm not sure yet."

"The folks and I can help you pack tomorrow."

"We're going to church in the morning. Perhaps on Monday."

Herman shrugged. "I have to work at the mill Monday morning. But I could pack your papa's books and things. I expect Mama will take care of his clothes for you."

"I'm not ready to talk about this, Herman. I suggest you go downstairs and prepare to sleep."

"It's too early."

"Then perhaps you'd like to choose one of Father's books and take it down with you."

"Maybe." He leaned back and eyed the engraving over the mantel. "Is that picture yours?"

"Yes." Emma walked over to her father's desk and opened the top drawer. She removed the slender key that fit the door and palmed it.

"His clothes are too small for anyone else in the family." Herman strolled to the bookshelves. "Mama said you'll probably donate them."

Aunt Thea had mentioned the prospect that morning, but Emma had asked her to let her put off those decisions until after the service. Tomorrow she would probably have to confront many issues she dreaded. "I'm not sure." She walked out and went to the lavatory.

When she returned, Herman was still in the den, seated in the desk chair examining a book.

"I'm going to retire now," she said. "I'd like to turn out the lights in here. If you wish to take a book downstairs, please do."

"I shan't be long."

"No, Herman. I want to close this room. I'd rather you left things as they are for me to go through tomorrow or whenever I get to it."

A scowl crossed his face as he rose. She stood back and let him pass into the hall. When he was halfway down the staircase, she went in and turned off the lamps. Then she went out and locked the door, pocketing the key.

* * * * *

Sunday, January 31, 1915

To Emma's surprise, Herman left immediately after breakfast the next morning. John called for her as promised and drove her and the Meyers to church.

Emma found it difficult to concentrate on the message. Thoughts of her father and the funeral flitted through her mind. The added distraction of John sitting beside her in his crisp navy uniform didn't help.

He offered to take Emma out for dinner, and she dearly would have loved to accept, but Aunt Thea insisted it would be improper the day after the funeral. And besides, they had so much food at the house; the lieutenant must come and eat with the family. John did not protest but returned to the house with them for dinner.

Bergen and Bold met them at the door, jumping and yipping. Uncle Gregory spoke sternly to them and put them outside.

Emma felt John's presence as a buffer between her and the Meyers during the meal. Each moment she grew more certain that she did not wish to go and live with them. Aunt Thea had treated her kindly when she'd stayed there as a child, but the cousins had alternately teased and ignored her. Uncle Gregory had barely noticed her presence except to correct her if she spoke up. She had soon learned to keep quiet in his house. Only when her father returned, more than a year later, had she found that she could freely express herself again, and her father had remained her closest confidant until his death.

"I do hope Karl and Gretchen got home safely. You'd think one of them would have called." Aunt Thea jumped up to fetch the cream for Uncle Gregory.

"Are your children all gone then?" John asked as Uncle Gregory passed him the dish of pickled beets. The leftovers from the reception made for a varied and unusual Sunday dinner, heavy on nut breads, cold cuts, and relishes.

"Yes, Gretchen and Karl left last night, and Herman this morning. It's only us and Emma now."

"And the dogs," Emma said, and John gave her a wry smile. At least the Alsatians were confined to the back yard while they ate.

John took his leave soon after the meal ended but managed to have a private word with Emma when she brought him his coat and hat. "Has everything gone all right here? You've had no disturbances since the gathering yesterday?"

"No, it's been very quiet."

"I confess I wondered if someone might come to the house while you were at church today."

"You mean…" Her neck prickled. "Father's papers?"

He nodded.

"Should I look upstairs now, to be sure?" She hadn't gone up to her room since they'd left for church.

"That's all right," John said. "But if you find anything has been tampered with, let me know. I expect those two mammoth dogs discouraged any would-be callers while you were out."

"Yes, you're probably right."

She felt John's absence keenly after he'd gone. She sat in the parlor with her aunt and uncle for an hour but escaped upstairs as the afternoon light waned. The den was still locked, and her own room was as she had left it. For the first time, she was glad Uncle Gregory had brought Bergen and Bold.

Again she wondered what, if anything, was missing from her father's college office. She also wondered if Herman had carried off anything from the den.

She unlocked the door and lit the small lamp on the desk. The inkwell and the engraving, at least, were still in place. Turning to her father's desk, she immediately missed the small photograph that had been there on Saturday evening. She yanked open the drawers with trembling hands and scanned the contents. In her mind she saw Herman sitting at the desk with an open book before him. She looked about the room, wondering if other small items had been taken. The den seemed undisturbed since she'd run Herman out last night.

"What are you doing?" Aunt Thea asked from the threshold.

Emma jumped. "Just looking at all the things we'll need to go through. I'll need to do Father's office in the science building first, though." She blew out the lamp. She didn't like to lock the door with

Aunt Thea watching. With Herman gone, it probably wasn't necessary, so she kept the key in her pocket.

"Are you too tired to go through some clothing? I thought perhaps we could empty out the dresser tonight."

A painful lump formed in Emma's chest. "All right. Then you and Uncle Gregory will have more room for your clothes."

* * * * *

Monday, February 1, 1915

"I'll go over to the college with you this morning," Uncle Gregory said as Emma dried the last of the breakfast dishes on Monday morning.

"There's no need," Emma said. "I have help coming."

"Oh?"

"Yes. I believe you and Auntie would do more good here, if you want to start sorting through things in the house. Mrs. Chatham brought some boxes that we can pack dishes and linens in."

"Well..." Uncle Gregory looked uneasily toward his wife and walked to the back door. He held it open and whistled for the dogs. They charged in from the fenced yard and pranced around him.

"Feed those animals," Aunt Thea snapped. "Emma, you go. We will start cleaning here. There is much to do, with all of Alfred's things to go through."

Emma's throat constricted. She didn't like the thought of their handling Father's belongings while she was away. Was she selfish to want a few hours alone with John? Her cheeks warmed, and she ducked her head. At least she'd removed the most sensitive papers from Father's den before they came and wouldn't have to worry about the relatives disposing of them. Before she'd retired last night, she'd locked everything pertaining to the cipher project in the wardrobe in her bed chamber.

Bergen and Bold rushed past her as Uncle Gregory went to the cellarway to fetch their food.

"I suppose I should begin cleaning out the cellar," Uncle Gregory said. "There's a lot of stuff down there, *ja*?"

"Yes, that would be a big help." Emma picked up her handbag from the table near the door. If Uncle Gregory could take care of the bric-a-brac in the basement, it would save her a lot of trouble. It would also keep him out of her father's more personal effects.

"Too bad Herman had to work today at the mill. I could have used his help lugging things up those stairs." Uncle Gregory set the dogs' full dishes on the floor, and the Alsatians plunged their faces into the food.

"You're walking this morning?" Aunt Thea asked.

"Yes. It's not as cold as it has been. I'll be fine. Oh, and I would like to wait on Father's den upstairs. His photographs and correspondence are in there. If you don't mind, I'd prefer we went through that room together, perhaps tomorrow or the next day."

"That's fine."

"Thank you, Auntie." Emma hurried out. A brisk walk across the campus kept her from feeling the chill. Classes had already begun, so the halls of the science building were empty. Several pasteboard cartons were stacked outside her father's office. She smiled when she saw them. Dr. Shaw had said he would ask the custodian to leave some for her, and he had not forgotten his promise.

A police officer came out of the office as she approached. "Miss Shuster, isn't it?"

"Yes. Good morning."

"We're done here, and you are free to clean up the room."

"Thank you. I don't suppose there's anything new in my father's case?"

"The chief will let you know if there is, I'm sure. There were a lot of fingerprints in the office, but that's to be expected at a school like this." The officer shook his head. "As I said, the chief will notify you when we learn anything new. Here's the key." He handed it over and nodded with a subdued smile. "Good day, miss."

"Good day." She watched him walk down the hall, suddenly dreading going into her father's office again.

CHAPTER SIX

John briskly mounted the stairs in the science building carrying an empty wooden crate. Was it wrong to feel so happy, just knowing he'd see Emma again soon? He ought to sober a bit before he greeted her, but he couldn't douse the anticipation.

A policeman was starting down from the third floor. "Morning," he said as they passed each other.

"Good morning." John looked through the railing's spindles as he mounted the last few steps.

Emma stood in the hallway in front of her father's office, looking toward him with a frown creasing her brow. The instant she saw him, her face lit. She smiled and took a few steps to meet him.

He quickened his pace, amazed at the strange tightness in his chest. He set the crate down and took her gloved hand. "Good morning, Miss Shuster. Did you sleep well?"

"Better than the last few nights, thank you."

He held her gaze for a long moment—longer than he should have. After all, he'd only be here another day or two, and his official duties would not likely bring him back to Maine soon. He might never see her again. And yet, she was special. Something beyond her intelligence and serenity touched him—perhaps the courage with which she faced this unnerving task. "I'm ready to work." He nodded toward the cartons. "I see you're prepared."

"Yes. I thought we could start with Father's books."

"Good. I've got this crate, and three more in the car."

When she opened the door, she stood for a moment on the threshold, gazing at the spot where her father's body had lain.

John was glad and a bit surprised to see that the police had cleaned the floorboards. At least Emma didn't have to deal with bloodstains, though he would probably do well to keep her from looking too closely. "Shall we begin here?" He stepped over to a ceiling-high set of built-in bookshelves.

"That will be fine." She removed her gloves and tucked them in her handbag.

John set to work with a rush of gladness that he could help her and perhaps distract her from her grief. Anything he could do to make this day easier for Emma would please him.

He routed out the custodian and borrowed a stepstool so he could climb up and hand the books down to her from the top shelves. Emma took them and packed them neatly into boxes then labeled the cartons carefully with the subjects of the volumes inside. Pure mathematics. Engineering. Statistics. Philosophy.

"Did your father have any books on cryptography?" He reached for the last two leather-bound volumes on the highest shelf.

"A few, but I don't think there are many in print on the subject—at least not in English. I believe he'd thought about writing one." She took a ragged breath. "He won't be able to now."

John took a step down. "Are you all right?"

She nodded, but her eyes glistened.

"Shall we do the next shelf then?"

"Yes, please."

"What will you do with all his books?"

"I thought of asking the school librarian if the college would like some of them. I think Father would like students to use his books. I'll take a few of them with me, but…"

"Where will you go?" The thought had troubled him, but he didn't like to ask, and Captain Waller had cautioned him to go slowly until they learned more about her. "Will you stay with your aunt and uncle?"

"They've asked me to, and so has Gretchen." She blinked rapidly. "I'd prefer to find employment. I'd like to earn my own income. I did consider teaching after I took my degree, but Father wanted me to come home for a while, so I put those ideas aside. I'm afraid I don't have a plan yet."

Beneath her words lay a weariness that hinted at unhappiness. He didn't know her well enough to ask, but he sensed that the time she lived with the Meyers had not been entirely pleasant for her, even apart from missing her parents. She shrank from going to live with them now.

"It would be nice if you could find a position that let you use your degree."

"Yes. Perhaps there's a school out there that needs a mathematics teacher. That's rare in the middle of the academic year, but I shall put out inquiries. And if I found a place, I might be able to rent some rooms…"

Again John wished he could speak of the matter he'd discussed with Captain Waller earlier, but it was too soon. Details needed to be worked out, and more information gathered, so he only said, "I believe you said you graduated from Smith."

"Yes. Bowdoin College doesn't admit women, or I'd have studied here. I matriculated as a literature major, but I found that I've inherited the mathematical bent from Father. After my freshman year, I switched to mathematics."

"And you came home immediately after you graduated?"

"That's right. I've lived here in Brunswick ever since."

John handed her several volumes and watched her pack them. "How did you start working on the encryption project with him?"

She looked up at him. "When the banking corporation hired Father to work on it, the college had just given him an extra class to teach. He was busier than he'd anticipated that semester. He found he needed an extra person to do some of the basic coding work for him, and he invited me to help him. I didn't mind. In fact, I enjoyed it. In the evening, we'd discuss the project and go over what I'd done that day. Those were pleasant times."

"I'm glad you have the memories. It makes me think of when I was at home with my family."

She stepped toward him, still holding the books. "Tell me about it. Where did you live?"

"My family has a farm in western Pennsylvania. Walnuts and vegetables. My brother still lives there, helping my father."

"What a wonderful place for children."

"Yes, and my parents are fine people. I was blessed."

"But you didn't like farming?"

He smiled ruefully. "I wouldn't say I didn't like it, but it's true I wanted to get beyond the cornfields and pastures."

"The navy was a good choice for you then."

"I think so. I've seen a lot of places, and I enjoy what I'm doing. But now and then I drive out into the country to look at the farms in Virginia."

She smiled at that.

John wished he could tell her more about his work, but most of his travels constituted classified information—carrying out confidential orders or observing procedures of the Allied military forces. "I look back on my days at the farm with grateful nostalgia, and I'll always love visiting home." He inhaled deeply. Enough of that—he'd be wishing for his mother's cooking next.

Emma had regained her poise, and they worked through the morning. When the books were crated, she began the daunting task of going through her father's files. "I need to decide what to give to the school and what will mean something to me personally."

"Take your time," John said.

As she reached the end of the papers in one bulging drawer, he ventured to ask, "How are things going with the Meyers and their dogs?"

Emma gave a resigned chuckle. "I can't pretend I'll be sorry to see the dogs go. We don't let them upstairs, but they have the run of the downstairs and sprawl wherever they like. They're so awkwardly large."

John laughed. "I like dogs, but those two look a bit much to handle."

"Yes." Her eyes focused suddenly, and her mouth sobered. "Lieutenant…"

"Please call me John."

She ducked her head, flushing becomingly. "All right, if you will call me Emma."

"I should like that."

"Well then, John, I have to say that I was thankful for the dogs after the suggestion you made yesterday, that thieves might come to the house."

"I hope I didn't upset you. I only wanted to put you on alert. If your father was killed because of his work on the cipher, the killer might hope to find more information."

"Yes. And I believe I have all the documents concerning that. I hope I can finish the work myself."

"I'm sure you can."

"Thank you." She frowned then looked over at him. "You're aware that my cousin Herman left yesterday."

"Yes." On Saturday, John had formed an impression of Herman being sly and greedy, supported by his repeated stealthy forays to the buffet table.

"He wanted to pack up the things in Father's den at home, but I wouldn't let him," Emma said.

"Good for you."

"He seemed more interested in knickknacks and small artworks than Father's papers."

That didn't surprise John. He'd seen Herman place his cup on the parlor mantelpiece, then pick up a china ornament and turn it over to peer at the hallmark on the bottom. Just as well that the young man had left the house.

"I haven't missed anything except a small photograph of me with my father. But I may have set it down somewhere and forgotten."

"And how long will your aunt and uncle stay?"

"I'm not sure. It feels a bit strange, having them there without Father, and knowing I must leave the house soon. Aunt Thea is a hard worker, and she'll help me pack everything and scrub the house from top to bottom…"

"But?"

She shrugged almost imperceptibly. "Uncle Gregory made a telephone call last night. He said he would pay me for the long-distance charges."

"Where was he calling?"

"I don't know, but almost the entire conversation took place in German."

John arched his eyebrows. "Is that unusual in your family?"

"It's his mother tongue, and he often speaks in German."

"And you think this telephone conversation was important?"

Emma frowned. "He said it was business."

"What line of work is he in?"

"He's an accountant. And immediately after the call, he went out. He said he went to pick up something at the store, but when he returned, I didn't see any packages. And Aunt Thea seemed worried."

"Hmm." John found the timing of the errand a bit suspicious. "You overheard the call."

"Part of it. The telephone is in the dining room. I didn't wish to eavesdrop, but as I was putting away the china, I did hear bits of it."

"Did you understand it?"

"Not really. I made out a few words—'work' several times, or maybe 'workers,' and 'no,' and something about money." She stepped over to the carton she'd been filling and laid some papers inside. "It's probably nothing."

"What do you think it might be?"

She chuckled. "If Aunt Thea didn't act so perturbed afterward, I'd probably think it was exactly what he said and nothing more."

John glanced at his watch. "It's after noon, and we ought to go and eat. Would you show me your favorite restaurant?"

"I have to call Aunt Thea first."

"Will she be upset if you don't come home for luncheon?"

"I hope not, but she is expecting me."

"Let's go downstairs, and you can telephone her from there."

* * * * *

Emma took him to a small, family-owned restaurant a few blocks from the campus. She and her father had dined together there only three weeks ago. Her new grief tugged at her as they entered.

The owner's wife, Mrs. Slate, showed them to a small table at the edge of the room, out of traffic. "Would you like the soup? It is very good today—chicken with vegetables and rice. Very good for this cold weather."

After they'd ordered soup and sandwiches, John asked, "Do you happen to have a telephone here?"

The woman pointed. "Yes, we do. It's around the corner."

John looked at Emma. "And would you excuse me for a minute or two? I need to check in with my superior, but it shouldn't take long."

"Of course." Emma watched him round the corner and noticed female heads turning to watch him. John did cut a dashing figure in his uniform.

Mrs. Slate brought a pot of tea and a pitcher of cream.

Emma fixed herself a cup and felt comfort seep through her with its warmth. John was like that. His presence this morning had lightened her burden and spurred her to work harder and do better. A morning spent packing and cleaning with Aunt Thea would have seemed drudgery, much as she cared for her aunt. But with John the time had flown.

Even the difficult topics they'd broached seemed less daunting now that he'd shared his thoughts with her. She'd have to be careful, though. She'd only known him a few days. She mustn't depend too much on him. He wouldn't stay long. He couldn't, even if he wanted to—and unless she was mistaken, he wanted to.

He returned to the table with a smile and another sincere apology.

"Think nothing of it. Would you like tea?"

"Yes, thank you." John turned his cup over, and she filled it. "There's something I'd like to discuss with you." He glanced about and leaned toward her, his face only a foot away across the small table. "Emma, would you be interested in a job in Virginia?"

She set the teapot down carefully. "You mean you know of a position I could apply for?"

"Yes. I told Captain Waller a little about your background the day I met you—your education and your work with your father. And now, after getting to know you better and learning more about your abilities and experience, I recommended that you be offered a job."

"But…the navy?"

"That's right. I'm attached to the Signal Corps, but we hire civilian workers to do clerical work and…other tasks." He cleared his throat and looked around again. "The job I'm speaking of would be an office position with several other civilians working on classified material." Before Emma could react, he sat back with a broad smile. "Ah, here's our lunch."

The waitress set their soup and sandwiches before them. "Anything else I can bring you?"

"This looks delicious. Thank you." Emma waited until she'd retreated then looked over at John. "I don't know what to say."

"Then don't say anything yet. Think about it, and when we're in private, we can discuss it more. Shall we pray?"

She bowed her head automatically. Once again, his firm, quiet voice calmed her, though her thoughts darted off to Virginia and military duties and a new home far from the Meyers. As John said "amen," the realization hit her that this might mean a possibility of seeing him again in the future.

She opened her eyes and found him eyeing her speculatively. The heat mounted from her collar, up her cheeks to her hairline. She reached for her spoon.

On the way back to the office, in the privacy of his car, he offered more information. "Captain Waller, who was your father's friend, approved my extending this offer to you. That's what my phone call was about. I couldn't mention it before, but in light of the things you told me this morning, I felt I could make a strong recommendation. The job is offered based on your knowledge of cryptography."

Emma had guessed as much, though she wasn't sure she was qualified. True, she'd achieved a certain expertise in the field, but nowhere as deep as her father's knowledge. "It would mean moving to the Washington area?"

"Yes. Northern Virginia. Our headquarters are there, and we have an office building. We don't really have a cryptography department, but the Signal Corps has traditionally handled naval and other military ciphers since Civil War days. The men in charge are gathering a few people who are good with ciphers."

"A need for this has arisen?"

"Yes." He pressed his lips together for a moment. "Emma, there have been several incidents lately where people have used ciphers to discuss committing crimes against the American people. They seem to be increasing in number and complexity. We need people who can unravel them quickly—people like you—so that people like me can go out and catch these thugs before they do their mischief."

Emma's pulse raced. Was he inviting her to take part in stopping espionage? It sounded like a kind of police work. "I'm not sure I have the qualifications…"

"I think you do. I can't tell you exactly where the office is, but if you decide to go down and interview with the people in charge of the program, we'll pay your travel expenses."

"That's kind of Uncle Sam."

"Yes. We don't do it for everyone, but I'm convinced that you have an extraordinary ability."

"You haven't seen my work."

"No, but you know so much…"

She raised a hand in protest.

"I mean it," he said. "You think you're a novice, but there are so few experts in this field, especially in this country, that it would be laughable if the international situation weren't so precarious right now. We need people who have a special type of mind, who look at things a certain way. We've discussed how to find them. Emma, they want to advertise for people who are good at crossword puzzles. You're so far beyond that!"

She stared at him. "Is that true?" When he nodded, she chuckled. "I'm very good at crosswords."

John smiled. "I suspected that. The navy is planning to send some bright fellows for special training, but we need to get more people working on the ciphers we have now. We need to stop these attacks."

"Attacks?"

"Sometimes it amounts to that."

"But why?"

No cars were parked on the street in front of the Searles Building. John parked and sat for a moment in silence with his hands on the wheel. "They don't want us to help England and her allies." He blew out a breath and smiled at her. "Let's not be so grim, eh? We have a lot more work to do." He got out of the car and came around to help her out.

"There's not really that much left for us to pack," she noted as they hurried up the snowy walk to the front entrance.

"No, I think we're down to files and the contents of the desk. We ought to be able to trundle everything over to your house in a couple of trips and be done by..." He glanced at his watch. "Oh, say three o'clock." He opened the heavy door and held it for her then walked beside her up the stairs.

Emma felt a little breathless when she got to the top landing. They turned toward her father's office, and she stopped short in the hallway. The door she had closed stood wide open.

CHAPTER SEVEN

John stepped cautiously to the threshold and peered inside. The hundreds of books they had so carefully packed were strewn about the room. Papers from the open file drawers and boxes littered the floor. A pile of small items on top of the desk suggested that the drawers had been upended there.

Emma touched his sleeve gently.

He pulled back, not wanting her to see the mess but aware that he couldn't keep it from her. "Looks like we had a visitor while we were gone."

She peeked into the room and caught her breath. "I should have locked the door, but I thought no one would bother anything with other people in the building. Should we call the police?"

"Let me look things over first. I won't disturb anything." He took two steps, which was as far as he could go without stepping on books or papers. "I don't suppose you can tell if anything is missing."

"That would be difficult."

"Yes." He looked back at Emma. "I'm sorry. I should have taken precautions against this. I assumed that your father's attacker took anything he wanted from his office at the time."

Tears glistened in her eyes. "This makes me angry."

"Angry enough to put in several more hours' work?"

"That might help me work some of it off." She took off her hat and pulled the door around to hang it on a hook. "Calling the police would just hold things up, don't you think?"

"Probably." John surveyed the mess, calculating how they could best use their time.

"Let's not call unless we discover something's been stolen," she said.

John hesitated. He understood her desire to keep the project quiet and bring it to a close, but he wondered if it would be a mistake not to involve the police again. Her troubled face won out. "If you want to start picking up the papers and sorting them, I'll gather up the books and repack them. I can carry the boxes right out to the car as soon as we fill them. When I have the car full, we'll take a load over to your house."

"All right." Emma set to work at once.

An hour later he had most of the books crated again and half the boxes in his car. Emma had sorted about half the files.

A timid rap at the door drew John's attention, and Emma swung around to look. The engineering student, Clark Hibbert, stood in the doorway holding a large wooden box.

* * * * *

"Hello, Emma. I have the machine here."

"Bring it right in and set it here, on Father's desk." Emma quickly pushed a small stack of books aside, ignoring his familiar use of her first name.

John stepped to her side to help clear a spot.

Clark eased the box onto the desk and looked around the room, blinking from behind his glasses. "So he died right here?"

Emma fought a surge of anger. "That's right."

Clark cleared his throat and flicked a glance at John. "Can I help clean things up?"

"We can handle it, but thank you." Emma turned back to her task.

"You sure? It looks like quite a job." Clark gazed over the disarray then cast another look John's way. "I'd be happy to fetch and carry for you."

"No, thank you. We'll soon be done." Emma smiled but spoke firmly. The last thing she wanted was Clark hanging about and prodding her for information about her father's death.

"All right then. If that company wants the machine finished, I'm sure I could get it done within a few weeks."

"I'll let you know if they want you to continue working on it."

"Good. Because I could just hang on to it and keep working until you hear…"

"Thank you, Mr. Hibbert, but I shall be moving before long, and I wish to have everything in hand when I go."

"Oh?" He took a step toward her, frowning. "Where are you moving to?"

Emma hesitated. She wished she knew the answer to that question, but if she did, she wasn't sure she'd tell Clark.

"Miss Shuster is still making arrangements," John said.

She glanced at him in surprise, grateful that he'd come up with a noncommittal answer. Hearing it from the lieutenant disturbed Clark—she could see that by the confusion in his eyes as he looked John over once more.

Clark shoved his hands into his pockets and shuffled his feet. "I'll be going then. I wish you the best."

"Thank you." After his retreating footsteps had echoed from the stairwell, she exhaled and said to John, "And thank *you*."

"You're welcome. I hope I didn't overstep my position."

"Not at all. I was at a loss how to answer him without seeming rude. Clark can be difficult to discourage." She reached toward the box he'd brought and lifted the lid. "Would you like to see the machine?"

"I'd love to."

She laid back the cover, and he peered into the box. "It does look nearly complete. In fact, I couldn't tell you what's left unfinished."

"Neither could I, but I see Clark put Father's plans in with it, as I asked him to."

"Tell me more about the project. What did your father hope to accomplish with this?"

"Father saw far-reaching potential for this device. When it's finished, the operator will type in his message and the machine will automatically change it to a different alphabet—or number substitution—and then do so again, effectively encrypting it twice in one step."

"So, it will save the bank a great deal of time and cut down on the chance of error."

"Yes. And the cipher messages will be nearly impossible to solve without the key. That, of course, will be the heart of the system. Father always said key distribution was the worst problem cryptographers faced."

"How did he plan to solve that?"

"He envisioned pads of paper with a different key on each sheet. Each person who has an identical pad can use the key on the top sheet for one message or one day, then dispose of it and use the next one. As long as the tablet lasts, they don't have to exchange new keys."

John nodded slowly. "Yes. They wouldn't have to distribute new keys for weeks at a time."

"He often said the government would take an interest if it served the bank well."

"Of course. And it's brilliant." John shrugged. "With the situation in Europe, we need all the advantages we can get in intelligence."

"Do you think America's entering the war is inevitable, as some people insist?" The thought troubled her on several levels. Her family was of German extraction, yet she couldn't countenance the tactics employed by the Germans and Austrians lately. If the United States declared war on Germany, men like Herman could wind up battling relatives in Europe. On the other hand, some days the news was so grim that she felt they'd already waited too long to step in and help the Allies.

John raised his chin and gazed at her thoughtfully. "I don't know what will happen, but frankly, I don't see how we can avoid it much longer. Emma, there are things going on..."

"Yes, I know it's terrible in Europe."

"Not just in Europe. Even here, on our soil."

"The crimes you hinted at in the car..."

Another knock came at the doorway. "Good afternoon," said the dean. He looked at the disarray on the floor. "Oh my."

"Quite a mess, isn't it?" Emma said.

He stepped over a few papers. "I telephoned your house, and your aunt said you were here."

"Yes. Have you met Lieutenant Patterson, sir? He's helping me pack up Father's things."

"I believe we met on Saturday." The dean took another careful step and shook John's hand.

"I wondered if the college would like to have Father's mathematics books." Emma glanced at John, realizing her mind was more than half made up. "It appears I'll be moving out of the area soon, and it would be difficult for me to take his entire library."

"I'm sure the college would be glad to accept his books." The dean peered at the empty shelves and the files dumped on the floor.

"There's been a bit of devilment going on here," John said.

"Oh? Vandalism?" The dean frowned, and his chin nearly disappeared inside his coat collar.

"Yes," Emma said. "We went to lunch, and someone came in and undid all our hard work of this morning."

John stooped to retrieve a folder spilling papers on the oak floor. "We've got most of the books boxed up, however, and about half of them are down in my car. If you'd tell me where to deliver them, I could drive them around there now."

"Why yes. The library is open today." The dean harrumphed and nodded in Emma's direction. "I can walk around there now and alert the library staff that a large donation of books is coming."

"That would be very helpful," Emma said. "Thank you. Was there something else I could do for you?"

"No, I just wanted to make sure you were all right."

"That's kind of you, sir."

He nodded. "Well, then, I'll see the librarian."

The dean left, and John patted her shoulder. "You must be exhausted. Why don't you come along and tell me which boxes to leave at the library? We can collect the rest of this tomorrow morning."

Emma gazed about the room. "I hate to leave his papers. What if someone comes in here again?"

John nodded. "Well, you've sorted a lot. What if we just gather up the rest in these last two boxes for now? We can take the papers to your house, where they should be safe. In the morning, we'll come back and clean up the odds and ends."

"And I'll sweep this room and scrub down the woodwork."

"I'll help you. Come, my dear."

Emma shot a glance at him. John's lashes hid his eyes, and she wondered if he'd meant to let the words slip out. "Thank you. By the time we deliver the books to the library, it will be nearly suppertime."

"Emma."

She waited, savoring his gentle tone and anticipating comfort from him. She barely knew him, but already he'd become important to her.

"I'm at your service this evening," he said. "If there's anything else I can do to help you, please let me know."

"You are too kind. I'm so tired I can't think straight. But if I retire early tonight, maybe tomorrow I'll be less addled and can consider the intriguing proposal you've brought me. Right now, it's all a whirlwind of college faculty and Alsatian dogs and vandals and…" She looked about hopelessly. "Virginia is looking rather attractive."

* * * * *

Tuesday, February 2, 1915

On Tuesday morning, Aunt Thea had already retrieved the newspaper for her husband when Emma entered the kitchen. Uncle Gregory unfolded the paper while his wife spooned up a bowl of oatmeal for him.

Emma smiled and laid the folder she carried on the table. "Good morning! What's in the headlines, Uncle Gregory?"

He grunted.

Aunt Thea turned from the stove with the ironstone bowl in her hands. "The British have captured another American ship, that's what! I don't know how they get away with that. We're a neutral country. Neutral. That means we don't fight."

"Maybe not for long if the British keep this up," Uncle Gregory said.

"That's right. We'll be fighting England soon." Aunt Thea thumped the bowl onto the table. "You want some oatmeal, Emma?"

"Thank you. That would taste good." Emma bit back a comment on the tense situation between the United States and Britain. England saw intercepting cargoes to combatants as an acceptable act of war, even when the ship flew under the flag of a neutral country. At least they hadn't sunk the ship or killed the crew.

"I hope you slept well?"

Emma smiled at her aunt. "Yes, thank you. I believe I'm catching up on my sleep."

"I dreamed about Alfred last night." Her aunt went to the cupboard for another bowl.

Emma walked over to the ice box and took out a quart of milk. "I hope the dream didn't upset you."

"Not nearly so badly as those English do."

Emma sat down and closed her eyes for a moment, offering a silent blessing. When she opened them, Aunt Thea had brought her oatmeal. Emma poured milk on it and reached for the sugar bowl. "I don't understand why the United States is aiding Germany anyway. That's why the British are intercepting our ships—we're aiding their enemies."

"Emma!" Her uncle lowered his newspaper and scowled at her. "Are you forgetting that we are of German heritage?"

His belligerence startled her. "No, sir, I'm not."

"Well then. Remember, you still have relatives living there."

"Yes, sir."

"You don't want us to go to war with our own families, do you?"

"No, of course not, Uncle, but neither can I countenance some of the things Germany has done lately."

"Is your young man going to come around today?" Aunt Thea asked.

"Who, Lieutenant Patterson?" Emma swiveled to look at her. Although she was glad for the change of topic, she didn't want her aunt and uncle to misinterpret her relationship to John. "He's hardly my young man, Auntie."

"Nonsense. He's hung about here for three days when I expect he could have had better things to do."

Emma sprinkled sugar over her oatmeal. Were her aunt and uncle upset because she'd formed a friendship with a military officer? Certainly she was old enough to choose her own friends—and suitors, too. "Well, he did say he'd help me finish up at Father's office."

"What needs to be done?" Aunt Thea asked.

"Not much. There are a few more things to collect, and then I'll scrub it down."

"I will go with you."

Emma opened her mouth and then closed it. No doubt Aunt Thea considered her time spent alone with John in the office scandalous.

"What do we need?" her aunt asked. "Broom? Mop?"

"Yes, and rags. Castile soap and the scrub bucket."

"Fine, then. After we eat, we go and scrub."

Emma finished her breakfast in silence, thinking about what Uncle Gregory had said. In an ideal world, there would be no war. President Wilson seemed to think America could stay out of the turmoil in Europe and trade with both sides. Emma wasn't so sure. It would be horrible if America did get mixed up in the war, and yet, how much more horrible if they stayed neutral and watched countries like England and France beaten down and overrun? And what about the job opening in Virginia? If she went for the interview and was offered a position, what role would she play in the hostilities?

The thought that war might actually come to the United States caused her heart to pound. It couldn't happen—or could it? John had implied that already things were going on within the borders of the United States that could lead to warfare in the near future. She'd always considered herself a serene academic, like her father. Yet during the conflict with Spain, he hadn't hesitated to serve his country, and neither would she. If America had to fight, she would wrestle and claw with all her strength. But she would risk another stern lecture if she voiced these thoughts before her uncle.

The phone rang in the dining room. Emma hurried to answer it, wiping her hands on her napkin as she walked.

"Is Mr. Meyer there?"

"Yes. One moment please." Emma let the earpiece dangle and walked back to the kitchen, marveling at the rudeness of the man on the phone—calling without identifying himself. "The call is for you, Uncle Gregory."

He grunted and shoved his chair back, using the table to lever himself to his feet.

"You are finished?" Aunt Thea reached for Emma's dirty dishes.

Emma looked at the clock. It would be another half hour before John met her at the office. "Yes, thank you. I think I'll have a cup of tea."

A moment later, she carried her cup and papers through the dining room.

Uncle Gregory's voice rose in protest as he spoke to the caller. "*Nein*, you mustn't let him do that."

Emma kept walking and sat down in the parlor. The papers were some she'd brought home from the campus office. She hoped she could sort through them before it was time to meet John.

Uncle Gregory's voice again grew louder, and she winced. His obvious agitation made her wonder if the "he" under discussion was her cousin Herman.

He hung up the earpiece none too gently and stomped into the kitchen. Emma could hear him clearly. "Althea! I must go."

"What? What is happening?"

"Business. I must leave at once."

* * * * *

John entered the science building as classes changed. He walked up the stairs against a wash of students flowing downward. On the third floor, all was quiet, though a couple of doors stood open. Professor Shuster's was closed and locked. He took up his post beside it in the hallway and waited for Emma.

Five minutes later, he heard labored breathing and footsteps on the stairs. He hurried forward.

Emma and her aunt had paused at the landing between floors. Mrs. Meyer panted and fumbled with the buttons of her coat.

John scurried down the steps and reached for the mop Emma carried over her shoulder. "Good morning, ladies. Allow me to help you." Emma surrendered her mop, and he stooped and retrieved the bucket beside Aunt Thea. "Let me carry these. Are you all right, ma'am?"

Aunt Thea nodded. "Just catching my breath, young man."

Emma smiled at him. "Good morning, John. As you can see, Aunt Thea and I came prepared to work."

"Then we shall be done in short order."

Emma glided ahead of them and unlocked the door. John stayed near her aunt. When he and Mrs. Meyer reached the office, Emma had opened the door. She took a quick look inside then stood back to let Althea enter. "Uncle Gregory left this morning," she murmured.

John arched his eyebrows. "Is everything all right?"

"He took a call and said he was needed on business matters. Auntie will stay a few days longer."

John nodded, wishing they could discuss it in private. Emma seemed more disturbed by the incident than her words revealed. "Let's get at it, then."

In the next hour, he finished packing up the professor's belongings and carried the remaining boxes out to his car. He scrubbed the top bookshelves, and Aunt Thea did the lower ones, while Emma polished the desk, chairs, and oak filing cabinets. The women had him help move the furniture to one side so they could wash the floor. John and Emma had just pushed the desk across the room when a young woman entered.

"Excuse me, are you Lieutenant Patterson?"

John straightened. "Yes. May I help you?"

"There's a telephone call for you downstairs, sir."

That couldn't be good. He'd left the college switchboard number with his superiors and told them he'd be at the Searles Science Building all morning. No one else would call him here. He put on a big smile. "If you'll excuse me, ladies, I promise to return as soon as possible."

He hurried down to the office, where an older woman gestured toward the telephone. John put the receiver to his ear. "Lieutenant Patterson here."

"This is Captain Waller. You're still in Maine then, Patterson."

"Yes, sir." Even though his captain was hundreds of miles away and couldn't see him, John stood at attention.

"How far are you from the New Brunswick border?"

"Uh—I'm not sure, sir, but I can ask someone here in the office."

"No, don't do that. Here's the deal: the bridge over the St. Croix River at Vanceboro, Maine, was bombed early this morning. I want you to get over there and find out what's going on."

John swallowed hard and glanced around. The three women in the room weren't even pretending to work but were watching him. "Could you give me any more information about that, sir?"

"Some fool German sympathizer tried to blow up the railroad bridge between Maine and Canada. No one was hurt, but they tell me a lot of windows in the town shattered, and there's minor damage to the bridge."

"All right."

"The police nabbed a suspect. I'm authorizing you to question him. I expect the Justice Department has men on the way, but you're close enough that you might beat them to it. I'll alert the civilian authorities that you're coming."

"Very good, sir."

"And, Lieutenant, phone me as soon as you have any information. This fellow wasn't working alone."

"Yes, sir."

"Oh, say, Patterson, any progress on the other matter?"

John couldn't speak frankly about Emma's situation with the office workers listening, so he simply said, "I believe so, sir. I'll report to you on that in full when I get to the destination you just mentioned."

"All right. I hope you've urged her to join us."

"Yes, sir."

"And will she bring her father's coding machine?"

"I'm not sure yet, sir."

"Well, get over to the border as quickly as you can."

John hung up and thanked the woman who seemed to be in charge of the office, then hurried back upstairs. He wasn't ready to leave Emma behind, but he was probably within hours of the bombing site. The navy brass made the logical choice in sending him. A few other attempts to disrupt railroad lines between the United States and Canada had been reported, but those were farther west. The saboteurs had turned their eyes on new targets.

When he reached Professor Shuster's office, Emma was on her knees in one corner while her aunt wielded the mop in front of the filing cabinets.

John hurried to Emma, being careful not to step on the portion of the floor they'd already scrubbed. "I'm afraid I'll have to leave you ladies."

Emma stood and gazed at him, the scrub rag dangling from her hand. "Immediately?"

"Yes. At least, I need to call the train depot and find out whether it would be more efficient for me to take the hired car or ride a train, but either way, I must go at once."

"Where are you going?" Aunt Thea asked.

"I'm sorry, ma'am. I can't tell you that."

Emma gave a quick nod. "If you'd like some privacy for your telephoning, you could go over to our house. There's nobody there right now except the dogs."

"Thank you." He considered that for a moment. "Perhaps I'll do that, if you don't mind. And I need to have your decision and leave you a contact number."

Emma smiled up at him. "I've made my decision, and it's yes. I'll go."

He couldn't hold back a grin. "Wonderful. I'll give you full instructions on what to do when you reach Washington."

"What?" Aunt Thea strode across the wet floor and glared at him. "What is this? Emma, going to Washington? You mean Washington, D.C.?"

Emma placed her hand on her aunt's shoulder. "It's all right, Auntie. Lieutenant Patterson told me yesterday of this opportunity for a job in northern Virginia."

"You didn't tell us."

"I'm sorry, but I wanted some time to think it over before I let you know." Emma looked back at John. "When will I go?"

"As soon as you are able." He reached into his uniform pocket and handed her a small card. "This is the captain's address and the phone number at his office. I'll inform him of your decision, and he will contact you. In light of my new orders, perhaps I'll let his office tell you what to do, but I expect when you go, you'll take the train from Portland to Washington, and someone will meet you there."

"Who?" Aunt Thea's frown would have wilted an oak tree. "Who will meet her? What will she do? Where will she stay?"

John held up a hand. "I don't know precisely, but I assure you it's all right. She'll be in good hands." He retrieved his coat and hat from the hooks on the back of the door. "Miss Shuster, just go about what you're doing—closing the professor's office and your house. When you are ready to go, telephone the captain, and arrangements will be made."

"All right." Her blue eyes teemed with questions, but she didn't speak.

"I could drive you ladies home…"

"No," she said. "We're nearly done here. I'd like to know the job is finished. But let me give you my key." She went to where her coat hung and took it from the pocket.

"Thank you. If you arrive home before I've finished, I shall see you. If not…where shall I leave this?"

She hesitated only a moment. "There's a ledge above the porch stoop. If you put it up there in the center, I'll be able to reach it."

"All right. Good-bye, Emma." He glanced toward Mrs. Meyer, who watched with narrowed eyes. Did she think Emma trusted him too easily? If she only knew, the suspicion between them was mutual. He wasn't at all happy leaving her in her aunt's care. John gave Emma's hand a quick squeeze and hurried out the door.

CHAPTER EIGHT

Monday, February 22, 1915

Three weeks later, the navy ensign who'd met Emma at Union Station in Washington drove up before a four-story stone building flanked by others much like it. "This is your boardinghouse."

Emma looked the house over, enjoying the balmy air. She could hardly believe it was still the month of February. She could wish for a less urban setting and some lawn, but she must take what they handed her, at least until she got her feet under her. Perhaps later she would have the option to find more pleasant lodgings. "And what is the name of the town?"

"Fairfax, ma'am. You can take the trolley into the city anytime. The electric cars run several times a day. Come, I'll take you in, and we'll see if young Draper's around to help unload your trunk."

"Young Draper?"

"Mrs. Draper owns this building. She's a widow, but she has a strapping son who helps about the place when she nags him."

They walked up to the front door, and Ensign Belton rapped on it.

A stout, middle-aged woman opened the door. "Well now, this be the young lady I'm expecting, for certain. I'm Mrs. Draper."

Emma held out her hand, and the landlady took it. "How do you do? I'm Emma Shuster."

"I gave you the back room on the second floor, though Louise Newton wanted it." Something about the way she hiked her chin told Emma that Mrs. Draper was not overly fond of Louise Newton. "The rent be five dollars a week. Three dollars more if you want board. I make lunches for my boarders to take to work."

"That will be fine."

"One week in advance, please."

Emma found a five-dollar bill and three ones in her purse and handed them over. Her remaining cash supply was quite meager, though she had about two hundred dollars in the bank, back in Maine. It was all that remained of her father's pay from the college and her own small savings.

Mrs. Draper nodded and slipped the money into her apron pocket.

"We've got a trunk to take up a flight of stairs," Belton said.

Mrs. Draper frowned. "I'll see if Lonnie can help with it." She backed into the entrance hall. "Come in, miss. Now, all my renters are nice young ladies what work for the government. In fact, military men such as the one yonder"—she nodded after Belton, who had retreated down the steps toward the car—"brung the better part of them. Don't know what the military wants with them all. They don't wear uniforms, the ladies don't, but they go to their jobs every morning, regular as clockwork. Secretaries, likely. Is that what you're doing?"

"I'm not sure exactly what my duties will be yet." Emma felt her face color and hoped Mrs. Draper didn't think ill of her. She simply didn't know what to expect yet. "You see, I am interviewing for a position tomorrow, and I believe they'll tell me then."

"Ah." Mrs. Draper gave a sage nod. Without further warning, she turned her head and shouted, "Lonnie!"

Emma flinched and took a step backward.

"Lonnie! Come help the gentleman with the new boarder's trunk!"

A large young man with a rounded belly and puffy cheeks shuffled into a doorway down the hall. "What, another one?"

"You mind your manners," said his mother. "Come now. The captain's waiting for you to help him."

Lonnie trudged toward the front door, casting Emma an appraising glance as he passed her. He looked out at Belton, who had the suitcase out of the car and waited near the rear tire. "That ain't no captain, Ma. The man's only an ensign."

"Well, he's got more braid than you. Go on now."

In the second floor hall, Mrs. Draper took Emma to a closed, white-painted door and opened it. The landlady stepped back and let her new boarder enter first.

Looking about, Emma smiled. Two large windows let sunshine in, and the bare branches of a couple of trees could be seen outside. There must be a backyard out there. The single bed had maple head and foot boards with decorative spindles, and a cheerful green and yellow quilt topped the mattress.

"I provide clean sheets and towels every Saturday," Mrs. Draper said.

A nightstand, a white-painted bureau, a desk, and two straight chairs completed the furnishings. Over the desk hung an etching of the Capitol building, and on the opposite wall, near the closet door, a spring landscape added a bright note to the pale, gray-striped wallpaper. The braided rug on the floor by the bed echoed the green in the quilt, muted with black and gray. Simple and plain, but comfortable.

"You can use your own decorations if you like," the landlady said. "The bathroom is down the hall. You'll share that with three other ladies."

"I think this will do nicely."

Mrs. Draper let out her breath in a puff. "Well then, that's settled. Don't pound nails in the walls, and report any damages immediately. Supper is at six. If you're kept late at work, I keep a plate for you until eight. Later than that, and you're on your own. Breakfast from six to seven, and luncheon at noon if you're here. The sack lunches will be ready at breakfast time for those that take them. Do you want one tomorrow?"

"Uh—I'm not sure." They heard heavy footsteps on the stairs, and Emma said quickly, "I have an interview with my potential employers tomorrow."

Belton's tall, straight back appeared in the doorway, followed by her trunk. Lonnie entered last, holding up the other end of the burden and puffing as he staggered forward.

"Where to, miss?" Belton gasped.

"Right there beside the closet door." Emma pointed, they complied, and everyone sighed. "Thank you, gentlemen."

Lonnie said, "I'll fetch your suitcase, miss."

"If you're satisfied then, Miss Shuster?" Belton arched his eyebrows and waited.

"Yes, thank you."

He nodded. "You will excuse me, then. I or another driver will fetch you in the morning at eight o'clock. If you're hired, you'll find your own transportation after that."

"I expect the other young ladies can tell you the best trolley and such," said Mrs. Draper.

When the two men and the landlady had left her alone, Emma sat on the edge of the bed. She was tempted to undress and take a nap, but she was afraid she would sleep through the supper hour. She forayed into the hall and found the bathroom. The fixtures were up to date, with running water in the taps on the porcelain tub. Most satisfactory, and she wouldn't have to go down to the cellar to feed the furnace, as she and Father had done in Maine.

She felt better about her venture. The lodgings weren't bad, and if things didn't work out… No, she wouldn't think that way. But if they didn't, she would accept Vivian's invitation and return to her friend's home in Connecticut, where job prospects seemed promising.

She'd managed to avoid staying at the Meyers' house but had spent a few days with Gretchen and Henry and then had traveled to Vivian's house near Hartford. While staying there, she'd finished up her business with the banking corporation and delivered her father's project to them—minus the cipher machine, which they'd decided not to take in its unfinished state. When the final word came from Captain Waller, she had set out from Vivian's house for Washington.

As she headed back to her room, three women came quickly up the stairs, chattering without regard for anyone who might overhear.

"So, Mary's room is let already," said a red-haired girl with plain features and hazel eyes. "We'll have someone new to chum with."

"I wanted that room," said a tall dishwater blond with a pout to her lips.

"Hush, you two." The young woman in the lead had spotted Emma. "I suspect the object of your conversation stands before us."

The trio gained the landing and clustered about her.

"Hello." The redhead extended her hand. "I'm Doris."

"And I'm Louise," said the blond. Up close, Emma could see that she was a few years older than the other two. "This is Freddie. We're your hall mates, it seems."

The petite brunette smiled as she shook Emma's hand. "Welcome to Draper's Dormitory, as we've dubbed it."

Emma chuckled. "Thank you. I'm Emma Shuster."

"Where are you from?" Doris asked, eyeing her with a slight frown.

"No, wait. Let me guess," Freddie said. "But first, would you please say something else?"

"What sort of thing?" Emma asked.

"Just whatever you'd like."

"All right. Perhaps you ladies could tell me about working in the city, or trains, or government jobs—well, just everything." Emma felt her cheeks flush. "I'm sorry. I'm not usually so inquisitive. But the navy man who brought me here didn't tell me much, and I confess I wasn't comfortable asking too many questions."

"Navy man?" Louise grinned. "Was he handsome?"

"I suspect you're here to work for the Signal Corps," Doris said.

Freddie raised her hand in triumph. "And *I* suspect you're from New England. Massachusetts, maybe."

"Maine, actually."

Freddie snapped her fingers with an exaggerated wince. "So close."

Emma laughed. "A hundred years ago, it was part of Massachusetts, if that makes you feel better."

"It does. Much."

"I work for the Signal Corps," Doris said softly.

Emma turned to her and smiled. "Really? How wonderful."

"Yes, I'm a typist. There are two more ladies on the third floor who take the same trolley as me every morning, but they work in the Labor Department offices. Are you going to start work tomorrow?"

"I don't know," Emma said. "Someone's going to fetch me at eight in the morning for an interview. Oh, and should I have Mrs. Draper fix me a lunch?"

"Yes, take one," Doris said. "If they take you out to eat, you can save the bag lunch for a snack."

"Or feed the birds," Louise said.

The young women talked for a few more minutes, until Freddie looked at her pendant watch. "Dinner's in ten minutes, girls. Look sharp."

They scattered to their rooms. As Emma opened her door, Freddie called down the hall, "I'm here in number seven, if you need anything."

Emma returned to her own chamber and brushed her hair. This was almost fun. She'd had first-day-at-boarding-school butterflies, but the other boarders seemed like a pleasant group of hardworking young women.

Over the supper table, she learned that Freddie worked in the accounting division of Virginia's retirement department for state employees, and Louise was a stenographer for a law firm. Freddie seemed the most fun-loving. Doris was more earnest, but Emma liked her. If she received the job, she'd have Doris as a coworker—a pleasant prospect. Five other boarders joined them at the table, and Emma gave up keeping all the names straight.

She unpacked her suitcase after the meal, yawning all the while, and decided to let her trunk sit until morning. As she prepared for bed, she took her Bible from the nightstand and read a short psalm then closed her eyes.

Thank You, dear Father, for my safe journey here, for making my path smooth, for Ensign Belton and Mrs. Draper and the other boarders.

Trying to remember the names of all those she'd met at supper, she dropped off to sleep.

* * * * *

Tuesday, February 23, 1915

The next morning, the other boarders had all left the house when a car arrived for Emma. She hurried outside carrying her lunch sack and a leather carryall, noting that her knees trembled. She sent up a swift prayer as a uniformed man got out of the car.

"Miss Shuster?"

"Yes."

"Good morning. I'm here to take you to Captain Waller." He opened the passenger door for her, and Emma climbed in.

What would she do if Captain Waller didn't think she would perform well at the job? She bit her lower lip and tried to stop thinking about the uncertain future. Everything was strange here. Though the day was much warmer than what she'd been accustomed to in Maine Februarys, she still shivered. The city streets they traveled seemed to her cold and unforgiving. The job, which she only knew had some connection to cryptography, loomed before her as a huge unknown.

Heavenly Father, if this isn't where You want me, You'll have to provide something else.

The driver took her on a thirty-minute ride to a military compound and delivered her to an office. Emma sat on a hard bench for twenty minutes. The woman at the desk kept busy at a typewriting machine. Several times the telephone at the side of her desk rang and she answered it in ostentatious tones. A young man wearing a suit came in from the hall, spoke to the woman, and took a seat.

Finally a white-haired man in full uniform came out of the room behind the typist's desk, glanced about, and settled his gaze on Emma with a nod. "Miss Shuster, come this way, please."

Emma picked up her carryall and followed him into a smaller room that reminded her of her father's office—built-in bookshelves on two sides, a large desk, and several cabinets for papers. A painting of a ship of the line hung behind the desk, and two padded chairs awaited the captain's visitors.

He turned and faced her. "I'm Captain Waller. It's a pleasure to meet you." He shook her hand. "I had the utmost respect for your father."

"Thank you, sir."

"I'm sorry he's gone, and I hope that if you find yourself in need, you will call upon me."

Emma's eyes teared up, and a lump filled her throat. She nodded and tried for a grateful smile.

"Please have a seat."

Emma sank into one of the chairs.

The captain settled into the large chair behind his desk. "Lieutenant Patterson gave me a glowing report on your abilities, but also on your poise and deportment. In this organization, temperament can be as crucial as intelligence."

"Oh? I'm not certain what type of position is being proposed."

"Good. Patterson was under orders not to say too much. You must have gathered that we at the Signal Corps deal in communications."

"Yes, sir. I will go so far as to say that I felt my cryptography work with my father led directly to this expedition."

He smiled, the creases in his face sliding into pleasant lines of amusement. "It's true. We're not currently at war, but that could change at any time. We have of late concentrated on three goals in the Corps, ma'am. First, to help the Allies—that is, those we assume will be our allies if we join this great conflict. We in the United States have many reasons for wanting to see England and her friends come out the victors."

Emma nodded. "I feel the same way, though I realize all has not been amicable between us and the British."

"No, we've had some trouble with them where shipping and free trade are concerned." Waller shrugged. "However, we shall put that aside for now. Officially, we can't do much in that quarter at present, but if our activities bring us knowledge that will help the Allies, we'll share it with them."

He sat back in his chair and eyed her gravely. "Our second purpose is to gather all the information we can, so we'll be ready if this country should enter the war. There is much we can learn now to help us know the principal combatants better. And knowledge, as you know, is power."

"Yes. I can see that it would be helpful to enter a conflict armed with certain information about the enemy."

"Indeed. And our third purpose..." He paused and gazed for a moment toward the window. When he looked back at her, his face was grim. "Miss Shuster, during the past three weeks, I've had your background examined minutely."

She swallowed hard, wondering just what he had discovered. Did he know she'd been involved in a rather foolish prank in high school, or that she'd failed some of her examinations the year her mother died? That she'd visited her mother's grave weekly while she lived in Maine, or that she'd exchanged hundreds of letters with her girlhood friend, Vivian?

"I tell you this," Waller said, "so that you understand my confidence in you. I don't speak so frankly to all our candidates. But from what I've learned of your character, and I must admit, because of your father's character, I don't hesitate to tell you that we also engage in trying to stop espionage and destruction within these United States."

CHAPTER NINE

Tuesday, February 23, 1915

Emma inhaled slowly. The bridge at Vanceboro. She'd read about its bombing in the newspaper the day after John left. That was the type of activity Captain Waller wanted to thwart. "There was an incident a few weeks ago—when Lieutenant Patterson was in Brunswick," she said. "A bridge on the Canadian border…"

"Yes. That's precisely what I'm talking about. Bridges, warehouses, cargo ships. All are targets for those hoping to keep us at odds with our friends. They'd like us to wonder whose side we should come down on, to keep us so busy at home that we don't want to look beyond our borders."

"And the Signal Corps can help stop these saboteurs." She knew it even as she said it.

Captain Waller opened a desk drawer and took out several sheets of paper. He leaned forward and slid the top one across the desk toward her. "Do you know what this is?"

Emma picked it up and studied it carefully for several seconds. The groups of letters presented gibberish to the untrained eye. "It appears to be an enciphered message."

His eyes glinted. "And what type of cipher would you deem it to be?"

She perused the sheet again. "I can't say for certain without further study, but I would guess a simple substitution cipher. I see some pattern words. If it is a simple substitution, it wouldn't be difficult to solve."

"And this?" He handed her another paper.

The second sheet held columns of figures, all in groups of five digits each. "Ah. This is more complicated. If it is a cipher, I'd say it's a combination substitution and transposition, set up to be transmitted by telegraph."

"Oh, Miss Shuster, you have no idea the sweet music you've brought to my ears. If you think you would like to work for us, we would love to have you as one of our staff. The salary would be thirty dollars per week."

Emma pulled in a steadying breath. The pay was better than she had hoped. "Yes, sir, I would like to work with the Signal Corps."

"Wonderful. Do you speak any languages other than English?"

"I studied French in high school and college, and I learned some German as a child. I didn't want to lose that because of family ties, so I took two semesters at Smith."

"Ah, yes. Shuster. Very Teutonic. I don't believe your father spoke the language, though."

"No, he didn't—at least, not more than a few words. But I lived with my aunt and uncle for a time while Father was in the navy, and my uncle speaks it."

"Excellent." A gentle tap came at the door, and Waller called, "Yes, Miss Edson?"

The typist opened the door partway. "Lieutenant Patterson is here, sir."

Emma's pulse skyrocketed. John was here? She'd hoped to see him in Virginia but had no idea when their next meeting would take place.

"Send him right in," Waller said.

Almost at once, John strode into the room, taller and more handsome than Emma had remembered, and she recalled him as being one of the most dashing men she'd ever met. She jumped up and faced him, unable to rein in her smile.

John nodded first at Waller. "Sir." His gaze swung to Emma. "Miss Shuster, I'm delighted to find you here. I trust you had a pleasant journey."

"Yes, thank you." With John in the same room, she was ready to erase from her memory the many discomforts of her long train trip.

"Please sit down, both of you," Waller said. "There's one more thing we need to discuss, Miss Shuster, and then I'll send you over to meet Mrs. Harper and our senior cryptographer."

"Yes, sir?" Emma settled back in her chair and smoothed her skirt.

"I noticed the large bag you brought in with you. I hope I'm not remiss in thinking it might contain your father's work?"

"Why, yes, Captain. Lieutenant Patterson specified that I should bring my father's code machine with me if the bank didn't want it. I contacted them and they were appreciative of the encryption system my father had developed for them but said the machine was no use to them in its current state. It wasn't part of Father's original proposal to them, so they decided not to pursue it. I also brought copies of his work on that project."

"I am aware of the job your father did. I'm glad you were able to complete it for him."

Emma rose and lifted the carryall to the desktop. "The machine was commissioned as an afterthought—when Father suggested it, they told him to go ahead and develop it. But it's not quite finished, so they haven't seen it in action. I don't think they quite grasped Father's vision for it. So it's in here, along with my father's papers pertaining to it. There are more files in my trunk at Mrs. Draper's. I do hope they are safe there. She gave me a key to my room, and I've locked it, but…"

"If you wish, you may bring them here to be placed in our vault."

"Thank you. I've also included the sketches Father made. The young man who constructed the machine added some scale drawings of his own." As she spoke, she opened the bag and set the papers on the desk.

She reached in to lift out the apparatus, and John sprang to help her. "As I said, this is not quite finished, and I believe that in practice several machines would be required. Father said it was only the beginning and that he would have to develop and perfect it over time. Now he won't be able to do that, but perhaps someone else can."

Waller bent over the machine and examined it eagerly. "May we keep this to study?"

"Certainly."

Waller straightened and looked into her eyes. "Do you believe it is a practical apparatus?"

"It's awkward, and I don't think it carries the principles of encryption far enough. Father wanted to make a machine that would change the cipher key with each transmission, but of course, that means that the receiver must also know what the new key is in order to solve the ciphers."

Waller nodded. "That's the biggest dilemma we have for sending messages undetected. It's a boon to us that our enemies haven't mastered the problem yet, either. But if someone could come up with a device that would change the key randomly and yet let the recipient know what key to use…yes, that's a tricky problem."

"I'm afraid it would take a much larger, more complex machine on each end, and a better method of key distribution," Emma said. "This machine is not capable of that."

John cleared his throat. "I believe Professor Shuster also conceived of printing pads for the cipher makers, so that each had sheets of random keys in the same order."

"That's right," Emma said. "But the tablets of cipher keys would still have to be distributed, though not so often as individual keys would."

Waller nodded. "An interesting concept. I can see how it would save the risk of exchanging keys often, yet if the key pad itself were captured, that batch would be worse than useless. It would reveal all to the enemy." He lifted the machine back into the bag. "I'd love to continue this discussion, but I'm keeping people waiting. We must speak again soon."

"I should like that, sir."

"I did want to speak to you briefly about your father's death."

Emma's heart lurched.

"Please sit down again." They all resumed their seats, and Waller met her gaze across the desk. "We've made some discreet inquiries, and it seems to us that whoever killed your father hoped to gain possession of this machine and the encryption system he developed for the bank."

Emma swallowed hard and nodded. "I've had those thoughts myself. I can't imagine any other reason someone would kill him. But I didn't like to discuss the project with the local police."

"We appreciate that. Our investigators have gone at it from the bank's end. We believe that German sympathizers in this country are trying to arrange funding for their activities here from within Germany or Austria. This would necessitate a legitimate bank account here for them to draw upon to pay agitators and saboteurs to carry out their plans."

"And they are using the bank my father worked for?"

"We're not sure. But we believe that's how they learned of his project. There may be a sympathizer among the bank's officers, perhaps a board member, who told them about the cipher project. This would interest them, of course. They could pass the system on to their counterparts in Germany."

"Aren't the Germans already further advanced in cryptography than we are?"

"Yes, I believe they are. But your father's system was of necessity very secure, and very difficult to crack. That would be useful to them. And this machine, if it worked the way he envisioned, would put them into a new league of secret communication." Waller glanced at his wristwatch. "I have an important meeting, so I'll have Lieutenant Patterson take you back to Fairfax, to meet Agnes Harper."

John nodded as though he knew Mrs. Harper well.

"She will explain our procedures and protocols to you and give you a tour of our offices at Trafton House," Waller said. "We keep our cryptologists in a quiet place, away from the military bases. The public has no idea that this division of the Signal Corps exists. In fact, it hasn't for very long. We've just started pulling talent together to decipher intercepted messages of a political or military nature. In the past, the Navy has handled this as a routine part of the Signal Corps' duties, but the increase in volume of ciphers... Some of our best officers from the Signal Corps are detailed there now, with Commander Robert Howe in charge. You'll meet him, and..." He slapped his hand down on the desktop. "Well, enough for now. Trafton House will be your workplace, beginning tomorrow, if you're willing."

"I am, sir." Emma glanced at John, and he smiled at her. She turned her attention back to the captain for fear she would blush scarlet otherwise.

"Mrs. Harper will also see that you get signed up for your regular paycheck. For the next few days, you'll attend orientation sessions and some classes on specific methods of solving ciphers in English, Spanish, French, German, and Italian. Sound good?"

"A little intimidating, but I look forward to it."

Waller nodded. "That's the spirit."

Emma rose and extended her hand. "Thank you very much, Captain."

"Delighted to be of service, and to welcome you into our fold, Miss Shuster." He looked at John. "Patterson, take good care of this young lady."

* * * * *

They walked through the outer office where the stenographer had her desk. Several men appeared to be waiting to see Captain Waller.

John opened the door for Emma. With the office behind them, he fell into step with her. "The car is right here." He swallowed. "Emma, I must say you're looking well."

"Thank you. I had some trepidation in coming here alone, but I feel God has worked this out for me." She kept her eyes downcast, but he felt her excitement as she walked beside him toward the vehicle. "Lieu—John—I'm so glad to see you again."

He opened the car door for her. "I hoped you'd be here when I got back."

"How long have you been back in Virginia?"

"Only since Saturday. I was quite awhile in the North."

"You had something to do with the bombing in Vanceboro."

He smiled but avoided responding directly to her remark. Emma was quick at putting two and two together. She ought to fit right in with the code breakers. He cranked the engine and walked around to the driver's seat. "I'm shuttled about here and there, wherever they need me. I came most recently from Chicago."

"I see. I shan't ask why you were there."

He drove to the gate of the military compound then guided the car onto a busy street. "Trafton House, where they are setting up the cipher division, is much closer to your lodgings than this is."

She raised her eyebrows and stared in mock consternation. "Aha. So you know where my lodgings are."

John chuckled. "It's one of the first bits of information I ferreted out when I got back here."

"And do you know Mrs. Draper?"

"I've met her once, when it was my assignment to pick up one of her boarders. I believe the government recommends her to its employees because she's shown she can be discreet." He checked his mirror and turned left onto a quieter avenue. "So, how have you really been, Emma? Have the past few weeks been difficult?"

"I've missed Father terribly."

"Of course."

Her feathery lashes shielded her eyes as she gazed down at her gloved hands. "I got everything packed up and found a farmer who would store most of my things in a corner of his barn. Aunt Thea wanted the dining room table and chairs, and I let her have them, but I told her I wanted to keep the rest of the furniture."

"Good for you. Someday you'll have a home for it."

She grimaced. "I wonder."

"Where did you stay after you left Brunswick?"

"I went to my cousin Gretchen's for a few days, until I heard from my friend Vivian. She urged me to stay with her in Connecticut until it was time to come south, and that was a big relief. I loved visiting with Vivian again—we've been best friends since fourth grade. And she was near enough to the bank's headquarters that I was able to meet with their officers concerning Father's work."

She shook her head. "Vivian's invitation was such a blessing. I couldn't bear to stay long with Gretchen and Henry, but I didn't want to go to Aunt Thea's. I knew I'd be uncomfortable there, what with Uncle Gregory and the Alsatians and Herman."

John smiled grimly. "Not the pet I'd choose, either. The Alsatians, I mean."

Emma chuckled, and he noted how pretty she looked with her eyes bright and her cheeks flushed. "To be honest, the Meyers' home is not a happy one. Herman seems to be all the time at odds with his parents, but he doesn't take the initiative to move out and find his own place."

"He works in a mill, you said."

"Yes, there's a woolen mill a few miles away." She glanced over at him. "I had Aunt Thea with me several days after you left, and she insisted on looking through all of Father's papers herself. I was glad I'd gone into his study first and removed a few things."

"Like the papers concerning the cipher project?"

"Yes. And his checkbook. That's terrible of me to say, but meager as his funds were, I wanted to be the one to disburse them."

"I don't blame you."

She looked out the windshield. "What can you tell me about where we're going now?"

"We're nearly there. It's a graceful old building that no one thinks twice about. No sign or anything designating it as part of the navy, but a guard is on duty inside the front door all the time. No one goes in without security clearance."

"Do I have that?"

"They'll give you a temporary document until they have your badge made up. Then you'll show it each morning when you go to work."

"And the captain mentioned a Mrs. Harper. Who is she?"

"You'll like Mrs. Harper. Her husband's out to sea, and she works for the navy as civilian support. She's basically an office manager. Commander Howe runs the cipher-breaking outfit, and he's very good at it himself. Mrs. Harper tends to the mundane details. Payroll records and so on. She has a knack for administration." He drove into a gravel lot before a large stone building. "This is it."

John turned to observe her as she surveyed the place. He didn't want to take her in and leave her there without knowing when they'd meet again. He pulled in a deep breath. "Emma, could I possibly see you this weekend?"

She turned and studied him gravely. "I—think I'll be free. Actually, I have no idea what I'll be doing by then, but yes, if it works for both our schedules, I'd like that." Bright red spots stained her cheeks. She looked up at him, her dreamy eyes eager.

"Is there a telephone where you're staying?" he asked.

"I believe there is, but I don't know the number."

"I'll find it." Learning Mrs. Draper's telephone number would be child's play. He took a small card from his jacket pocket. "This is the number where I board. If for some reason you can't make it, call and leave a message. Otherwise, may I pick you up at ten Saturday morning? We could make a day of it. Take the trolley into the city if you'd like."

"I'd love to see the White House and the Capitol and some of the other sights."

"I thought you might. The view from the Washington Monument is especially striking. Shall we plan on it then?"

"Yes, thank you. But what if you're sent away with unexpected orders?"

"I'll get a message to you somehow. Now, are you ready for your next interview?"

She nodded, pursing her lips. "It's a bit nerve-wracking, meeting all these people, but I believe I'll find the work itself satisfying."

"I'll pray it is so, and that you make new friends here." He got out of the car and went around to help her out. They walked up to the door, and he rapped with the knocker.

A petty officer opened the door.

John showed his credentials. "Hello, Murray."

"Ah, Lieutenant Patterson. Who's your guest, sir?"

"Miss Shuster, to see Mrs. Harper and Commander Howe."

"Very good." Murray stepped aside and let them enter.

"I'll see you to Mrs. Harper," John said, and Emma threw him a grateful smile. He removed his hat and led her down a hallway and around a corner. In a daring moment, he reached for her hand and squeezed it, then let it drop before he knocked on the door.

"Enter," came a high-pitched voice from within.

John opened the door. "Miss Shuster is here, ma'am."

"Thank you, Lieutenant."

John stepped aside for Emma and reluctantly closed the door behind her.

CHAPTER TEN

"What's the meaning of this message I received? You still haven't found her?"

"That's correct, sir. She's not staying with her relatives anymore, and they insist they don't know where she went."

Kobold swore and crumpled the message he'd spent half an hour deciphering. Into the telephone, he said, "There must be a way to find out. What about that cousin of hers?"

"He got a new job and has moved out of town."

"She stayed with the sister for a while?"

"Yes. Only a few days though," his underling said. "Then she went off, purportedly to visit a friend. No address. Our man paid a call on Cousin Gretchen, pretending to be a friend of the old professor's, but if she knows Miss Shuster's whereabouts, she's a good actress. Connecticut. That's the most we could get out of her. And our fellow thought she was getting suspicious."

Kobold brought his fist down on the wooden case of the telephone. "Did she take the machine with her?"

"We don't know. I mean—our man can't go around asking people about that, now can he?"

"Well, it wasn't in the professor's office when he was killed, and he never sent it to the bank. We know that. So where is it?" He shoved the scrap of paper into his pocket and ran his hand through his thinning hair. "There was talk about a student who worked on the machine. Did that play out?"

"We're trying to find out more about it, but the professor was very tight-lipped about the whole thing. Nobody seems to know anything about it."

"Keep trying. There must be someone at the college who knows something."

"Yes, sir. But we don't want to get the police onto our people."

"No, of course not." The local police would still be in a dither over the professor's murder. Kobold let out a sigh. "You're correct, of course. Keep it discreet. Find some young fellow who can nose around among the math students. Somebody must know something."

He hung up the receiver and sat down heavily in his padded chair. He opened the top right drawer of his desk and lifted a stack of envelopes. From beneath them, he took out a small photograph that he'd received in the mail a week earlier. Professor Alfred Shuster and his daughter. Lovely girl. Too bad she didn't value her German heritage.

* * * * *

Agnes Harper took Emma by surprise. A small-framed woman in her mid-thirties, she wore a white blouse and a soft blue skirt. Her hair was pulled into a bun. Her only jewelry was a ring set on her left hand—a gold band and a modest diamond. Emma was drawn to her at once, captivated by her beauty and her gracious smile.

"Come right in and have a seat. Would you like a cup of tea?" Mrs. Harper turned to a small gas burner in one corner of the office, where a teakettle steamed cheerfully.

"Yes, thank you." Emma crossed to a Windsor chair with a patchwork seat cushion.

Soon they sat across from each other, using Mrs. Harper's desk as a tea table. The hostess pulled a tin of shortbread biscuits from a drawer and offered it to Emma. "Today I'm going to discuss procedures with you and show you around, and then Commander Howe will give you a cipher we intercepted to try, so he can see how you work. Everyone goes at these things differently, and you'll receive some instruction on how to attempt to solve more difficult ones, but sometimes it's best to just leave a person alone to analyze the cipher on his own terms."

"What sort of material do you handle here?" Emma asked.

"A lot of military messages. Some we intercept on purpose, some by accident. Our ships take in a lot of radio messages. If they're clear, of course we never see them. But naval orders are usually in code, not ciphers. Sometimes we're able to help them out with those. Sometimes other agencies send us ciphers they've received. In a nutshell, when any of our military branches or embassies get hold of a cipher or a naval code they can't solve right away, they send it to us."

Emma nodded. She knew that each nation's ships carried code books with lead covers, so that if the ship was in danger of being captured, the officers could toss the code books overboard to prevent the enemy from getting them. Each nation developed its own complicated system of coding words and entire sentences. It worked for the navy, because only a limited number of orders were generally given to ships. For other purposes, codes lacked the necessary flexibility, so ciphers were used where individual letters or groups of letters were replaced with other letters or symbols or were scrambled, or both. The recipient needed the key to be able to read the message quickly.

"We're keeping an eye on the fleets of the combatants for the safety of our own merchant ships," Mrs. Harper said. "I hear the British are seeing some very complicated, multiple alphabet encryptions coming out of Germany and Russia, but the naval codes we get here so far have been mostly straightforward."

"I understand. Are a lot of the messages I'll see in English?" Emma asked.

"Some. But we're getting some German, French, Spanish, and Italian messages too. Our navy sometimes intercepts radio transmissions in other languages. The British are keeping an eye on the Russians, and we don't get much traffic from them directly. Recently we've seen some in Japanese." Mrs. Harper waved a dismissive hand. "Of course, I don't do any of that. It's not my cup of tea, you might say. On the other hand, I'm told you have a gift for it."

Emma ducked her head as her color rose. "We shall see. I've only worked with my father on it. My exposure to ciphers is limited, and to codes almost nil, so I'm not sure where I'll fit into all this."

"I'm sure you'll adapt quickly. We have a large room upstairs capable of housing twenty or more staff. Right now we've only a few, but Captain Waller and Commander Howe are recruiting more people with expertise in cryptography—like yourself." She smiled at Emma and sipped her tea. "One of our best cryptographers has gone to Illinois to see what he can learn at a laboratory there."

"Not the Riverbank Laboratories?" Emma asked.

"Yes. You're familiar with them?"

Emma set her cup down and shrugged. "I was a literature major before I decided to switch to mathematics. I've been following the great controversy over Francis Bacon's codes and whether or not he actually wrote Shakespeare's plays. Recently I read that the people at Riverbank are doing some work on that."

"Yes. Our goal is to learn all we can from people who are making advances in the field. We may do some collaboration with Riverbank later if it seems advantageous. So, we have several people working on ciphers here, but not enough. I'll take you to the room where they work later. First let's talk about what you'll be doing."

Emma took a small notepad from her handbag. "Do you mind if I make a few notes?"

"No, but we don't allow you to take any papers out of this building. We'll give you a small cupboard, where you can lock your belongings while you work and leave papers and things before you go home each evening. We don't even like to tell people our address. This branch of the Signal Corps is almost unknown to the public—and we want it to continue that way."

Emma hesitated before poising her pencil over the notepad. She would take notes and leave them here, where she could go over them later if need be. She wouldn't trust her memory to store all the details after hearing them only once.

"The next thing I shall tell you is something you need to memorize," Mrs. Harper said. "It's the emergency telephone number you will call if a crisis occurs."

"What sort of crisis?"

"You will know when it happens."

Emma repeated several times the number she was given without writing it down. Woolrich 8-5917. Fifty-nine: her father's age when the killer struck him down. Seventeen: her own age when she left home for Smith College.

Mrs. Harper began a thorough explanation of how each incoming cipher message was classified and catalogued and the steps Emma would take to ensure that one person did not have to repeat work she had already done.

Half an hour later, they went to the bookkeeper's office, where Emma filled out several forms, then up the stairs. They stopped first in a room where three women, Doris included, were typing.

"These ladies make copies of all the ciphers," Mrs. Harper said. "Then three people check them for accuracy. They also underline patterns and repetitions of letter groups. This frees up the cryptographers to spend more time doing their actual decryption work."

Doris and the other two women greeted Emma and Mrs. Harper with smiles and then went back to their work.

"I understand you are rooming at Mrs. Draper's, where Miss Keating lives," Agnes said.

It was the first time Emma had heard Doris's last name, but the young woman glanced over at them at the mention of her name and gave Emma a distinct wink.

Emma nearly laughed aloud. "Yes, we met last evening."

Agnes nodded with approval. As they turned to the hallway, she said, "She's quiet, but she's a nice girl. I think you'll like her. She can help you learn how to get about the city. Of course, you mustn't talk about your work outside this place."

Next they entered Room 20, a large, open room with south-facing windows. Four men, one of them in uniform, worked at long tables with their papers and books spread out around them. Mrs. Harper led

Emma to a desk behind which a man who looked to be in his forties sat surrounded by paperwork, with a half-full cup of coffee in easy reach. He stood as they drew near.

"Miss Shuster, may I present Commander Howe," said Mrs. Harper. "He's the brains of this office, and he's generally here all day to supervise the staff and help out with difficulties."

Emma extended her hand. "I'm pleased to meet you, sir."

He shook her hand with a contained smile. "Thank you. I'm sorry about your father's passing."

Emma was surprised that he knew about her father. Perhaps Captain Waller had told him the circumstances of her recruitment. "Thank you. It's an honor to be here, sir."

"We welcome you. I'm sure you'll be an asset to our team."

Agnes Harper drew her to a corner of the room lined with bookshelves. "This is our meager library. You will be able to use any of the materials here, but you cannot take them from this room. We have most of the available works on cryptography, but only a few have been translated into English. We also have frequency tables for more than thirty languages. On the third floor, we have a room full of files. We keep copies of all the messages we've worked on there."

"Both solved and unsolved?" Emma asked.

"Yes. Even if a message is old, it may be useful. That's why we require you to catalogue each message you receive and classify it. If you discover the key to a new cipher, one of our clerks goes to the files and checks to see if any other similar messages came in that were not solved. If so, they will be brought to you or another staff member to see if they can be solved with the same key."

Mrs. Harper then showed Emma to a vacant table. "Have a seat.

I hope it won't bother you to work in a room full of gentlemen. I suppose we could get you a desk in the typists' room, but it's a bit noisy in there. These fellows are all well-behaved, I assure you. And before too long, you may have other female company."

"I'm sure I'll be fine," Emma said, though she felt a bit nervous being surrounded by men. Knowing Doris and Mrs. Harper were also in the building helped.

"Good. I'll ask Commander Howe to bring you the practice cipher he wants you to work on. And I expect I shall see you at noon."

Emma sat down and drew in a shaky breath. For some reason, she felt more nervous coming face to face with a real encrypted message than she had meeting her new employers.

"There you go." The commander laid a sheet covered with jumbled letters before her. "As you can see, this cipher has already been classified for our files. We're only concerned with whether you can solve it, not whether you've mastered our filing system yet." He smiled at Emma. "If you finish before noon, please bring it to me. If not, you can bring it to me at noon and I'll put it away while we take luncheon. I believe you'll be eating with Mrs. Harper and me today in her office. We're having food sent in, so that we can talk without fear of being overhead. If you have any questions about your new position, you may ask them at that time. We'd like to get you oriented and working on incoming messages as quickly as possible."

"Thank you."

Twenty minutes' study of the cipher assured Emma she could solve it, but she doubted she could reduce the entire message to "clear" before noon unless she got a little help. She rose and went to the library corner, where one of the cryptographers was browsing through a slender volume.

"Hello," he whispered.

Emma looked up into the pleasant face of a man who wore civilian clothes. His brown hair held a sprinkling of gray.

"Hello. Mrs. Harper said there are frequency tables here."

"Yes. What language do you need?" he asked.

"English."

"Of course." He shifted a step to his left and took down a sheaf of papers held together with brads. "This has letter frequency and also charts for digraph frequency—that is, the frequency of any two letters found together, and then letters found before and after other letters. Then it goes into trigraph frequencies."

"Oh." Emma stared at him. "I had no idea."

He chuckled. "It's a different world here, but you'll soon get used to it. And you'll find that all these charts and tables are your friends. I keep one of those volumes close any time I'm working on English ciphers."

"Do you do other languages?" Emma asked.

"When I have to. I'm getting quite good at German ones, they tell me, and occasionally I do Spanish. Did you know the Spanish alphabet doesn't include W and Y?"

"I'd never thought about it."

"They only use those letters in foreign place names, like 'New York.'"

Emma nodded slowly. "They won't throw a cipher at me in a language I don't know, will they?"

"Possibly. We have a couple of fellows who do Japanese, and they generally get the other Far Eastern languages when they come up, which is rare. They're looking for someone fluent in Arabic. But you'd be surprised—you don't have to know a language to solve their ciphers. I worked on an Italian one last month. I was new here, and they put me with one of the fellows who knew a smattering of the language. It took us three days, but we cracked it. It turned out to be a requisition for uniforms, but Commander Howe said it was useful in a minor sort of way—it told us Italy was outfitting a new batch of troops." He shrugged. "Anyway, I'll let you get back to work. I'm Martin Glazer, by the way."

"Emma Shuster. And thank you." She took the book back to her table and continued with her absorbing task. She soon realized the message concerned a labor rally to be held in Detroit, Michigan. The sender gave instructions to the recipient to "have at least a dozen of our men there to keep things lively. Discontent is the precursor of revolution."

She stared at the words she had deciphered. Revolution? In America? In 1775, yes, but in 1915? She thought back on things John Patterson and Captain Waller had said to her. If the German sympathizers could push American laborers into violence, might it not keep the United States government too preoccupied to enter the foreign war?

She puzzled out the last few words and looked at the clock. Ten minutes to spare. She rose and headed for Commander Howe's desk.

Martin glanced up and smiled at her as she passed.

"Well, Miss Shuster," Howe said as she held out her paper, "all finished?"

"Yes, sir."

He eyed it frowning.

She held her breath. Had she made some foolish mistake? What if the basic message was a code for something entirely different?

After a moment he met her gaze and smiled. "Nice work."

She exhaled. "Thank you, sir. I wondered—am I allowed to know when this message was intercepted? I found it…disturbing."

"You'll see many more distressing things than this if you work here, Miss Shuster. But I can tell you it came in a few weeks ago. Our people were able to stop the rabble rousers from disrupting the rally, and we arrested three men. It's the men giving the orders we'd really like to catch, of course. But perhaps that will happen if we keep on intercepting their communications in time." He smiled. "You mustn't fret about this one, though. All over and done with. I see Mrs. Harper at the door. Are you ready to go and eat now?"

"Yes, sir." The other workers were putting away their materials. Some opened sack lunches on their tables. As they entered the hallway, Emma saw Doris and the other two typists going down the stairs carrying their lunches. They must have a favorite spot to eat. She looked forward to joining their circle. Perhaps tomorrow, unless she had more orientation sessions to undergo.

With Commander Howe and Mrs. Harper, she retired to Mrs. Harper's office on the first floor. Spread out on the desk was an array of sandwiches and salads, with milk or hot coffee available.

"The delicatessen on Third Street is most obliging," said the hostess. "Would you please ask the blessing, Commander?"

Emma bowed her head as he thanked God for the meal.

When she opened her eyes again, Mrs. Harper handed her a plate. Howe opened the container of potato salad, and soon the three of them were engrossed in the food. Emma's nerves had kept her from eating much that morning, and she was glad for the hearty meal.

"Now then," the commander said after he'd eaten half a sandwich, a mound of potato salad, and a fair portion of carrot and raisin salad. "If you will excuse me for talking about you in your presence, Miss Shuster, I wish to brag to Mrs. Harper about your performance this morning."

"Oh?" Mrs. Harper arched her fine eyebrows. "I take it she's done well?"

"Very. She solved the cipher I gave her in less than eighty minutes. Of course, it had already been classified, but still—I found that remarkable. I've used it on three other candidates, and none of them cracked it in less than three hours. I can't wait to see what she'll do with a multiple alphabet cipher."

"Like the Viginère?" Emma asked. Immediately she wished she'd kept silent, as both of their heads swiveled and they stared at her.

"You know the Viginère Cipher then?" Agnes asked.

Howe grinned. "Of course she does! My dear Miss Shuster, how glad I am that we've found you."

Emma felt her cheeks flush. "Well, yes—that is to say, I've never solved any messages written in the Viginère, but I've read about it and even played around with encrypting a few short messages of my own that way. As an exercise. My father told me about it when he first explained his own system to me."

"Indeed." Howe shot a glance at Mrs. Harper. "I predict she will be our prodigy."

"Perhaps. But we have some excellent cryptographers here." Mrs. Harper poured herself a cup of coffee. "Would you like some, Miss Shuster?"

"No, thank you."

"But, Agnes, the most complicated messages we get are variations of the Viginère." Howe turned eagerly to Emma. "You will study under the best here. And you will work on some of the most important projects ever."

Emma felt the weight of his words on her heart. If she could help stop sabotage within her country, she would indeed feel she had done vital work.

CHAPTER ELEVEN

Saturday, February 27, 1915

On Saturday Emma couldn't calm the butterflies flitting about in her stomach. She'd had no message from John canceling their plans, but she had not seen him again since their brief meeting on Tuesday.

She put on a serviceable but attractive plaid dress and chose her gray wool cape to wear over it. The weather had already taken on the warmth of spring, and it was too balmy for the heavy overcoat she'd worn in Maine.

In Mrs. Draper's parlor, she waited for him and pretended to listen to Freddie and Louise's chatter about the moving picture they wanted to see that afternoon.

At last Freddie jumped up. "Let's go, Louise. I want to stop at the drugstore on the way." She glanced out the front window. "Oh, Emma, I daresay your young man is here. My, he's good looking."

Emma tried to calm her rioting pulse. Freddie and Louise bade her a teasing good-bye and went noisily into the front entrance just as the knocker sounded.

Emma heard Freddie's sugary greeting. "Hello there! You must be Emma's beau. I'm Freddie, and this is Louise."

"Good morning." John's voice, as always, was cultured and discreet, but Emma thought she heard an undertone of amusement as well. Would John be happier with a bubbly girl like Freddie?

Emma rose and twisted her hands together. She didn't consider herself timid, but she knew without doubt that Louise was prettier than she was, and Freddie would certainly take the medal for personality. Why would a man like John prefer her, out of all the young women he must meet?

"Oh, she's right in there," Freddie said. "Probably primping for you."

"Have a good time," Louise sang out, and the door shut firmly on their giggles.

Emma gulped and avoided the temptation to glance at the mirror that hung between the windows. She brushed her hands over the front of her skirt.

At that moment, John appeared in the doorway, immaculately clad in his service uniform.

"Hello." She stood rooted to the spot on the carpet as he advanced into the room smiling.

"Vivacious friends you have there."

"Yes. I don't know them well, but Freddie seems incorrigible." Emma laughed. "I like her." Perhaps she secretly wished she could be more like Freddie.

"I do too. By the way, you look lovely."

Emma's stomach stirred uneasily, but she managed a serene, "Thank you."

"Are you ready to go?"

"Yes." She reached for her cape.

He held it for her then offered his arm, and she took it. A spring in Emma's step matched her mood. She was walking out with a handsome naval officer. What a change from her drab life in Maine.

"How have things gone for you at Trafton House?" he asked.

"Quite well, I think. They put me with Martin Glazer on Thursday. Do you know him?"

"I don't think so."

"He's one of the best cryptographers, apparently. He's not in our generation, but he certainly knows how to go about solving more quickly than I do."

John laughed. "Learning from an old hand who's had experience in the field can be a bonus."

"Yes. He was patient and showed me how to make the most efficient use of the tools we have available. I was amazed at how quickly he deduced the cipher method. And the message was in German. Once we knew how to unravel it, the two of us made short work of it. And, John, it had to do with another of our ships leaving New York."

"Let me guess. The enemy planned to plant a bomb in the cargo."

"It certainly sounded like it. I asked Commander Howe what would happen, and he said some of the navy's best men would go at once to look into it. He said we may never know if they are successful in stopping the bombers. All of that is hushed up unless the newspapers get hold of it. We can only solve the messages and pass them on. It's a bit frustrating, not knowing the result."

"I agree, but the fewer people who know the details of an operation, the better its chance of success."

"I can see that. At least they didn't send you to New York." She glanced up at him. "Is that the type of work you did in Chicago? Oh, don't tell me if you're not supposed to."

John drew in a deep breath and glanced about at the other pedestrians before answering. "I actually crossed into Canada to consult with officials there about a recent rash of sabotage along the border."

"So, there's trouble in Canada too."

"Yes. We don't know if the German embassies are involved or not. Perhaps some lower-level diplomats. But someone is giving the orders for these disasters. The Canadians are determined to root him out."

"How do they expect to do that?"

"The Canadians claim to be as tenacious as we are. They're also starting to gather cryptographers, but I think we have the jump on them there. We'll share information if it's pertinent to their security." They reached the trolley stop, and he grasped her hand firmly in his as the car approached along the track. "They've given him a nickname."

"Who? This shadowy person giving orders?"

John nodded. Several other people hurried toward them to catch the trolley. He leaned close to Emma's ear and whispered, "They call him Kobold."

* * * * *

Squiring Emma about the capital gave John one of the most pleasant days he could remember. Her delight at seeing each new sight was contagious. He felt anew a deep-seated pride in his country.

They ate lunch at a small restaurant near where the area to be known as the Mall was under construction. Afterward, he splurged on a horse-drawn carriage to take them around the city.

"I hope I'm not embarrassing you," Emma said. She had leaned out the window to better view the Washington Monument.

"Far from it."

She settled back on the seat and grinned at him. "I suppose I'm the classic tourist from the hinterlands. But I want to see everything. I love being here."

He took her hand and nestled it on the seat between them. "I'm proud to be with you, Emma. You can gawk all you want."

She laughed again. "Thank you. I'll try not to be too gauche. Did I tell you that they gave me some codes of my own to work on yesterday?"

"No, you did not."

"Navy codes. Our people have figured out some of the German code words, but not nearly enough." She kept her voice low so that the carriage driver could not possibly hear her. "The commander gave me three new messages, along with some that they'd partially decoded over the last month. They've figured out a few basic words just by the position in the messages, and they've learned the codes for a couple of place names by seeing where the German fleet turned up. But apparently much of it is still a mystery. I'm afraid I didn't make a lot of headway."

"Aren't the British tracking the German fleet?"

"Yes, but at least one German ship has shown up in Rio de Janeiro, and then it went on up to Caracas."

John frowned. "We don't want them in Western waters."

"Exactly. So we're trying to discover what they're doing puttering about South America."

John thought about that for a few minutes as the carriage rolled slowly along. The Germans had been stirring up trouble in the United States and Canada. If they decided to muddy the waters even more by spreading their activities to Latin America, things could heat up quickly. He hoped he wouldn't be sent down there, but if his duties took him to South America, he would go. The fleeting day with Emma seemed even more precious with that prospect in mind.

"You'll probably go away again soon, won't you?" she asked.

He grimaced. "You're a mind reader."

"Do you have new orders?"

"Not yet. Perhaps we can attend church together tomorrow."

"I'd like to. Doris Keating asked me to go with her, but I didn't promise. She's another of my fellow boarders, and she's a typist at Trafton House."

"If I can, I'll come around for you. If Miss Keating wants to go with us, she's welcome."

"And if you can't?"

"Captain Waller told me to take today off and call him this evening. If something's come up, I'll call you at the boardinghouse." It was the best he could do.

"This leader of theirs," Emma said tentatively, her frown puckering her brow. "Do we know anything about him except that he tells the saboteurs where to go and what to do?"

"Not much yet. But he's got to be drawing on at least one bank account to fund all of this activity. We've got several men working on that angle."

"That may be a good way to trace him. You said the Canadians call him Kobold. Doesn't that mean…"

"Goblin," John said.

"I thought so. My aunt Thea used to say it if something went wrong. If I spilled my glass of milk on the table, she'd say the kobold did it."

John smiled. "If only this one pulled such harmless pranks."

They rode on in silence. Two strong passions struggled within John's mind and heart—his growing feelings for Emma and his need to stop the sabotage. The only thing that could take him from Emma's side now would be a lead on Kobold.

* * * * *

The hall telephone rang about eight o'clock that evening, and a moment later Freddie dashed up the stairs and tapped on Emma's door.

"Emma? Are you still up? Your lieutenant's on the phone."

Emma opened her door. "John? Now?"

"Yes, ma'am. He's so polite, isn't he?"

"Thank you, Freddie."

"It's no trouble. I was just playing Old Maid with Louise and her caller and his friend—" She leaned close and whispered, "Who's boring."

Emma smiled. Freddie turned and walked quickly with her to the stairs. "Next time Louise suggests a foursome, I think I'll tell her no thanks."

At the bottom of the stairs, Emma hurried to the telephone. Freddie rejoined her party in the parlor but left the door open. Emma wondered if they'd be able to hear every word she said.

"Hello?"

"Emma, it's John. I'm sorry, but I won't be able to make it tomorrow."

Her spirits sagged, but after their near-perfect day, she couldn't feel too depressed. "That's all right. I'll go with Doris."

"Thank you for understanding."

"How could I not?" Her lips curved in a bittersweet smile as she pictured his drooping shoulders and anxious brown eyes. "We had a wonderful day today, anyway."

"Yes. Well, I need to pack a few things. I'll take the midnight train. I can't tell you where I'm going, but I'll be in touch as soon as I can."

"I'll be thinking of you. Be safe, John."

As she turned away from the telephone, Emma reminded herself that she barely knew John. She ought not to trust him so quickly. On the other hand, how could she not trust a man as patriotic and dedicated to his job as John Patterson? After all, Captain Waller and the navy had no doubt put him through all sorts of tests and checks. She and John were even fighting the same enemy.

She raised her chin and mounted the stairs. Today she'd toured Washington with perhaps the most trustworthy man in America. And she liked him enormously.

* * * * *

Thursday, April 1, 1915

Emma and Doris came home from work together one showery evening. As they entered the boardinghouse, Doris spied a letter on the hall table.

"Look! You've got a letter."

Emma seized it eagerly, thinking the missive was from Vivian. She'd written frequently to her friend, always careful not to disclose the nature of her work but dismissing it simply as "clerical," but the return address and handwriting told her this letter came from Aunt Thea's pen.

Incoming mail for the boarders arrived via a post office box, where Mrs. Draper collected it. Soon after her arrival, Emma had sent one postcard with no return address to the Meyers, to assure Aunt Thea that she was well and hadn't gone astray in the wicked city. No doubt her aunt fumed over not having her address, but Emma wasn't ready at that time to reveal her whereabouts. Not until the end of March did she feel secure enough to send the post office box address to her aunt, requesting that she not give it out to anyone else.

She took the letter to her room and opened it before going down to supper.

Dearest Emma,

At last I can send you word. Why haven't you let us write to you before this? There is so much to tell you. Gretchen is expecting another little one next fall, and Herman has a new job. But wait—there is more urgent news.

It distresses me to tell you that your things have been rifled. The man who stored them for you called this morning and said someone had broken into his barn last night. He assured me that he had padlocks on the doors, but the burglar must have been determined. Mr. Stevens said some of your crates were opened and upended. He doesn't think the furniture is damaged. My dear, I'm so sorry and very alarmed. We have no idea who would do this. Mr. Stevens called the police, but they were not much help, he said. If you would like me to bring the parlor furniture to our house, I would be happy to ask your uncle to fetch it for safekeeping.

Emma clenched her hands, crumpling the letter. First Father's papers, now her belongings. Would this never end?

She wished John was on hand to discuss it with, but she'd soon learned that his erratic schedule kept him away from his base in Virginia more often than it allowed him to be home. She didn't question him too closely, but it became obvious that his service under Captain Waller placed him in an irregular category. His assignments changed quickly and often. She never knew when he'd be called away, or when he'd be home again. They snatched brief meetings when they could, and he revealed little of what he'd been doing.

With his frequent absence, Emma did not depend on John. She'd fallen into a pattern of work and leisure time. Since he was rarely in town on weekends, she began regularly attending church with Doris. The volume of enciphered messages coming to Room 20 at Trafton House increased, and some days she worked into the evening to solve a stubborn one. But John was not the person to go to with Aunt Thea's disturbing news. She had better report this to Captain Waller.

* * * * *

Friday, April 2, 1915

The next morning, she phoned Waller's office and left a message with the yeoman on duty before leaving for Trafton House. The shock of the news had worn off, and she reread her aunt's letter, shaking her head over the offer to keep the parlor set for her. Aunt Thea had wanted the sofa especially, but Emma had told her that she wanted to keep it herself. Maybe she should let all the furniture go to the Meyers' house. It could be stolen or ruined at any time, and Emma's prospect of having her own home to use it in anytime soon looked slim.

About ten o'clock, Agnes Harper called her into her private office.

Captain Waller waited for her and stood as she entered. "Miss Shuster, I received your message. I'm very sorry."

Emma clasped his hand for an instant and sat down with him and Mrs. Harper. "I can only believe that my father's killer is still looking for the rest of his notes and perhaps for his cipher machine."

"I'm afraid that must be the case. Did you bring your aunt's letter with you?"

"No, I'm sorry, but I didn't."

"May I send a man by your boardinghouse tonight to fetch it? There may be something that can help us, although I doubt it, since your aunt was giving you secondhand information."

"You may certainly have the letter. But, Captain, what should I do?"

"Nothing. The positive side of this incident is that they have no idea where you are. It took them a while to ferret out where you'd placed your things in storage."

"You don't think they'll keep searching and follow me down here?"

He frowned. "I hope not. I'll ask the Department of Justice to look into this. They're spread very thin right now, but since it's connected to the murder of a patriot, they may spare a man to evaluate the case and cooperate with the local police."

Emma pulled in a shaky breath. Since she'd come to Virginia, she'd gone through loneliness, anxiety, and renewed grief, but now she trembled. "They must want it badly."

"Yes. You gave your address to your aunt?"

"Only the post office box, but now I wish I hadn't. She might give it to anyone. If they learn I'm in Fairfax, I suppose it would be simple to find me."

"You had to let your family know you were safe," Mrs. Harper said. "Besides, if you hadn't given her a way to reach you, she couldn't have told you about this burglary."

"I could have phoned and told her I was all right. That's what I should have done—phoned her every week or two." Emma buried her face in her hands for a moment. "What have I done? I may have exposed the entire Signal Corps."

"No, don't think that," Waller said. "It's true we keep a low profile, but anyone who is determined can find us. And no one told you not to give family members your new address. Our other employees don't hide their addresses from the world. Mrs. Draper maintains the post office box at my request, as a layer of security for you ladies, and she says all her female boarders appreciate that."

"I've been very careful not to name Trafton House or say exactly what type of work I'm doing," Emma said.

"Good. Oh, and it may encourage you to know that Werner Horn, the man who bombed the bridge in Maine, was indicted this morning."

"Will he be put away for planting that bomb?"

Waller gritted his teeth. "Not exactly. Since the bomb was planted on the Canadian side of the bridge, they can't make that charge stick here. Our authorities in Boston are charging him with transporting explosives on the train. If all goes well, he'll serve some time here, and then we'll extradite him to Canada. They may be able to convict him of attempted murder there. Certainly something more than our flimsy charge. Or I suppose they might deport him. But our Justice Department wants to be sure he serves some jail time in the United States."

"Thank you for telling me." It made Emma feel a little better to see at least one saboteur facing the consequences of his actions.

* * * * *

Monday, April 12, 1915

The staff at Trafton House grew. Four more cryptographers joined Emma and the others in Room 20. She was delighted when she heard that another young woman would soon become part of the group. Muriel Ainsley had enlisted in the Navy Nurse Corps, but Howe told the group she had been recruited as a cryptographer because of her interest in the field and her skill at mathematics. She would arrive as soon as her current assignment ended. Emma looked forward to having another woman working in the same room with her.

Mrs. Draper was using the telephone in the hall when Emma entered the house on the evening of April 12. When the landlady saw her, she said, "Just a moment, please," put her hand over the mouthpiece, and called, "Miss Shuster, this call is for you."

Surprised, Emma hurried toward her with her pulse rocketing. Was John back from his latest mission already? "Hello?"

Mrs. Draper disappeared through the doorway that led to her private sitting room.

"Miss Shuster, is that you?" asked a shrill female voice.

"Yes. Who is calling, please?"

"This is Olive Starbuck, at the Bowdoin College switchboard."

"Oh. Hello." Emma frowned, trying to think why the college would telephone her. She had written recently with her new address and Mrs. Draper's telephone number, in case the school needed to contact her regarding her father's academic affairs, but she hadn't really expected to hear anything from that quarter.

"One of our graduate assistants, Mr. Clark Hibbert, insists that he needs to get in touch with you right away. You requested that we not give out your address, but I told him I'd try to reach you and see if you wanted to speak with him."

"Oh. Well, I..."

"He's here now, if you are willing," said the woman. "If not, I shall tell him you declined."

Emma swallowed hard. Clark was the last person on earth she wanted to talk to, but the fact that he'd gone to a significant effort to find her made her curious.

"All right."

After a few moments of rustling, Clark's voice came on the line, loud and sharp.

"Emma!"

She gulped and decided now was not the time to remind him that she'd never given permission for him to call her by her first name.

"Emma, are you there?"

"Yes."

"I had to let you know—someone accosted me last night. There was a public supper at the town hall. When I left it, a man followed me back toward my lodgings."

Emma frowned, trying to follow Clark's tale. "Why did he do that?"

"You may well ask. I was about a block from my rooming house when he called out to me. I turned and saw that he had a pistol."

The strap of Emma's handbag slipped through her fingers, and the purse slid to the floor. "A gun? Did he rob you?"

"No. He asked me where the code machine was."

Emma gasped and clutched one hand to her chest, where it felt as though a rock had struck her. "He—he wanted the machine?"

"Yes. Your father's work. He said if I didn't give it up, he'd shoot me. There was no one else about, or I'd have called out for help. I didn't know what else to do. Emma, I'm afraid I told him that after your father passed away, I gave it back to you."

An even heavier rock seemed to settle in her stomach. "You told him I had it?"

"Yes. Emma, my dear, dear Emma, I'm so sorry! I didn't mean to put you in danger, but the more I think about it, the more likely it seems that I've done just that. He demanded to know where you'd gone, but I told him quite honestly I didn't know. He shoved me down, and by the time I'd collected myself, he'd run off. I went on into the rooming house and discovered that my rooms had been thoroughly tossed. He must have gone there first, while I was at the supper, and searched my lodgings for the machine."

"Oh dear." Emma raised her hand to her temple and rubbed it, trying to think what to do. "You're certain they don't know where I am?"

"Positive. And I didn't know, so I couldn't tell him. After pondering it all day, I realized it was possible the college had a forwarding address for you, so I came here to inquire. They wouldn't give me your address, which is proper of them, but I did persuade the switchboard operator to try to locate you. It took her awhile, but she found that the dean's office had a telephone number on file. I felt I ought to warn you about what's happened."

"Yes. Yes, thank you." Emma tried to think what to do next. It seemed very likely that Clark had stood by while the operator attempted to get through to her by telephone, and he may well have gained a clue as to where she now lived. How did she know Clark was telling the truth? What if the people who had killed her father had persuaded Clark to work for them? If they thought she had the machine, they would come after her next. "Clark, I want you to know that I don't have Father's machine with me now."

"You don't? Then you gave it over to the bank?"

"I…" She gulped and sent up a swift prayer for wisdom. "It's in safe hands now, and that man won't be able to get it."

"All right. But you be careful, Emma. I don't like to think this ruffian might come around and scare you, especially after the way your father was killed."

Emma winced. "If he shows up again, tell him that you heard from me that the machine is no longer in my possession. Will you do that?"

"Yes, of course."

"Thank you. And thank you for letting me know about this. Good-bye."

"Emma, wait!"

She paused with the receiver halfway back to its hook. He sounded so desperate, she couldn't ignore his plea. Reluctantly, she returned the instrument to her ear. "Yes? What is it?"

"Emma, please, won't you give me your address? I hate to lose touch with you."

"I don't think…"

"Please! Or give the college permission to release it to me."

"No, Clark. I can't do that. Good-bye." She hung up before he could say more.

She stood in the hallway, breathing quickly, staring at the phone. Her hand shook as she picked up her handbag. What did Clark's call really mean? She snatched up the receiver again. "Yes, I'd like Woolrich 8-5917."

CHAPTER TWELVE

Monday, April 12, 1915

"Can you recall anything else that he said?" Captain Waller asked.

Emma sat across from him in his office in the military compound. Waller had sent a car to Mrs. Draper's for her immediately after she'd called. "I don't think so. But he was talking openly about the machine. There were people in the office who must have heard him."

"And you're certain he doesn't know you're in Virginia?"

"No, I'm not certain at all. He begged me at the last to give him my address, but I've no way of knowing how much he overheard while the school's operator was trying to reach me. I had given Bowdoin College the number at the boardinghouse. The woman at the switchboard might have had to give it aloud to another operator, or perhaps even ask for my town and state. I'm not sure how that is done precisely, but Clark lives and breathes mathematics. If he heard the number, he'd surely be able to memorize it."

Waller made notes on a pad of paper. "To tell you the truth, Miss Shuster, we were thinking of asking this Hibbert fellow to come down here."

"What?" Emma stared at him.

"Your reaction to that statement makes me hesitate." Waller shifted in his chair. "You see, we've found that the machine he was building for your father might be very useful for us. We could get someone here to work on it, but Hibbert knew exactly what was needed and how your father envisioned it would work—and truthfully, we haven't an engineer who can be spared to work on it at present. It would be much quicker if we had him complete the job."

"I—don't know what to say."

"You obviously don't like this fellow."

She brushed back a strand of her hair. "He's been a bit of an annoyance in my life, nothing more. He seems to have feelings toward me. I've always discouraged him. But now…I'm not sure I can trust him, Captain. How do we know he told me the truth this evening?"

Waller sat back in his chair and swiveled gently left and right a few times. "I wasn't going to tell you this, but I don't want you to be frightened unnecessarily. We began looking into Hibbert's background weeks ago—in fact, not long after Lieutenant Patterson met him and described him and his relationship to your father in his report to me. We wanted to make sure Hibbert was indeed on the right side, so to speak. And to be certain he wasn't a menace to you. Patterson didn't think the police considered Hibbert as a suspect in your father's murder, but just to be certain, we conducted an investigation of our own, unknown to the Brunswick Police."

Emma was speechless.

"I regret that we had to keep you in the dark, Miss Shuster, but we found nothing to connect Mr. Hibbert with any known saboteurs, nor anything suspicious in his behavior. He has an ironclad alibi for the time of your father's murder. Hibbert is a scholar engrossed in his work and a bit awkward socially, but beyond that, I have reason to believe he spoke the truth to you this evening."

"Oh?"

Waller nodded. "As I said, we've been watching him and thinking of recruiting him to finish the work on the machine. So our man kept watching him and followed him last night to the supper at the town hall. When Hibbert left, our man hung back, quite certain he was headed home. The usual dull evening. He was surprised when he saw another man fall in behind Hibbert. After a short time, Hibbert turned and began talking to the unknown man."

"Exactly as he described to me," Emma said. "Only he said no one else was about."

"Our fellow ducked behind a tree. By the time he realized the man had a gun, he feared it was too late. He stepped out to aid Hibbert, but just then the other man pushed Hibbert down. When the thug saw our man, he bolted. Our fellow let him go, since he thought it was more important to be certain Hibbert was all right. He walked innocently past where Hibbert was pulling himself together. The young man appeared to be unharmed, though a bit disoriented, so our man said 'Good evening' to him and passed by. He fetched up behind the porch of the rooming house and watched Hibbert go inside. When the police came a short time later, our agent hung about and learned that Hibbert's rooms had been ransacked while he was out. That's about it, but it fits with what Hibbert told you."

"Precisely." She swallowed hard. "Are you really thinking of bringing him down here?"

"Yes. And in light of this recent attack, he might be safer if we get him out of Maine. We planned to wait until the end of the academic year. Hibbert will have finished his advanced degree. We didn't want to disrupt his education, and it's only a short time."

"I understand your wanting him to finish the job, but—does he have to be—here?"

Waller eyed her thoughtfully. "Are you frightened of him?"

Emma sighed. "Not really. I don't so much dislike *him* as I do his attitude toward me. Perhaps I flatter myself, but he seemed last fall to take an almost proprietary air toward me."

"Did he pursue you openly?"

Emma clasped her hands tightly in her lap and looked down at them. "Yes. In fact, he asked my father to allow him to court me. Father left the decision up to me, and I declined. Even so, Mr. Hibbert issued invitations to me, and he often seemed to place himself in my path and find reasons to contact me. I grew to dread seeing him."

"I see." Waller picked up a pencil and tapped the edge of the desk. After a moment he looked up at her. "I'm not sure what to tell you, Miss Shuster. The machine—I've been calling it the Shuster machine—could be useful to our military for sending and receiving ciphers, but Commander Howe thinks it might also help in deciphering messages sent by other entities. I'm not sure he's right about that, but I'm certain of one thing—it won't be long before all the major powers will be using similar devices. Your father can't have been the only man in the world to conceive of such a machine."

"Father was sure he was not the only one. He said they might already have something similar in Europe. He'd have given a lot to know, and to see how closely his idea resembled theirs."

"Hmm. Interesting. Well, this is the first one we've seen, and in fact, the first one we're sure has actually been built. Every cryptographer in the world would drool over it. We'd really like to bring it to the operational stage."

Emma nodded slowly. "And you feel bringing Clark Hibbert here is the fastest and surest way to do that."

"Yes." Waller laid the pencil down and leaned toward her. "I assure you, we've raked through his background, his contacts, everything. If I learned this man has connections with German sympathizers, I'd be shocked. He's smart, but he's not all that clever, if you understand me. I don't think he'd be able to hide it that well."

"What about the break-in where my things are stored? Could he have anything to do with that? The more I think about it, the more certain I am that the burglar was searching for the machine."

"As a matter of fact, I had some news on that front just this afternoon. I had planned to come to Trafton House to tell you about it tomorrow."

Emma caught her breath. "What is it?"

"The Justice Department agents think they've caught the man who went through your belongings."

"Oh?"

"Yes. Someone saw him leave the scene, and they got a description. That, along with some information I passed to them about your father's funeral, helped them find the suspect."

"What information?" She frowned at him. What could Waller possibly know about the funeral that would lead to a burglar's arrest?

"Do you remember a man who came to the reception at your house after the service? Lieutenant Patterson reported to me that a man you didn't know came to the gathering and spoke with your cousin, then left without speaking to you. We both thought that odd, since you were the chief mourner."

"I remember. John followed him outside. I meant to ask him later if he'd learned anything, but it never came up, and I'd forgotten about it."

"Well, he did learn something. He got the license number of the car the man left in. Our people have located the man who owns the car, and Patterson has since identified him from a drawing made by a police artist. I suggested that the Justice Department investigate him, and they were able to link him through the eyewitness's testimony to the burglary of your belongings."

Emma let out a long breath. "That's amazing. Who is he?"

"Edward Klaussen. He's a second-generation German-American living just outside Portland and a known German sympathizer. He may very well have been commissioned to steal your father's work. The police and federal agents will keep me informed if they learn any more from him."

"Could he be connected to my father's death?"

"It's possible."

Emma shivered. The murderer had perhaps been in her house the day of the funeral. "He's in custody, you said?"

"Yes. They hope to put him away for a while. The burglary of the barn storage isn't a very weighty charge, since it's not known that he actually stole anything. But they're trying to connect him to other incidents in the area."

"Well, have them speak to the Brunswick police chief about a prowler who came around my house the day after Father was killed. Chief Weaver will remember."

"I'll do that." Waller made a note. "So, back to Mr. Hibbert. We found no connection between him and this Klaussen fellow. All the time we shadowed Hibbert, there was no contact between them. You didn't see them speak the day of the funeral, did you?"

"No." Emma pulled her shoulders back and raised her chin. "All right. You think it's best to bring Clark here. Just—please, Captain, if you're going to do that, will you give me a little notice? I'd like to prepare myself mentally and not just run into him one day at Trafton House."

"I understand. And I doubt we'd take him to Trafton House. More likely, we'd find him a place here in the navy compound or at Fort Myer to work. Perhaps assign a couple of mechanically inclined sailors to help him." Waller stood. "Now, unless there's something else, I'll ask the driver to take you back to your lodgings."

Emma rose and shook his hand. "Thank you, sir. And thank you for taking me seriously when I called."

"You did the right thing."

She walked out to the waiting car, pondering this new development.

Outside of work, she fought off loneliness. Homesickness was not the right word for it, since without Father there was no home. Her loss settled in as a permanent dark rift in her life. Many times she wished her father was there to confide in. She cultivated her friendships with Freddie and Doris and put her energy into mastering the art of decipherment.

During the last six weeks, she had spent only two afternoons and one Friday evening with John. He joined her and Doris once for church services. She hoarded those meager times with him in her heart. As spring unfolded, she puttered about the town of Fairfax, learning every cranny, and took several forays into Washington with the other boarders. The cherry trees, sent as a gift by the Japanese people just three years earlier, bloomed magnificently in early April. John found a rare Sunday afternoon to stroll with her and Doris and admire the blossoms.

But now, Clark Hibbert might be coming to Virginia. This collision of her old world with her new one felt wrong. The old upset stomach returned—the same one she used to get when she knew she'd be seeing Clark.

* * * * *

Monday, May 3, 1915

"Did you see this?" Martin Glazer tossed a newspaper on Emma's table one morning three weeks later.

"What?" Emma scanned the page quickly.

He pointed to a small box at the bottom of the page. "This ad."

Emma read the first lines aloud:

"Notice. Travelers intending to embark on the Atlantic voyage are reminded that a State of War exists between Germany and her Allies and Great Britain and her Allies; that the zone of war includes the waters adjacent to the British Isles..."

She glanced quickly to the bottom of the paragraph where bold letters proclaimed the signature: Imperial German Embassy. "This is outrageous."

"It certainly is." Commander Howe came from his desk to join them. "It's a blatant warning. 'Any vessel flying the flag of Great Britain or her allies is liable to destruction.'"

"More like a threat," Martin said.

Emma read the next line. "Travelers sailing in the war zone do so at their own risk."

"Why are we putting up with this?" Martin asked.

Commander Howe shook his head. "If it were up to me..."

"Right." Martin turned and plodded toward his station. "Let's get back to work, kiddies. Something tells me it's going to be a busy week."

Emma wondered where John was. She hadn't heard from him in ten days. Was he investigating a new plot to sink an Allied ship? She tried not to worry about him when he went away for weeks at a time.

As she opened the folder Howe had given her that morning, she silently gave John over to the Lord. It would be difficult to keep her thoughts from returning to him constantly throughout the day, but that was her best strategy.

* * * * *

Saturday, May 8, 1915

Kobold paced his opulent office with a cigar in the corner of his mouth. An American ship had left Philadelphia with four bombs in its cargo hold yet had made it through to Marseilles unscathed. The bombs had not gone off. Worse yet, the French customs officials had discovered them.

His phone rang and he seized the receiver. "Yes?"

"T says the bombs were operational. He has no explanation why they did not explode."

"He's lying."

"No, I think he speaks the truth."

"Then he is stupid. We won't use him again."

"Stupid or careless, who is to say? He is ready to do another job."

"No."

"He needs the money. His wife and children are hungry."

Kobold puffed on the cigar for a moment, thinking. It seemed that when his men performed their assignments, the government learned of their plans and interfered. It was those code breakers. Emma Shuster and her infernal machine. Had to be. And when his men's plans weren't discovered, their equipment failed or someone fell down on the job. "One more chance. We pay him only when we see the results."

The man on the other end of the connection grunted. "This failure will be forgotten. All anyone is talking of today is the sinking of the *Lusitania.*"

"Yes. The U-boats do their job. Too bad our people don't." He slammed down the receiver.

* * * * *

Monday, May 10, 1915

Mrs. Harper called Emma to her office in the middle of the morning.

Captain Waller was there, enjoying a cup of coffee with the office manager. "Good day, Miss Shuster." The captain rose and shook her hand. "I dropped by Trafton House this morning to bring you some news."

"Oh? That was good of you." Emma took the chair he indicated.

"I must speak to one of the typists," Mrs. Harper said. "Please feel free to use this room as long as necessary, Captain. And, Miss Shuster, help yourself to coffee if you wish."

"Thank you, Agnes," Waller said. When Mrs. Harper had left and closed the door behind her, he sat down across from Emma and gazed at her soberly. "Mr. Hibbert arrived in Washington last night. I wanted to be certain you knew."

Emma puffed out a breath. "Thank you for telling me."

"He asked if I was acquainted with you, and I told him that I am and that I also knew your father. He had much praise for Professor Shuster and his work."

"But you didn't tell him my whereabouts."

"No. I did, however, promise to tell you that he is in the area and would like to contact you. I told him that if you did not wish to see him, I would tell him and that he would be under orders not to try to locate you."

"Thank you." She gripped the arms of her chair, fighting the dread again. In reality, what was so bad about Clark? He was a pest, that was all.

"Our plan is to have him complete the work on the Shuster machine within the next four to six weeks."

"He told me it wouldn't take more than a couple of weeks."

"We want him to thoroughly train two of our ensigns to use and replicate the machine."

"Ah." So they would have Clark work himself out of a job. "And then he'll be discharged and sent back to Maine?"

"Something like that."

"Would you tell me when he is no longer in the area?"

"Yes, I can do that."

"Thank you."

"Pleased to be of service." Waller smiled, and she noticed for the first time the fatigue lines at the corners of his eyes.

"You've been working hard."

"Oh, yes, everyone has, especially since the *Lusitania* incident."

"Sir, I'd be interested in your personal opinion about America's position and—well—the likelihood of us declaring war."

He studied her gravely then sighed. "Unofficially? I think it's only a matter of time. But the President still feels we should maintain neutrality at all costs."

"Even at the cost of American lives?"

"The *Lusitania* was a British ship," he countered. "Though there were a hundred fifty-nine Americans on board when she sank, it is true."

"And the steamer *Gulflight* was American."

His face fell. "Yes. Three souls on board lost."

"So, what will it take?" Emma asked. "How many torpedoes? How many bombs in our ships' cargo holds?"

"Ask me again the day we declare. Then I'll know."

Tears filled Emma's eyes. "I pray every day…"

"Don't stop," he said. "Though it seems to us very black just now, God is still in control. I firmly believe that."

She raised her chin and managed a shaky smile. "So do I, sir. Thank you." She stood and held out her hand. "I appreciate your telling me about Mr. Hibbert, and your encouragement."

"And I appreciate you, Miss Shuster. We've saved ships, and we've saved the people on them. Your work is important. Don't ever doubt that."

CHAPTER THIRTEEN

Tuesday, May 11, 1915

Commander Howe strode to Emma's work table with a sheaf of papers in his hand. "Miss Shuster, this just came in from one of our men in New York. I've given it a quick once-over. It doesn't seem to be the same type of cipher as any of the others that have come from New York lately. Either the agents there are getting craftier or there's a new kid in the class."

Emma spent the entire morning trying different configurations of the message to find out what method had been used to encipher it. At last she was fairly certain it was a shift cipher with embedded code words. After lunch, she attacked it afresh. Each letter of the message had been "shifted" to a letter in a different part of the alphabet. If all the letters were shifted three places, then the word "and" would read "dqg" in the cipher. However, she couldn't find one shift that made sense, leading her to believe that different degrees of shifting had been used in rotation. Trial and error helped her discover one of the shifting intervals, but the rest eluded her.

"Miss Shuster, will you be staying late tonight?"

She looked up to find Commander Howe standing near her work table. A glance toward his desk told her that Lieutenant Bullock, who often supervised an evening shift of a few cryptographers, had arrived to relieve him.

"It's well after five," Howe said. "If you wish to stay late, ask one of the gentlemen to see you at least as far as the trolley station. If you'd like to go now, I could drop you there myself."

Emma hesitated, but she knew she couldn't finish solving this message tonight. "I'll go with you. Thank you, sir." She quickly returned the folder to the file room and retrieved her handbag and cloak.

On the way to the station, she found herself confiding in Howe. "I get so frustrated some days I think I'll explode. Then my spirits plummet. I think I'll never be able to solve another cipher again. Either they've come up with some new, ingenious method that's unbreakable, or I've lost some of the ability I had a few weeks ago and my brain is growing feeble."

"This new one is tough," Howe said. "I looked it over and couldn't see an obvious method to solve it."

"Yes. I don't want to waste a lot of time working on something I can't crack. On the other hand, I don't want to give up on something when I may be only a step away from blasting it wide open."

He smiled. "I'll put one of the others on it with you tomorrow. Tell him everything you've tried so far. Perhaps he'll have some insight."

By this time, Emma had come to realize that pride had no place in this work. If two heads could reveal the message faster than one, then by all means, two should attack it together or from separate quarters at the same time. The conceit of solving a cipher alone was not worth the lives that could be lost in the delay. "I feel as though I ought to have stayed tonight," she said. "What if the message is of vital concern, and I went home to sleep?"

"Everyone must sleep," Howe said. "Even our enemies. That message may be nothing, or it may be of utmost importance. We've no way of knowing."

"What sort of things have we been getting from New York?" she asked.

"Recently we've intercepted several communiqués from the stock market floor. We believe one of the brokers is sending coded messages to his counterpart in Italy. I've given them all to Martin, and he's made some progress. We think they're using regular financial lingo to pass on word of ship movements."

"Ship movements? That could be very important."

"Yes." His brow furrowed. "These ship sabotage incidents are increasing. Whenever one of our ships, or an Allied country's ship, leaves our shores laden with munitions or other war supplies, I always wonder if it will make it to Europe. Well, here we are, Miss Shuster. I'll see you tomorrow."

"Thank you, sir." Emma hurried down the platform for her trolley car.

That evening, Doris and Freddie invited her to go to the movies with them, but she declined. She read for a while and went to bed early, praying for wisdom in her work and also for John's safety. This time he'd been gone a week, and she'd had no word from him.

During his last brief visit to the Washington area, they'd managed one evening out and had attended church with Doris on Sunday. Their relationship progressed so slowly that Emma had begun to wonder if John was truly the one for her. Or perhaps she wasn't the one for him. Would John prefer a woman more animated than she was, more outgoing and fun-loving? Perhaps they weren't as well suited as she'd first imagined.

* * * * *

The next morning when Emma arrived in Room 20, Commander Howe rose from his desk and came to meet her. "Miss Shuster, this came here for you, marked 'personal.' Since it was enclosed with the report of a certain lieutenant we both know, I trust it's not a security risk, so I haven't censored it."

She felt her face flush as she reached eagerly for the small envelope. "Thank you, sir. I hope it's not against regulations. I assure you, I didn't request that it be sent this way."

"On the contrary, it's probably safer than if he'd addressed it to you at your lodgings."

Emma quickly went to her usual table and opened the envelope. She smiled as she gazed down at the slip of paper with a short enciphered message:

GOHTT XPTUD SSGDO VYGMM CAJNP BDWNP OCDVX

"Hmm, not a simple substitution. Looks like the Playfair Cipher to me."

Emma jumped and stared up at Martin, who was reading over her shoulder and smiling. "That's not polite, you know."

"Of course it's not, but it's irresistible for one of our kind." Martin scowled. "Dear me, could the sender be such a rank amateur as that? Using the Playfair with no code word? Tsk, tsk."

Emma looked down at the message again and then covered it with her hand.

"At least he's not afraid to admit he misses you, though he felt he had to put it in cipher."

She felt her cheeks go scarlet. "Would you stop it, please?"

Martin chuckled. "All right. Whenever you're ready to work, come over to my station. I came in early, and I've got the file you began yesterday. I think I'm on to something." He walked away.

Emma sat for a moment trying to regain her composure. *Lord, give me grace!*

She shoved John's message into her pocket. Martin had her so flustered now that if she tried to read it she'd probably waste time fumbling to solve what he'd proven was a simple encryption. Better to wait until this evening when she was alone in the privacy of her room.

She walked over to Martin's table and sat down across from him. "So, have you solved that without me?"

"Not completely. I went over your work sheets, and you were almost there. You've done excellent work."

"Thank you."

"So, with a little more trial and error, I unraveled the rest of their basic cipher. They used a key for the shifting of the letters—eighteen fifty-nine. The first letter was moved one place in the alphabet, the next eight, the next five, then nine, then repeat."

"Why eighteen fifty-nine?"

He shrugged. "Don't know. Does it matter? We have the key."

Emma squinted, trying to recall things she had read. Loose ends always bothered her. "The year the Kaiser was born?"

Martin cocked his head to one side. "Perhaps."

"So, if you've deciphered the whole message, what does it say?"

"Well, that's the tricky part. I've got the cipher, all right, but as you suspected, some of the words are in code. Here's the plaintext." He passed her the top sheet of paper from his file.

She scanned the message, which consisted of several lines of text. "I see what you mean. 'Fisher sent fifty dollars to Nigel. Prayers for wagon and copper twilight.' This is gibberish."

"Mostly. I'd say Fisher and Nigel are code names for people they don't want identified, and fifty dollars is probably shorthand for some amount—maybe fifty thousand. 'Wagon' and 'copper' could be places."

"Yes," Emma said. "Or commodities or names of ships. Twilight—that could be code for a time, like the end of the year or a certain month."

"Or any agreed upon time."

"And prayers?"

Martin frowned and wagged his head from side to side. "A generic for ships leaving? Or troops? That's doubtful, but still…"

"Payment, maybe?" Emma hazarded. "Or agents?"

Other cryptographers came in and went to their stations. Howe moved about the room handing out assignments and talking to each man about his work.

"How do we figure out what it means?" Emma asked.

Martin scratched his chin. "We should have the clerks check to see if any other ciphers have come in with an eighteen fifty-nine shift."

"Yes, there could be some no one solved yet. But Commander Howe seemed to think this was a new system that we hadn't encountered before."

"It probably is. They've changed their method to make it harder for us. But we should still check. And there may be others coming in soon that use it."

She nodded. "I'll go and ask the clerks to check the files if you'd like. I'll tell them to look for these code words too. It's possible that 'copper' or some of these others appeared in other messages, and we can use the context to help us classify them."

As she neared the door to the typists' room, a man in uniform raced up the stairs and across the hall. A minute later, when she re-entered Room 20, he was leaving.

Martin strolled over to her work table. "Did you see that fellow? He just brought in new dispatches, and he told Howe that a steel mill has been bombed near Pittsburgh."

Emma caught her breath. "Was anyone killed?"

"Don't know yet. Several injuries, at least."

Emma's lower lip trembled, and she bit it. "Martin, do you think the message we worked on could have anything to do with that?"

"I don't know."

"If only we'd solved it sooner. I should have stayed last night."

"Wouldn't have mattered. We can't know what their code words mean because we don't have their codebook."

She let out her breath. With his calm demeanor, Martin sometimes reminded her of her father. "Yes, but just think—if we got another message with 'wagon' or 'copper' in it and another factory was hit, we'd know something, wouldn't we?"

"Well, yes. That's the hard way to crack a code, though."

Commander Howe walked over to them. "Miss Shuster, Mr. Glazer, I think this will interest you. It was in the batch of messages just brought in. From New York again. The others were military ciphers, and I've given them to other people to work on. But this one…" He put a folder in Emma's hand. "Good luck."

By lunchtime they had reduced the new message to plaintext or "clear." Again, several words and names seemed senseless.

"The one thing that stands out is 'Nigel,'" Emma said.

"Yes. He shows up again in this message." Martin chewed on the end of his pencil for a moment. "We can have our intelligence boys check every list they've got for that and the other names we're collecting, but it has to be a code name."

"Then we've gone as far as we can with this."

"Probably. Let's get some lunch. Maybe something new will come in this afternoon."

Emma had arranged to eat with Doris and her friends. Most days she met them in the drab room downstairs furnished with a table and wooden chairs to give the workers a place to eat away from their desks.

Emma's curiosity got the better of her. Before joining the other women, she ducked down the hall to the "comfort room." There she could be sure of not being interrupted. She pulled John's crumpled message from her pocket and smoothed it out. It took her less than a minute to decipher it.

I miss you terribly. Will be home by Monday.

She smiled. John would be back in five days.

* * * * *

Tuesday, May 18, 1915

"We're sure Kobold is behind at least half of the German espionage and sabotage going on in this country. If only we could pin him down." John walked along the street with Emma in the warm evening air. Being back in Virginia boosted his spirits—he was near Emma. But it also tended to make him feel lazier than when he was out in the field.

It was far warmer here than in Ontario, where he'd spent the last three weeks tagging along after Canadian officials who were pursuing a ring of saboteurs. The railroad bridges and tunnels up there were all considered at high risk these days.

He'd taken dinner with Emma at the boardinghouse—she insisted he not spend money to take her out every evening he was in town. John would gladly have spent every cent of his pay on her, but he could see the sense of putting some by for the future.

Now they walked along a wide, tree-lined avenue among old houses. Did they know each other well enough for him to hold her hand as they walked? Perhaps not in public like this. He wouldn't want to embarrass her, though he longed to feel the warmth of her touch.

"Can you get a location on where the orders come from?" she asked.

"We're trying. Kobold must have underlings in different cities. We got several messages coming out of New York and Washington, but now there seem to be more in the Midwest, and even California and Seattle. It's maddening, the way he's running things, and we can't get a handle on him. He must have funding out of Germany, but we don't know how they're getting the money into our banks for him."

"Perhaps some wealthy German-Americans are making the transfers for him. Do you still think he's connected to a consulate?"

"I don't know if this individual is, but one of the main conspirators must be. Either within the German or Austrian embassy in Washington or one of their consulates in this country. I don't see how they could do all this without someone in authority being in on it."

"And he's either getting around quickly, or he has a large band of followers helping him," Emma said.

"Yes. Being here in the United States, they have almost unlimited freedom. We don't have the laws and restrictions other countries have. And their people can move freely into Canada and out again. They're wreaking havoc up there, demolishing railroad lines and communications centers then ducking back over the border."

Kobold, the unknown German leader, had to be snugly settled in America, giving orders for destruction to dozens of eager sympathizers. But there were tens of thousands of German-Americans, and most were loyal to the United States. How could they tell which ones found their heritage more important than their citizenship?

He smiled down at Emma. "Let's not talk about that anymore, all right? We both need to give our minds a rest from it."

"All right. Have you been by where they're building the monument to President Lincoln lately?" she asked.

"Not for several weeks."

"You ought to see what they're doing. It's going to be magnificent."

"Maybe we can go next weekend, if I'm in town."

"I'd like that. It's exciting to see the progress on the building." Emma told him about her recent outings with her fellow boarders and her letters from home. "Aunt Thea says Herman got a job in Portland, and he's moved there."

John hesitated but decided to bring up a topic Waller had briefed him on. "Speaking of your Maine connections, I guess you're aware that Clark Hibbert is down here now."

"Yes. I haven't seen him, and I've no desire to. The captain agreed not to tell him how to reach me."

John nodded, somehow comforted by that. According to Waller, Hibbert was housed on the navy base and so far stuck pretty much to business.

They walked in silence for a minute, and then Emma said, "Our ciphers have changed, too. They're more complicated now."

He chuckled without mirth. "So you can't put it out of your mind, either."

* * * * *

Tuesday, May 25, 1915

By late May, ten men worked alongside Emma each morning, and Muriel Ainsley's arrival caused a stir. The daughter of a navy captain, she spoke French well and had studied German and Spanish, in addition to her nurse's training.

Emma's excitement at working with the young woman was somewhat dampened by her sense of inferiority. Would the new cryptographer be better at the job than she was? She rebuked herself inwardly for having such a thought. She would rejoice that another code breaker had come to help them.

"Do you suppose she knows anything about codes?" Charles Tallie asked Martin the next morning as they poured themselves coffee.

"I certainly hope so," Martin said. "Her orientation seems to be taking longer than most."

"Maybe they're training her for something new."

"Newer than what we got off that German U-boat this morning?" Martin asked.

Charles shrugged. "She'll have to be really good to outshine the people we've got, right, Miss Shuster?"

Emma arched her eyebrows at him. "I don't think outshining us is the idea, Mr. Tallie. She's here to save lives, the same as we are."

As she turned away, she heard Charles mutter, "Pretty soon we'll be overrun with females."

The remark stung. Did the men resent having women cryptographers invade their territory? She'd felt welcome up until now, especially by Martin. Some of the younger men smiled at her and hurried to open doors for her, but most of them were quiet, studious fellows who concentrated on their work. When she'd responded to their overtures with impersonal courtesy, they had settled down, and she seldom felt that her gender caused any disarray in the office.

Commander Howe brought Muriel to Emma's table mid-morning, and Emma stood. "Miss Shuster, you'll be working with Miss Ainsley today. She's still learning our system, but we want to put her to work as soon as possible. She'll need some guidance in solving multiple alphabet and numerical ciphers. I thought working with you would help her advance quickly."

"Thank you, sir. I'll do all I can to help her." Emma smiled at Muriel and got a tentative smile in return.

"If you don't mind, I thought perhaps you ladies could attack this new text together." Howe handed Emma a folder.

"Of course," Emma said. She could put aside the one she was working on—an older message they had failed to solve. "We'll do our best."

He nodded and went to his desk.

"I'm pleased to be working with you." Muriel extended her hand.

Emma couldn't help but notice her willowy figure and her cultured tones. The young woman wore her starched navy nurse's uniform, and

Emma felt her drab brown skirt and cream blouse looked a bit dowdy by contrast.

"Thank you. Won't you sit down?" Self-consciously, Emma opened the folder and took out the cover sheet. "You've been trained in the cataloging system, I suppose."

"I'm still a bit fuzzy."

"I'd be happy to answer any questions you have." Emma studied the notations made by the man who had filed the message initially and by Captain Howe when it reached his desk. "This seems to be a variation of the Viginère Cipher."

"Oh dear," Muriel said. "Isn't that a rather complicated one?"

"Yes and no," Emma said. "It will take awhile, but we can crack it. Have you ever used the Viginère Square before?"

"I've seen it, but no."

Her lack of experience surprised Emma. She'd assumed anyone Commander Howe hired would know at least as much about ciphers as she did. She took two sheets of paper that had the cipher matrix already typed on it. "The typists make dozens of these for us, to save us time. You see how the alphabet is typed in order across the top, and again down the left side of the square?"

"Yes."

"The top row is the plain text alphabet. The side column is the cipher alphabet. Each row has the alphabet written out again, starting with the letter in the column on the left. So the second row starts with B, the third with C, and so on. Basically, this square shifts the alphabet over one place on each line, giving the user twenty-six possible alphabets. They often use a code word and repeat it over and over. For instance, if the code word was 'dog,' the first letter of the message would be enciphered using the alphabet on line D, the second using line O, and the third on line G, then the person enciphering the message would start over."

Muriel nodded slowly. "I think I understand."

"It will make more sense when you do it. Of course, this message may not be in English. I see on the cover sheet that the police reported the man they arrested was of Austrian heritage."

"My German's not that good." Muriel gave a nervous chuckle.

"I'm no expert myself, but I've worked on several messages enciphered from the German. In German, E, N, and I are the most frequently used letters. But if the clear message is put into an alternate alphabet, or multiple alphabets, the frequency tables won't help much, at least not at this stage."

They worked at the problem for two hours. By the time they were ready to break for lunch, Emma leaned toward the opinion that the message had started out in English, not German.

"All this time to decide what language," Muriel said. "We still haven't started on what it actually says."

When they came back from lunch, Emma retrieved their papers and frowned down at her work sheet. "I think we're on the right track. Sometimes walking away from the job for a little while helps. It seems to me the frequencies are right for a message in English, or nearly."

She took Muriel through the most successful method of solving a Viginère cipher, and by the middle of the afternoon they were able to turn in the plaintext.

"Rather boring on the surface," Emma told Howe. "I'm not sure why it's even in cipher. Looks like a routine diplomatic report."

"Very good, ladies." Howe grinned up at them. "I knew putting you two together was a good idea. Are you ready for another file?"

"Why not?" Emma asked.

Muriel looked at her and shrugged. "I'm willing, but I'll be the first to say that Miss Shuster did most of the work on that one."

"You certainly helped with the drudge work," Emma said. "The next one will go faster."

"Well, the next one is not a Viginère," Howe said. "This was taken off a man who was arrested in New York. The police have found bomb-making materials in his apartment. Since he had this cipher on his person, the police believe he had a partner or someone bank-rolling him. They'd like to find out who. Take a short break, make yourselves a cup of tea if you wish, and come back for this folder. See what you can make of it. It's a shorter message than the one you just cracked."

A few minutes later, Emma and Muriel settled down with the new cipher. The typists had done a letter count, and Emma consulted the frequency tables for English and German.

"It's not a very long message," Muriel said.

"Only a hundred eighty letters, so the frequencies may be distorted," Emma said. "If it were put into a different alphabet first, the frequencies would be way off, and these are close to normal for English. I think we should try it in rectangles of different dimensions."

Emma took several sheets ruled off in rectangles, choosing first a ten-by-eighteen grid. "Ten rows of eighteen each. I'll try this first because the largest rectangles you can make for the number of letters in the message often turn out to be correct."

Muriel watched her closely as she worked. "What can I do to help you?"

"Take a six-by-ten grid and do the same, but use three of them. Set it up and see if you can get anything by reading back and forth, up and down, or in a spiral."

"I'll try." Muriel set to work with her pencil and the grid Emma had indicated.

After half an hour's silent labor, Muriel laid her pencil down with a sigh. "Maybe it's German after all."

"Or maybe we just haven't looked at it through the right glasses yet. I'm going to try digraphs. There's no Q, but look for T and H together, or E and R." Emma began to copy the message again, this time in three rows sixty characters long. "Muriel!"

"What? You found something?"

"Yes. Look at this." Emma leaned eagerly toward her. "Right here. June one. That's next Sunday."

"What about June one?"

"Let's see. Alternate diagonals. I'll spell it out and you write it down for me."

A few moments later, they sat back and smiled at each other. "I believe that's a success," Muriel said.

"I agree. Let's take it to the commander." They walked together to the supervisor's desk.

Howe looked up from his own paperwork. "Well, ladies, what do you have for me? You look like two kittens with cream on their whiskers."

"We solved the message, sir." Emma held out a copy of the clear. "I put periods in where they made sense to me."

"SHIP LARKIN LEAVING CHARLESTON JUNE ONE. TAKE TRAIN STAY STJOHN. BEAR WILL SUPPLY CONTACT AND YOU DELIVER ON EVE OF LAUNCH. MAKE SURE ANONYMITY

MAINTAINED. POPPY WILL PAY ONLY AFTER SUCCESSFUL MISSION. DO NOT CONTACT." Howe lowered the paper and looked up. "What do you make of it?"

"He was to go to Charleston and sabotage a ship leaving the first," Muriel said.

Emma nodded. "That seems the most likely interpretation. His employers have taken steps to distance themselves through two or three layers of contacts. And the man who received the message was warned not to try to contact them. I suppose Poppy is a code name for his employer."

"The big boss, maybe." Howe scrutinized the message again. "And 'Bear'?"

Emma brushed a stray lock of hair back from her forehead. "That could be a code name for the contact. St. John could be, too."

"I disagree on that point," Howe said, rising. "There's a hotel called the St. John in Charleston."

"Really?" Muriel said. "Then we can stop him."

"Perhaps. So far as we know, this man's contacts don't know we've pinched him. Good job, ladies. I must send this message off to our naval staff in Charleston as quickly as possible."

"Make sure you code it well," Emma called after him.

Howe laughed and turned back. "No fear. I shall have it hand delivered by a trusty messenger."

Emma's heart sank. She had a feeling she knew who the Signal Corps counted on as their most trustworthy courier for messages of that ilk. No doubt she would find a message from John at the boardinghouse saying he could not see her that evening, as he was being sent out of town. This time, she thought she knew where.

CHAPTER FOURTEEN

Friday, May 28, 1915

John waited at the hotel, hoping his trip from Washington to Charleston wouldn't be wasted. He'd taken a room under the name of the man arrested in New York—Kurt Schwartz. Unless the New York police were wrong and Schwartz's friends knew of his arrest, John ought to receive a visit soon. That, or a message bearing instructions of some sort.

Captain Waller had prepared him to receive an enciphered message. Solving ciphers was not John's forte, but he had carefully studied the message Emma deciphered two days earlier, and he thought he could untangle one scrambled in a similar manner. If not, he would telegraph the message by a pre-arranged method from the hotel directly to Commander Howe, who would have his cryptographers drop everything else to solve it quickly.

Waiting was the hardest part. It was now Friday, and the ship would sail on Tuesday. It would be unrealistic for the contact to approach him too close to the sailing time. They would need time to transfer the supposed bomb to the cargo hold of the ship.

A courier had dashed down from New York, bringing him a suitcase from the prisoner's apartment. It contained a homemade bomb—minus the TNT that would have made it lethal. Instead they had substituted a harmless look-alike material. Officers in New York were now backtracking on Schwartz's trail to find out where he obtained the TNT.

John had put a few civilian clothes in the suitcase with the apparatus and shed his uniform and identification. Only Waller knew the real identity of the man waiting to meet Kurt Schwartz's contact in Charleston. While he had alerted navy officials in Charleston, they had decided to keep the details of John's meeting under wraps for fear of scaring off the man who was to make the contact.

On his arrival Thursday evening, John had visited the waterfront first and located the *Larkin* in its berth, loading cargo. Word had reached Washington just before he left of another American steamer hit by Germans. The *Nebraskan* was struck by a torpedo or a mine— the authorities weren't sure which—forty miles off Ireland. The ship had limped into Liverpool without loss of life. John was determined to save the *Larkin* from a worse fate.

He'd gone from the harbor to the St. John Hotel. He didn't dare leave the room for long, lest he miss the contact, so he had dinner and breakfast sent to his room. He'd brought along a crime novel, but the story couldn't hold his attention. His thoughts kept turning to Emma. Was she thinking of him?

By noon Friday he was ready to climb the walls, so he decided to pop out for a quick meal down the street. The pot roast and gravy tasted good, but John couldn't stop fretting while he ate. Was he foolish to leave the hotel, where the saboteurs planned to reach him?

He paid his bill and carried a slice of pie back to his room in a small box. Entering the hotel lobby, he scanned each person in the room. To one side, ostensibly reading a newspaper, sat a man in a worn suit, with a fedora resting on one knee. John walked to the stairway and turned to glance back as he opened the door. The man folded his newspaper and rose from his chair.

John pulled his room key from his pocket and hurried upstairs. At the landing, he looked carefully down the hall before stepping out of the doorway. It seemed empty except for two women walking together toward the stairs. He passed them with a nod and quickly unlocked his door and slipped inside.

He had been in the room for less than two minutes when someone knocked on the door. John glanced at the suitcase on the bed and walked over to the door.

* * * * *

Kobold answered the phone, though he wanted to ignore its ringing. He'd told the secretary not to disturb him while he met with the Italian ambassador. "Yes?"

"I have urgent news."

He flicked a glance at his guest. "I cannot speak now. Can you call later?"

"No, I think you need to hear this now."

"All right. Hold on." He placed his hand over the mouthpiece and gritted his teeth. The ambassador did not look happy. "I beg your pardon, sir. You will have to forgive me for this interruption, but I'm told it is urgent state business."

"Of course." The ambassador rose and walked to the window and stood there back-to, jingling the coins in his pocket.

"Go ahead," Kobold said into the telephone.

"Our man in Brooklyn was arrested Wednesday."

"What? Impossible. He took the train to the next location yesterday."

"I don't know about that, but I got the word from one of his neighbors. Double checked it, and it's true. The feds took him away quiet-like Wednesday evening."

Kobold sat still for a moment. The pain over his breastbone that plagued him during stressful moments had returned. "I understand. Send word to the contact. Now."

"Yes, sir." The other man hung up.

The Italian stood rigid by the window.

Kobold wondered what his guest had made of the conversation. Had he given away anything? He took his handkerchief from his pocket and dabbed at the perspiration on his brow. Pulling open his bottom desk drawer and reaching for the bottle he kept there, he plastered on a smile. "Now then, where were we? I tell the girl not to interrupt, but she still lets calls through. Most distressing. Would you care for a drink?"

* * * * *

John touched the knob on the door of his hotel room. "Who is it?" he called.

"Bear."

Against all his instincts, he opened the door.

The man from the hotel lobby slid past him into the room and turned to face him.

"Where is it?"

John nodded toward the suitcase. The man walked over to the bed and opened it. He tossed out the clothes covering the disabled bomb and eyed the apparatus. "All right, you'll hand it over tonight to the one who will get it onto the ship."

"Where? Here?"

"No. You'll take the suitcase to a bar down near the docks. It is near where the *Larkin* is docked."

"All right."

"You will go into the Tin Spoon and order beer. Your contact will find you there. He wears spectacles, and he has gray hair. He will sit beside you and lay a book of matches on the bar. You will leave the suitcase, and he will take it away."

"All right," John said. "Then what?"

"Then you are free to go home. When Poppy hears that the ship has sunk, he will send you your pay."

John pursed his lips. "Can't I get a little something in advance? The train ride, the hotel…"

Bear scowled but reached into his pocket. He pulled out a roll of bills, peeled off a twenty, and tossed it on the bed. "Don't ask for more until the job is done."

John nodded. He wished he could stop Bear from leaving, but that would present problems. If he took the man into custody, it would ruin his chances of learning the contact's identity. But if he let Bear go, would they ever learn who "Poppy" was and who was funding this operation? In a crowded bar, he wouldn't have the option of arresting the contact. Maybe he should take Bear into custody now, turn him over to the police, and still meet the other man tonight. He made a quick decision. With no one to back him up, he had to act fast. He reached under his jacket and pulled out his pistol. "You're under arrest. Put your hands up."

Bear moved faster than seemed possible. He shoved into John and raced for the door.

John regained his balance and aimed at the fleeing man but hesitated. What if an innocent person was passing by in the hall? He didn't pull the trigger but raced to the door after Bear.

By the time he got out into the hall, the man had disappeared, and the stairway door was closing.

John pocketed the pistol and ran after him. When he reached the bottom of the stairs and burst out into the lobby, the desk clerk looked up in surprise.

"Did a man in a fedora just run through here?" John asked.

"No."

John sighed and went slowly back up the stairs. He had never made such a serious mistake in his military career. How would he explain to Captain Waller?

* * * * *

"This may be a crucial one." Captain Howe laid a folder on Emma's table and walked on to place another before Martin and one before Muriel. He made his round of the room, until each of the twelve cryptographers had a folder.

"We all get the same cipher?" Martin asked.

"That's right. Time is of the essence."

Emma opened hers and took out the cover sheet. "What do we know about it?"

"We intercepted some letters yesterday from the German Embassy. We've seen several telegrams that went out from there in a new configuration this week. We think they may have changed their main cipher."

"It was bound to happen," said Charles Tallie.

"Yes, unfortunately for us," Howe said. "We'd done pretty well solving their messages for the past three weeks. The message Miss Shuster and Miss Ainsley solved earlier this week was not in the main cipher, so I don't think their key will crack this one, but I'll have Miss Ainsley try that first."

Muriel nodded.

"Yesterday we managed to get hold of a mailing that went out about one in the afternoon," Howe said. "We'd been watching a certain party, but it's nearly impossible to keep tabs on him once he's inside the embassy's compound. Our agent decided it was time to read their mail. Three letters were sent to three operatives in different locations. The envelopes were all the same, with the diplomatic franking on them."

Emma raised her eyebrows. Tampering with the U.S. mail was a crime.

"Oh, the addressees will receive their messages, never fear. But not until Monday. We steamed them open, made copies, and sealed the originals up again in their envelopes. We managed to delay them by twenty-four hours or so. That's to give you time to work on it. We have the weekend. Are you all willing to put in extra hours if needed?"

"Of course," said Martin.

Several of the others answered in the affirmative, and Emma nodded when Howe looked her way. With John out of town, working long hours would keep her occupied.

"Good," Howe said. "I need not remind you that you are to say nothing of this business outside this room. I'd like each of you to go at it with your individual expertise. If you think you've made some progress, share what you've found with the others. I looked this over, and I think it may be another Playfair variation, but I could be wrong."

Emma decided to explore that possibility first. Howe was not their quickest solver, but he had a deep understanding of the work involved. He'd seen so many incoming messages that his first instincts for classifying them were often correct.

Three hours later, Martin had the first breakthrough. He had tentatively identified a letter group. He sent a copy of his work sheet to the typists' room so they could reproduce it for all of the other cryptographers.

Howe asked Mrs. Harper to send out for lunch for the entire staff so they could keep working. At half-past three, he called for their attention. "Folks, we've worked hard all day, and we're not finished yet, though this cipher seems to be showing some cracks. I suggest we take a half hour off and go out onto the back lawn and have a game of baseball."

"Baseball?" Emma looked over at Muriel.

Howe opened a desk drawer, took out a ball, tossed it into the air, and caught it. "It will be good for everyone to get a little fresh air and stretch our limbs." Without warning, he fired the ball at Charles Tallie, who caught it and tossed it to Martin. "Right," Howe said. "I'll lock this room. Let's go!"

Emma hadn't played ball for years—not since her stint living with the Meyers as a child. Herman and Karl had pressed her and Gretchen into backyard games with them and a few neighborhood children. Martin and Commander Howe quickly chose teams, and she found herself on Martin's side. They went to bat first, and she nervously awaited her turn. One of Howe's young men caught Charles's fly ball, and Muriel struck out.

Martin picked up the bat and placed it in Emma's hands.

"Oh, I'm not sure…" She looked up into his laughing eyes.

"Come on, Emma. You can do it."

She pulled in a deep breath and turned to face the pitcher, Larry Crane, one of their newer members.

The first ball flew past before she was ready.

"Strike!" Howe had appointed himself umpire as well as catcher for his team.

Emma squared her shoulders.

"Go, Emma," Muriel called.

Larry threw the ball again, slower this time. She swung at it.

The bat connected, to her surprise, though not nearly hard enough. The ball flew forward a couple of yards and hit the ground, rolling toward Larry.

"Run!" Martin's shout brought her out of her shock.

She tore for first base, a folded newspaper guarded by Rory Ingersoll. Halfway there, she realized she still gripped the bat and let it fall. Just before she reached the base, Rory stretched, and the ball smacked into his hands.

"You're out!"

Emma skidded to a halt, profoundly disappointed.

Rory laughed. "You made a good try, Miss Shuster."

They switched positions and played the other half of the inning. Howe's team managed to score two runs. They trooped back inside laughing and promising each other a rematch soon.

Not long after they'd settled again into their almost silent work, Emma noticed a repetition in the cipher message that had eluded her earlier. If CR stood for EN and YR stood for ON, then...

She shoved back her chair and stood, still staring down at her paper. "Commander."

"Yes, Miss Shuster?" Howe hurried to her side.

"I've got something." She showed him her conclusion. "This could be Trenton, and if it is, then this…"

"Is TNT. Quick," Howe said, "copy it off for the typists. I think you're right."

Emma took a fresh sheet with the ciphered message on it and wrote in the letters she had tentatively identified.

Howe dashed for the typists' room.

"Keep working, boys and girls," Charles said. "If Miss Shuster's got a firm clue, we'll have it in minutes. But we need to keep on, in case it doesn't pan out."

"That's right, Mr. Tallie." Emma smiled at him. "If I'm correct, it's ten rows of twenty-one, twice over, for a total of four hundred twenty letters." She sank into her chair, certain about her findings. All around her, pencils scratched on paper. She seized a clean paper with a blank grid and quickly rearranged the columns.

The key word didn't have to be ten letters long, but it seemed likely, given the few repetitions she found. She numbered the columns she had juggled. Yes, the second rectangle of rows and columns would be rearranged in the same order as the first. She wrote the numbers of the order in which the rows belonged. Number six first, then ten, then eight, then seven… It gave her the alphabetical order of the letters in the key word. The result was 6 10 8 7 5 9 2 4 1 3.

The alphabetically earliest letter in the key word—very possibly A—was in the sixth position of the ten letters, and the second letter was in the tenth position.…

Howe reentered the room a few minutes later with a sheaf of papers. "Here we go, folks. Miss Shuster, anything to add?"

"Yes, sir. I think I've found the key."

Howe came instantly to her table and looked over her shoulder. "Tourmaline?"

"Yes, sir." Her arms prickled, and she began to shake. She hugged herself to still the tremors.

"What is it?" Martin called from across the room.

"Tourmaline," Howe replied.

"What's that?" Larry asked.

Emma looked up and caught his gaze. "It's a semi-precious stone."

Larry blinked. "Whoever would have thought it?"

"Obviously Miss Shuster would," said Howe.

Rory Ingersoll rose and hurried to the library corner.

Emma looked up into the commander's face. "Sir, it's not so valuable as a diamond, but it's somewhat rare. In fact, so far as I know, it's only found in a few places."

Howe's chin rose a fraction of an inch, and his dark eyebrows hiked up. "Where would that be?"

Emma gulped. "Well, Maine for starters."

Rory called, "She's right. It's a crystal that comes in a variety of colors and is used for jewelry. It comes from Ceylon, Brazil, and various locations in Africa. It's also found in Maine, and recently some has turned up near San Diego, California."

"So…" Howe tapped a finger to his lips then focused once more on Emma. "You're thinking there's a Maine connection."

"Possibly."

He nodded. "One of the three letters was addressed to a man in Harpswell, Maine."

"That's near Brunswick, where I lived with my father."

Howe nodded. "The others were going to the Pittsburgh area and Seattle."

"So the use of the key word may be a coincidence."

"It may. A person familiar with the stone may have chosen it. Or he may have picked it from the dictionary as a likely key." Howe strode toward his desk. "I'll call our people in Boston. They've already sent someone to look into this Harpswell man's background and activities. Perhaps they've found something. Meanwhile, let's get those letters unscrambled."

Emma seized her pen. Martin was probably halfway through the first of the three intercepted letters, now that he had the key. She flipped to the third message and took a fresh grid sheet. Quickly she wrote out the alphabet with the word tourmaline first, followed by the remaining letters, minus J. She used five rows of five letters, as was standard for the Playfair Cipher.

```
T O U R M
A L I N E
B C D F G
H K P Q S
V W X Y Z
```

The first two letters of the cipher message were R and M. Since they were in the same row of the alphabet square, she wrote above them the letters that preceded each: U and R.

"Martin, have you got the first word of the first message yet?"

"Yes. It's 'urgent.'"

Emma smiled and quickly checked the next pair of letters. GE in the clear had been transformed into SG in the cipher, since G and E came in the same vertical column of the alphabet key square.

"I'm getting that in message three as well," she called.

"Good," Martin said. "I'm well into the first one, and Rory is helping me. Charles and Larry, take the second one."

For several minutes all was silent but for the scratching of pencils on paper.

"Done," Martin called, shoving his chair back.

"Excellent." Commander Howe stood and took the paper from him.

A few minutes later, Emma put her plaintext in his hands, and Charles brought his soon after.

"Good work," Howe said. "These are very similar in nature, but they vary in details. I'll contact authorities in each city immediately."

Emma let out a long, slow breath and looked across the table at Muriel.

"They're bombing factories," Muriel whispered. "Here in America."

"Yes. Let's pray our forces can stop them."

CHAPTER FIFTEEN

Monday, May 31, 1915

"Don't punish yourself so severely," Captain Waller said. "We prevented one of our ships from being destroyed at sea."

John sat straight and tall in the chair, as much as he wanted to let his shoulders slump. "Yes, sir, but their man got away, and now they know we're onto their cipher."

"True. They probably won't use that one again, and we'll have to start from scratch with the next one. Sometimes that happens, Patterson."

"Yes, sir." John gulped. He hadn't seen Emma since his return from the botched assignment. She was probably at work, and he'd come first to his commanding officer, as was right. "What should I do now, sir?"

"Take a few days off."

John lowered his gaze. The contact in Charleston had not shown up at the bar. John hadn't supposed he would, but he'd kept the assignation, in case Bear hadn't reached his counterpart in time. No one had made any contact with him, and he'd taken the night train north, bringing back the useless bomb in the suitcase. Now it seemed Waller would have him put aside for a few days. The captain might call it a rest or a leave, but it felt like recompense for bungling a sensitive operation. "I'd rather keep working, sir."

"Would you? Hmm." Waller frowned then reached for a file folder on the edge of his desk. "Sit down, Patterson. There is something you could do. I daresay it will seem trivial and perhaps boring."

"I'm sure that if you deem it important, sir, then it is."

Waller smiled. "It's indirectly connected to Miss Shuster, and I believe your interests lie in that direction."

John wasn't sure what to say. He made no secret of his admiration for Emma, but neither did he flaunt it.

The captain's expression slackened into a slight frown. "Of course, discretion is important. We've brought a fellow down from Maine to work on a cryptography project. You've met him—Hibbert. The one who was working on the Shuster machine."

"Yes, sir."

"He's been here three weeks or so, and until now he's kept to himself. He's gone to a picture show with a couple of fellows from the base, and he's done some shopping and other errands in his free time. But yesterday he broke his pattern."

John arched his eyebrows and waited.

"He took a trolley to Fairfax."

John caught his breath. "To what purpose, if I may ask?"

"You may, indeed. He wandered about and made a few inquiries in diners and hair salons."

"Hair salons?" John's pulse quickened. That weasel.

Waller nodded. "At half past four, he took up a post at the trolley stop, as though watching for someone. Stayed there until six o'clock then hopped a car back here."

"He's searching for Miss Shuster."

"My opinion as well."

"You've had him shadowed?"

"Yes." Waller tossed the folder onto the desk. "My fear is that in his inquiries he will expose Miss Shuster and perhaps even the Signal Corps' Cipher Division. Our enemies have started hearing rumors about us—that we've got a crackerjack unit breaking their codes and ciphers. If they learned the location of that organization, it would be a simple matter for them to wipe out our best cryptographers. One large dynamite charge—or a bomb similar to the one we disarmed and sent to Charleston with you."

John's pulse pounded in his temple. "You want Hibbert silenced?"

"Only in the metaphorical sense. I called him in here this morning and asked him what he was up to. He claimed he'd only gone sightseeing yesterday. But he admitted he hoped to catch wind of Emma's whereabouts. I told him I'd get in touch with her again and ask if she would see him, but in return, he had to promise to stop looking for her. I forbade him to speak her name or anything connected with cryptography outside the base."

"And what do you want me to do, sir? Follow him about and make sure he complies?"

Waller eyed him pensively. "I thought perhaps you could strike up a friendship with him. Run into him by accident, so to speak, and befriend him. Keep it unofficial, so far as he knows. Maybe he'd tell you what his real interest is in Emma Shuster."

"You think it's more than a crush?"

"Maybe. I hope I haven't made a mistake in bringing him here."

John's mind darted off in several directions, chasing ramifications of Hibbert's presence. "Surely he won't tell me if he's here to carry out espionage."

"No, but he might be more frank with you than he would with me."

"I'm not so sure about that."

"Because Emma likes you?"

John shrugged. "He seemed a bit wary of me when we met in Maine."

"I can understand that. You're taller, better looking, and you wear a uniform. Rather hard for a man like Hibbert to compete. But you'd be a familiar face to him."

"And a possible connection to Emma?"

"Yes. I don't think he'd turn down a supper invitation from you, if only to talk about her. Maybe you can spend some evenings with him and keep him out of mischief. During the day, I'll use you as a courier. In the meantime, I'll speak to Miss Shuster again and see if we think it's in the best interest of our Cryptography Division for her to see him."

John hesitated. He didn't want to become Clark Hibbert's new best friend. And even more, he didn't want Emma to be pressured into spending time with Hibbert.

* * * * *

Sunday, June 6, 1915

"May I sit here?"

Emma looked up, and her pulse accelerated. John stood at the end of the pew she shared with Doris. "Of course." She slid over. As always, he was impeccably groomed in his uniform, but his usually animated brown eyes held a shadow today. As he took his place beside her, breathless awareness of him washed over her.

Doris leaned forward and smiled at him across Emma. "Welcome back, Lieutenant."

"Thank you."

He tipped his head toward Emma and said quietly, "May I take you to dinner after the service? I'd like a chance to talk to you."

"Well…" Outwardly Emma sat as still and serene as the eighty-year-old dowager at the far end of the pew. But her pulse jumped and careened, and each breath brought her the scent of his shaving lotion and a sense of unreality. She looked straight ahead. How could she have entertained the idea that they weren't suited for each other?

Careful, she told herself. *Emotion is not the basis for a permanent liaison.* Trust. That was a major requirement. Could she entirely trust John? One glance at the stalwart young warrior beside her, and she would shout, "Yes! Of course I can." And yet…

He'd been home nearly a week, she knew, but he hadn't called her. Instead, he'd opted to spring into her Sunday morning routine without warning. Now he expected her to shelve any plans she had made with Doris and join him for the afternoon. Should she turn him down? Of course, she and Doris only planned to go back to Mrs. Draper's and eat the dinner they had already paid for.

The very fact that John hadn't called her in the last week seemed a deviation in character from all that she knew of him. He'd always been courteous in the extreme and eager to see her when he came home from an assignment.

"How was your trip?" Let him wonder a little longer whether she would accept.

His lips compressed for a moment. "Disappointing. I'll tell you later—some of it, anyway."

"Excuse me."

They both looked up. In the aisle at the end of their pew, hat in hand, stood Clark Hibbert.

* * * * *

John leaped to his feet. "Hibbert. How extraordinary."

"Not really. Delighted to see you again, Patterson." The two men shook hands, but as they did so, Clark's gaze slid past John and landed on Emma.

John turned and looked at her, his stomach roiling. Would she think he had arranged this? On Tuesday he'd followed the captain's wishes and "bumped into" Clark on the navy base, rather than calling Emma and arranging a date with her. All week he'd been at the beck and call of the captain's office, running errands any sailor could handle. Evenings he'd spent with the indefatigable talker, Hibbert—a movie, a game of chess, a shopping foray. He couldn't remember a more boring week, and this was his payment.

He'd stayed away from Emma for fear of bringing Clark into her vicinity—or so he'd told himself. If he were honest, he'd admit he'd avoided calling her because he still felt the shame of having failed in his important mission. She knew about the Charleston setup. She'd solved the cipher that sent him there. She'd want to know what happened. He could plead security as an excuse not to tell her, and she would accept that, but he would feel the constant humiliation.

"Emma." Clark used a tone so reverent that John winced.

Emma's cheeks paled. After the slightest hesitation, she said, "Mr. Hibbert." She didn't rise or offer her hand.

"I've been hoping to see you," Clark said.

John considered reminding him of the condition Captain Waller had imposed on him, but he didn't want to embarrass Emma further. Apparently Clark felt the opportunity to see the woman he adored was worth facing the captain's wrath.

Clark stood awkwardly in the aisle, waiting for a response from Emma or an invitation to sit down from John.

Emma's jaw twitched, but she still didn't speak.

John looked steadily into Clark's eyes, hoping he would take the hint. "It's good to see you again. Perhaps we'll talk later." Mentally, he kicked himself for not being more careful this morning. He shouldn't have let his guard down, but he'd thought only of getting to where Emma would be and breaking the awkward silence between them, never suspecting he would be followed.

Strains from the organ hushed the whispers throughout the auditorium. The minister had risen and approached the pulpit. Clark gave a curt nod and walked to a vacant seat across the aisle.

"Good morning. Let us turn to number twenty-three," the pastor called.

John exhaled and sat down again. He threw Emma an apologetic glance, but she earnestly thumbed through the hymnal, avoiding his gaze.

She barely looked John's way during the entire hour. His heart sank lower and lower. He would have to explain that he had not engineered the encounter. But could they get out of the church without speaking to Clark again?

At last the final hymn died away and the minister intoned the benediction. Emma sat down with a plop.

John sat beside her, casting an anxious look at Doris, who bent over her friend.

"Are you all right, Emma?" Doris asked in a hushed voice.

"I don't wish to see him."

"I'm so sorry." John leaned forward, hoping his back would shield her from Clark's view. "Perhaps we can go out through a different door and—"

"Do you folks have plans for lunch?"

Too late. Emma touched John's sleeve and pushed him back.

"Hello again, Mr. Hibbert," she said firmly. "I'm afraid we do have plans. That is, Miss Keating and I do. I'm not sure about Lieutenant Patterson."

So. She was disowning him. John tried not to let his hurt show. She must be angry with him but didn't want the others to see it. He wouldn't add to her discomfiture.

"Oh," Clark said. "I'd hoped we could catch up. Did you know I was in the area? Captain Waller said he would tell you, but I wasn't sure if he'd done that."

Emma's face flushed a rosy hue. "Yes, he did. I hope you're enjoying the South."

"I'm working for the navy now. In fact, I'm thinking of enlisting."

"Really?"

John could see her struggle to give only noncommittal answers. He stood and turned to face Clark. "I don't think this is the best time to try to speak to Miss Shuster."

"Well, when is a good time?" Clark looked past him at Emma.

"May I telephone you, Emma? Or pick a time, and I'll call on you. Or I could meet you someplace, if you wish."

"No, I don't think so." Emma stood and gathered her Bible and crocheted purse.

"But—but you're the only person here that I know from Maine. And—do you know about—" He darted a quick glance around at the flowing crowd. "About my work?"

"I believe I know that to which you're referring," she said. "But we're not to discuss it."

"Oh." Clark's posture sagged, and his expression wilted.

Doris put a protective hand on Emma's sleeve. "I believe Miss Shuster and I will take our leave now. It was a—" She swallowed hard. "A pleasure to meet you, sir. And to see you, Lieutenant."

"No, wait," Emma spoke softly and took a deep breath. "Mr. Hibbert, if it is so important to you, I will take luncheon with you, if Lieutenant Patterson and Miss Keating will join us."

John turned away from Clark and whispered, "Are you sure?"

She nodded. Her training in etiquette wouldn't let her snub the man.

"Where?" he hissed. "You pick the place."

"Anywhere that's not near…" She didn't finish, but he thought he understood. Not near Mrs. Draper's. She wanted to prevent Clark from learning where she lived, if at all possible.

"There's a diner that's open Sundays not far from here." Doris smiled at all of them as though they were four friends planning a picnic. "And the prices are reasonable." She turned wide eyes on John, as if the fact that someone would have to pay the bill had just occurred to her.

"I'd be happy to treat you ladies," he said quickly.

"We can split it." Clark smiled from ear to ear. "It sounds grand."

* * * * *

The diner was crowded, and they had to wait for a table. As they stood squished together inside the door, Emma wished she hadn't given in.

The air in the enclosed space grew warmer and warmer, and Clark talked almost nonstop. "Do you remember Professor Rideout from the college? He's resigned. Going to teach in Arizona. Can you imagine? Going from New England to the desert."

"Perhaps he dislikes the long winters you have in Maine," John said.

Clark was not to be distracted. Still gazing at Emma, he continued. "Say, we had a student from Mattawumkeag last semester—a freshman—who died of appendicitis. It was awful."

Emma winced. "I'm sure it was." She noticed other waiting patrons eyeing them curiously and whispering. She cast a pleading gaze at John.

Once again, the lieutenant rose to the occasion. "Say, Clark, why don't we see if we can get a glass of water for the ladies? It's getting warm in here."

"That would be nice," Doris said. "I hope a table outside will open up for us."

Clark went off with John, and the errand kept them away for five minutes.

"Are you terribly uncomfortable?" Doris asked.

"I'm still not used to this heat, but it could be worse," Emma said.

"I meant because of Mr. Hibbert."

"Oh. I decided it was pointless to try to avoid Clark. If I didn't talk to him today, he would manufacture another encounter. I'd rather choose the time and place than have him spring it on me again."

"Is he such a bad fellow?" Doris glanced over her shoulder and dropped her voice. "I mean, I can see that he's a bit boorish, and he's not much to look at, but you don't think he means you any harm, do you?"

"Not really. It's annoying, though, to think he's prowling about, watching me, and apt to pop up wherever I go. When I left Maine, I thought I was through with that."

"So, he bothered you a lot there?"

"The college community kept him accountable, I think. He needed to keep a good reputation with the faculty. But here, it's as though he's renewed his—his—oh, I don't know what to call it."

"His passion for you?" Doris giggled and slapped a hand over her mouth to contain it.

"Oh, please don't start that." Emma looked up and saw the young men returning with tumblers of water. "Hush now. They're coming. I'm trying to be civil. If he won't take hints, then I shall have to be forthright."

"Here you go, ladies." John handed Emma a glass, and Clark offered his to Doris.

"Took us awhile to get a waitress's attention, they're so busy." Clark peered at Emma through his spectacles. "They say we'll be seated soon."

"Good," Emma said. "Thank you very much."

A minute later, a young woman in a gray dress and white apron approached them.

"I've a table for four on the back terrace."

"Thank heaven," Doris murmured.

They edged through the crowded diner in the waitress's wake, to a door at the rear. Outside, a dozen tables were spaced about the cobbled terrace. They claimed the only vacant one. Clark hurried to pull Emma's chair out before John could get to it. While he seated her, Doris slipped into the chair on one side of her, and John took the other. Clark frowned but walked around to the seat opposite Emma. They immediately gave the waitress their orders for sandwiches and cool drinks.

"Isn't this weather something, Emma?" Clark asked. "It's more sultry here the first week in June than in August up in Maine."

"Yes, it's very warm." She sat with her hands folded in her lap, not meeting Clark's gaze.

John cleared his throat. "So, Mr. Hibbert, you mentioned to me last night how the college had lost several students to the war effort."

"Yes, that's true. Several quit school to take jobs. The factories in Portland are paying quite well now, and one or two have gone to the ironworks."

Emma raised her chin and eyed him cautiously.

Clark went on, "Then there were a couple of fellows who went to Canada to try to join their military. They can't wait for the States to get into it." He shook his head. "A bit shortsighted of them, I'd say. And one was an engineering student."

"That must be a fascinating field of study," Doris said.

Clark turned eagerly toward her. "Oh, it is, Miss Keating. I love building things. And last summer I took some special training in demolition. Engineers have to know about that as well."

"Demolition?" Doris blinked at him, and he seized the invitation to continue. "Yes. Lots of times before a new building or bridge can be built, earth and rock have to be removed. Even old structures."

Emma caught her breath and made herself not stare at Clark. Instead, she looked at John.

He, too, had taken note of the topic and sent her a sidelong glance.

She tried to reassure herself that Clark would not boast of his expertise in demolition if he intended to use the skill for sabotage. Or would he?

CHAPTER SIXTEEN

Thursday, June 10, 1915

Captain Waller visited Trafton House on Thursday and detailed the good that had been done because of the cryptographers' recent work. He especially praised them for solving the cipher that foretold the attempts to bomb factories.

"Your work is far from done, however. There seems to be a renewed effort on the part of the Germans to buy legitimate passports. A lot of their reserve army officers were caught on the wrong side of the ocean when the war broke out. Some were here in the United States, but dozens seem to have been in South America. Lately quite a few who couldn't get to Europe from Brazil and Argentina have come up here hoping to find a way home from this country."

"Why would it be easier to get to Germany from here?" Charles asked.

"It wouldn't be, except that scores of American citizens—most of them with German or Austrian ties—have willingly sold their passports to help the Kaiser. The displaced reserve officers are using them to sail back to Germany. They're getting through our customs using other people's legitimate documents. Some belong to Danish or Norwegian citizens, but quite a few are genuine American passports."

"That's incredible," Muriel said.

"Not really. Many immigrants still consider themselves Germans, even second-generation Americans. And they know they won't be able to travel to Europe for a while, so they see it as an act of patriotism—not to mention a source of income—to sell their passports to German agents. It's disappointing, but it's happening. A lot. I'm telling you this so that you'll be on the alert for messages concerning passport fraud."

After discussing a few other points with the dozen cryptographers on duty, Captain Waller asked Emma to join him in private. "I understand you've had a run-in with Clark Hibbert."

She grimaced. "Yes, sir."

"I apologize. He was told not to contact you. He tells me that he only followed Patterson because he was at loose ends Sunday morning and thought he'd go to church with him. If you believe his story, then he started out too late and the lieutenant was already in motion, so he simply followed him to the church."

"I *don't* believe that, but it's done," Emma said.

"Was it so awful?"

"I suppose not. He's the same old Clark. I do hope I can keep my address and Mrs. Draper's telephone number private. It's probably only a matter of time before he gets them, though. And Lieutenant Patterson told you that Clark said he'd had demolition training?"

"Yes. That is of concern. Again, I assure you we've done a thorough check into his background, and the course he mentioned is standard for engineering students. We've found no connection whatsoever between him and the German sympathizers in Maine or in this region."

She nodded, thinking that over. "So he's not a threat, just an annoyance to me."

"I'd say so. And he won't be more than a few more weeks working on the cipher machine. After that, either he'll join the navy—and go off for basic training—or we'll turn him loose, and I expect he'll head back to Maine. He's told me he applied for a couple of teaching positions for fall."

"All right."

Waller smiled ruefully. "Perhaps I made a mistake in bringing him here. My biggest fear is that he'll be a security risk because he talks so much."

Emma smiled at that. "You've hit it, sir. I'm a quiet person, and I do find his chatter tedious."

"Well, if you see him again, perhaps you can steer the conversation around to who his friends are and where his loyalty lies. He might tell you something he wouldn't tell me or another military man."

Emma hoped she would have no occasion to do that, but given the circumstances, it was entirely possible. "We shall see. And of course I'll tell you if he lets fall anything suspicious."

* * * * *

Though Emma had hoped for a chance to talk things out with John, his commanding officer kept him busy, and they didn't manage to get together in their leisure hours. All she knew of his trip to South Carolina was that things had not gone as planned. For some reason, that had created a barrier between them. Whenever she thought about John, sadness crept over her, so she tried not to think about him too much. If he truly wished to make things right, he would contact her.

The following Friday, Commander Howe summoned Emma and Martin to his desk as soon as they arrived at work. His eyes glittered as he gestured for them to follow him into the hallway. "I know it's been a long, tough week, but I've got a new cipher for the two of you to work on."

"Why all the secrecy?" Martin asked. "What are we doing out here in the corridor?"

Emma wondered that too. Howe usually made the assignments inside Room 20, with all the cryptographers in earshot.

Howe closed the door and eyed them gravely. "This one's from Kobold. Our men in the field intercepted it. We're sure where it came from. If this message contains incriminating data, we may be able to arrest him."

"You know who he is?" Emma's pulse tripped.

"Not exactly. But we're certain he works at the German embassy in Washington. There are a couple of dozen men working there who might fit the bill. He's one of them."

"What if they're all in it?" Martin asked.

"They may well be. But Kobold has high-level contacts in Germany and Austria. He's given the orders for many acts of sabotage and arranged payments to the men who have carried them out. We believe he's also behind some of the propaganda campaigns sweeping our factories and promoting unrest in the labor ranks. He's the one we want most. Within the United States, he is possibly the most dangerous enemy we have at this moment."

Emma inhaled slowly. Their shadowy enemy would finally take form. She and Martin had it within their power to put a name and a face on the elusive Kobold.

"Our unit works well together," Howe said, "but we've got a lot of people working in there now. We have some new information from our friends in England about the dictionary codes Germany is using for their naval dispatches, and I'll put most of the other cryptographers on that. But this one…it's critical. I feel it. And it's different. So I'm asking you two to give it everything you've got, and I'm putting you in an empty office downstairs, so you can concentrate better. Take your dictionaries and frequency tables along and be prepared to spend the day on this one."

Emma gathered grid sheets, pencils, a binder of German frequency tables, and a pad of plain paper. She and Martin went with Howe to the first floor and into a small room across from Mrs. Harper's office. It held a plain wooden table near the window and two straight chairs. Against one wall, a small stand held a pitcher of water and two glasses.

"If you find you can't work here—if it's too stark and quiet—why, come on back to the farmyard," Howe said with a smile. "I know everyone has different styles of working."

Emma thought she would like the seclusion. Having worked with Martin several times before, she was confident they could divide the work with no jealousy or wrangling over tasks. Her worst problem would be forgetting about John and Clark for the day. She had to put them both out of her mind and focus on the task.

All morning the two of them worked without a break, trying various tactics to break the cipher. She appreciated the way Martin methodically attacked the problem, eliminating one possibility after another. At noon they brought their sack lunches to the room and ate while talking over the methods they'd tried and ones yet untested.

"They're sure it's in German," Martin mused. He took a bite of his sandwich and leaned back in his chair.

"I think they're right about that," Emma said. "We've had a few in English come out of the embassy before, but most have been in German. This one feels like a German message to me."

Martin nodded. "All our attempts to squeeze it into an English mold have failed."

"Commander Howe thinks the entire German embassy is suspect."

"Yes, but our agents must have narrowed the field more than that for Kobold's identity. I'll bet they have three or four diplomats they're looking to pin it on."

Emma finished her lunch, rose, and stretched.

"We ought to take a walk and get some fresh air," Martin said.

"Let's work awhile longer. I feel ready to go back at it. When we get tired again, we can take a break and get outside for a few minutes."

"Agreed." Martin crumpled the waxed paper from his sandwich and tossed it into the wastebasket.

After another ninety minutes, Emma flung her pencil down. "We're no closer to the solution than we were at eight this morning."

"Oh, I don't know. We've eliminated a whale of a lot of possibilities." Martin's rumpled hair and loosened tie belied his optimism.

"What if it's gibberish? A red herring to waste our time while they do their dirty business?"

He shook his head. "There's got to be some meaning to it."

She sighed and stared down at the grid before her. "I've looked and looked for a clue. Multiple alphabets. It must be." She lowered her face into her hands.

"The only way to crack these things is by brute force, and that can be exhausting. Let's take that walk." Martin stood and reached for the jacket he had discarded hours earlier. "We can stroll over to the bakery and get one of those newfangled Danish pastries. My treat."

Emma tucked her badge inside the neckline of her dress and grabbed her sweater. The walk would clear their heads, and the snack sounded tempting. She'd only tasted the flaky pastries once, and she wasn't against repeating the experience. "I can pay for mine," she said.

"Nonsense, let me be a gentleman."

Though it felt a bit odd, Emma said no more. Martin was a coworker and friend, and he'd never made advances toward her. Always the gentleman, he treated her with respect and deference. Besides, no one would misinterpret a simple walk with a man who was nearly her father's age. They took their folders up to Howe for safe-keeping. When they reached the front door at the bottom of the stairs, the guard opened it for them.

Outside, she shook her head, sending her hair swirling about her shoulders. She'd followed Freddie's lead and begun wearing it loose, instead of in the stern up-do she'd worn in Maine. She regretted donning the sweater—it was almost too warm for this humid June day.

Several customers stood in line ahead of them at the bakery. When their turn came, Martin procured the sweets and they carried them outside. "There's a bench down there, on the edge of the park," he said.

They walked a little farther down the street and sat down in the shade.

As Emma bit into her pastry, sweetness burst from the sticky layers. "Thank you, Martin. I'm sure I'll work much better after this."

He chuckled. "Perhaps, but I already wish I'd gotten us some coffee to go with it. Pardon me." He licked the glaze from his fingers. "Messy, aren't they?"

She laughed and took another bite.

"I hope we're able to solve this cipher. I need a day off."

"Yes," she said. "I hope we have tomorrow free."

"So do I. A friend invited me to his home for lunch." Martin frowned as he gazed toward the street. "Do you know that fellow? He's staring at us."

A man in a brown suit, wearing spectacles and carrying a paper sack, stood on the sidewalk surveying the park.

Emma sucked in a breath and nearly choked on a bit of pastry. "Wasn't he in the bakery?"

"I thought so, but I wasn't certain." Martin shook his head. "I've gotten too complacent. Out strolling with a lovely young lady, and I let my guard down."

"Do you think he's following us?"

"One way to find out."

"What—lead him on a wild goose chase?"

"Yes. See if he tails us across the park."

"Or we could split up." Emma watched his face to gauge his reaction.

"No, if we did that and he followed you, I might not get there in time to prevent mischief. Besides—what if he has a friend we haven't spotted yet, and they each followed one of us?" He popped the last of his pastry into his mouth and pulled out a handkerchief to wipe his hands on. "Ready? Come on."

He rose, and Emma quickly ate her last bite of Danish and pulled her gloves on. Martin seized her hand and struck off across the park.

"This is almost comical," Emma said.

"Don't look back."

"Then how will we know if he's following us?"

"See that shed over there? We'll duck behind it and wait—see if he comes nosing around."

Martin set a quick pace, and they soon gained the sidewalk on the other side of the park. He turned her to the right, and as soon as the shed screened them from anyone behind them, he pulled her off the walk and up against the shingled wall.

Emma couldn't help chuckling. "Are you going to peek around the corner?"

"Too bad we don't have a periscope."

"Ha. You have 'retired navy' written all over you."

"I'm glad you're amused." He went to the far corner of the shed and cautiously poked his head around then looked back at her. "Can't see anything unless I go around the side."

"Don't," she said, suddenly not wanting to lose sight of him. "Let's go back the way we came. Either we'll bump into him, or he'll be gone."

Martin returned to her side, but before they could emerge from their hiding place, Emma saw the man in the brown suit leaving the park near the place they had reached the sidewalk. She seized Martin's wrist, and they stood still. When the man reached the pavement, he looked left then right.

"He's afraid he's lost us," Martin whispered.

"Well, he'll find us when he turns around."

He tugged her arm and slipped three cautious steps toward the corner of the shed with Emma in tow. Once they'd gained the edge, he yanked her around the side. "Come on! Let's get out of here."

"Do you think he saw us?" She ran to keep up.

"Not sure."

"If he did, he may follow us now. We don't want to lead him to Trafton House."

They reached a grove of trees, and Martin slowed his steps. "You're right. Maybe you should go on, and I'll go back and confront him."

"No." Martin was too valuable to risk his getting into a fracas, but she didn't want to say so. He would scoff and set out to prove to her that the man following them was no match for him. "There's a bank next to the bakery. If they're still open."

Martin checked his watch. "They should be."

"They're bound to have a telephone box," Emma said. "We can call the police."

"Why? Because a man looked at us and then crossed the park at the same place we did?"

"Then we should call Commander Howe and ask him what to do. He wouldn't want us to go straight back if a spy were watching."

Martin opened his mouth as if to protest her casting of the man as a spy but then closed it. After a moment, he said, "All right."

They hurried to the street, with Martin casting frequent glances over his shoulder. Emma concentrated on the pedestrians along their route, but she saw nothing suspicious. When they reached the bank, they hastened inside.

A uniformed man smiled at them as they approached the telephone booth in the lobby. "Would you like to place a call?"

"Yes, thank you." Martin reached into his pocket for some coins.

"I'll watch the door." Emma positioned herself where she could see anyone entering the bank.

Martin made his call and walked over to where she stood. "Howe says to walk west two blocks. A car will pick us up there in fifteen minutes."

"Even if that man follows us?"

"Yes. The driver will take a roundabout route and make sure he's lost him before he takes us back to Trafton House."

They went out into the sunshine and hurried along the street.

"No sign of him, so far as I can tell," Martin said as they approached the rendezvous point.

A black car pulled to the curb just ahead of them. Martin hurried to it and flung the door open. He gave Emma a hand, and she climbed in beside John.

CHAPTER SEVENTEEN

Friday, June 18, 1915

At last, John got to see Emma, and she couldn't get away. True, there was another man in the car. First things first, but he was determined to fix a date with her before leaving her at Trafton House.

"Are you folks all right?" He looked at Emma then turned to glance at the man who had climbed into the back seat.

"Yes, we're fine," Emma said. "I don't believe you've met Martin Glazer."

"How do you do?" the man in the back said.

"This is Lieutenant Patterson." For some reason, Emma flushed when she made the introduction.

"Ah, pleased to meet you. Aren't you some sort of aide to Captain Waller?"

"I carry out many errands for him, yes." John tried to glimpse Glazer in his mirror, but the angle wasn't right. Was Emma embarrassed to introduce him to one of her coworkers? If so, was it simply because they were seeing each other, or did she have another reason? "What happened this afternoon? Someone followed you?"

"Yes," Glazer said. "We'd been working all day and decided to step out for a break. Clear our heads, so to speak. We stopped at a bakery then walked on to the park to eat our goodies. I noticed a man watching us, and Miss Shuster confirmed that he'd been in the bakery when we were there."

"And he followed us across the park," Emma said. "We hid until he went by, and then we went to the bank to call Commander Howe."

"Good thinking." Traffic thickened, and John kept the car inching along the street among automobiles, carriages, and wagons.

Glazer continually looked out the back and scanned the sidewalks. "I haven't seen him since we left the bank."

"My orders are to give you a roundabout ride and then take you back to Trafton House." John glanced over at Emma.

"But he must know we came from there," she said. "I don't think a customer in a bakery would suddenly decide to follow someone, do you? He had to have been tailing us when we came out of Trafton House."

"That's my thought too," Glazer said. "I don't like it, but what other explanation is there?"

Emma touched John's sleeve. "If our enemies—and I don't use that term lightly—have discovered our headquarters, they could do us enormous harm."

"Yes, we've thought of that. Captain Waller plans to increase the guard at Trafton House. We may need to provide escorts for you ladies who work there."

"Quite a logistical problem," Glazer said. "Costly, too."

"Yes, but we must protect our people."

"Have they considered moving us to a new location?"

John turned onto a quieter street. "I'm sure they must be thinking about it, but whether that's the best option, I don't know."

"Yes," Martin said. "That would be even more expensive. I suppose they could put us all on the naval base. Then we'd be inside an enclosed, guarded community."

"I'm sure the brass will consider all options." A few minutes later, John pulled up before Trafton House.

"Thank you, Lieutenant," Glazer said.

"You're welcome. I'll see you inside." John jumped out and hurried around the car, but Glazer was already out and helping Emma down.

"We'll be fine," Martin said to John.

"Oh—well, I wished to speak to Miss Shuster if I might. Perhaps inside. I don't want to keep either of you out here on the street."

"Of course," Emma said.

They walked to the door. A marine opened it, and another stood inside the entry. John removed his hat as they went in. He wondered if the new security concerns demanded a guard posted outside—or would that be like a gaudy billboard: TOP SECRET GOVERNMENT OFFICES HERE?

Glazer turned and extended his right hand, and John shook it.

"Thanks again."

"Anytime," John said.

Glazer nodded at Emma and went up the stairs.

Emma darted a glance at the marines. "There's a room down the hall where we work sometimes. Well, not sometimes. Martin and I worked there today, but we're usually upstairs with all the others. But the commander—" She stopped short, her face scarlet. "I'm sorry. Just—follow me, please."

Emma turned and walked swiftly past several closed doors and entered a small, stark room. She turned to face him. "The commander put us here this morning so we'd have quiet to work on a sensitive message. I expect Martin will retrieve our materials so we can go back to it."

John stepped closer to her. "Emma, I've hoped all week we'd have a chance to talk. I need to explain some things to you. I haven't meant to neglect you."

She looked directly into his eyes and pressed her lips together. He waited for her to speak. At last she said, "I'm glad. I didn't really think you had, but..."

"Oh, Emma. I've been rather blue, wondering if I'd ever get to sit down with you and talk things over."

"I'd like the chance."

His heart soared. "Let's, then. Tomorrow?"

She gritted her teeth. "The cipher we're working on is very difficult, but Commander Howe thinks it's urgent, so if we can't crack it today, we'll probably have to come in tomorrow."

"On Saturday?"

"There's always someone working here on Saturday, just not usually me." Her face pleaded for understanding. "We've had such an influx of ciphers lately."

"Of course." He, of all people, knew that matters of national security took precedence over social engagements, sleep, and many other things.

"Perhaps you could phone me later," she said. "I expect to be home by—well, by eight, certainly. And by then I should know whether I'll be free tomorrow."

"They'd keep you that late and expect you to work Saturday?"

"Well, if we're close to making a breakthrough, we hate to leave off. It could mean lives, John."

"I understand." His own failure again crossed his mind. "I'll call you then. At eight."

She smiled up at him and nodded.

Firm footsteps came down the hall and paused at the open doorway.

John turned.

Glazer stood there holding a bundle of papers. "Sorry to interrupt."

"It's all right," Emma said. "We've just finished."

"Yes, I need to report to Captain Waller that you're safely back in your nest. But when you're ready to leave here—no matter what time that is"—John shot a meaningful glance at Emma—"make sure you have an escort. Especially if it's after sundown."

"I could see Miss Shuster home."

"I imagine Waller or Howe will arrange for someone to drive her. You should be careful too, sir."

Glazer nodded, and John sensed that they'd marked their territory. Odd that he felt the older man was more of a threat than Clark Hibbert. Perhaps it was because Emma seemed to like and respect Martin Glazer. That and the fact that she'd worked all day alone with him.

He glanced around again. The room's wallpaper was faded, and the lack of comfortable furniture or decorations made it seem a rather bleak workplace. Even the large room upstairs, where a dozen people labored over their paperwork at the same time, would be more cheerful. But Emma didn't seem to mind being down here with Glazer and working on the baffling cipher.

"I wish you success on your project," he said.

"Thank you." Glazer walked around the table and laid the papers down.

"Yes, thank you, John." Emma held out her hand, and he squeezed it. Her smile cheered him somewhat, but he still hated to walk away.

* * * * *

Kobold sat down across from his contact and looked around the dimly lit restaurant. He didn't like business meetings outside his office, but it was getting harder to keep suspicion at bay and to get his intermediaries into the building without proper credentials. An eatery owned by a loyal German family might offer as much safety as the embassy.

A waiter placed glasses of water on the table and left two menus.

"What now?" Kobold took out a cigar and lit it.

"When our fellow in Maine was arrested—Klaussen—we got his friend out. The one called Ritter."

Kobold shrugged. He couldn't keep track of all the small-fry operatives.

"He's down here now, and one of our best men took him around to the place where we'd thought the navy might have a secret unit. It's over in Fairfax."

"Right. You find anything?"

"Several naval officers went in, but so did a raft of civilians."

Kobold grunted.

"Then a man came out with a lady."

"What man?"

The contact shrugged. "He wore a suit, but he walked like a military man. Retired, maybe. But the woman—she's the one we want."

"What do you mean?"

"Our boy recognized her. She's the daughter of the code man from Maine."

Kobold took the cigar out of his mouth and stared at him. "Shuster's daughter?"

"She's the one. She's got to be working for the navy now."

Kobold swore. "Probably gave them her father's machine."

"I expect so. That's why we never found it in Maine. They're probably using it on us now, to read our messages."

"No wonder they're onto so many of our schemes. I wonder just how good that machine is."

The waiter came back and smiled at him. "May I take your order, sir?"

"No." Kobold flicked a glance at the contact, who scowled down at the placemat in front of him. "Oh, bring us some chicken and potatoes. You want anything else?"

The contact's face perked up. "Coffee, please, and some rolls and butter."

"Vegetable of the day?" The waiter scribbled on his pad.

"Yes. Now go away." Kobold frowned as the waiter scurried toward the kitchen. "Do you know where she lives?"

"Not yet, but it shouldn't be too hard to find out. We just have to watch the building where she works and follow her home. They're suspicious, so we'll have to do it carefully."

Kobold sighed. "And why are they suspicious?"

"They saw Ritter tailing them. They lost him in a park over there. But we know where they work. It's just a matter of time."

"Yes." Kobold felt suddenly more optimistic. "Well, if the plans for

Monday go off well and if we figure out a way to get hold of that code machine, maybe things will start going our way."

The contact grinned at him. "That's what I say."

* * * * *

At 6:30 Emma was ready to call it quits. The letters danced before her aching eyes.

"Martin, I hate to admit it, but I'm exhausted. I keep trying the same thing over and over. Four times now. And it's still not working."

His brow furrowed. "You need to sleep."

"So do you."

"Yes, I suppose so." He rubbed a hand across his chin. "Shall we tell Commander Howe we need some rest?"

"I'm willing to come back in the morning."

"So am I."

Emma sighed. "Thank you. I fear if I don't stop now, everything I do tonight will be worthless."

Martin pushed his chair back. "When do you want to meet in the morning?"

"Eight?"

"Let's make it nine."

Emma nodded. "If you think that's all right."

"I think we're humans, not machines. I'll tell Howe we'll be in at nine a.m."

"Thank you."

They trudged up the stairs and handed in their folders.

"I'm sorry I don't have more stamina," Emma said to Commander Howe.

"That's all right. It's been a trying day."

Martin said, "Miss Shuster and I have agreed to meet back here at nine in the morning."

"That's good of you. Thank you both."

"Will you put someone else on it tonight?" Emma asked.

Howe shook his head. "We've only got two men who'll be here tonight, and they're already working on something important. Look, Lieutenant-Commander Nash will be here in the morning. I'll try to check in later and see how you're doing."

"You don't need to come in, sir," Emma said.

"I think this one's worth it."

She frowned. "Then we should stay now."

"No. Go home, rest, have a good meal. Come back refreshed. I'll call now for an escort. I don't want you riding the trolley home tonight, Miss Shuster. Glazer, they can drop you off too."

"I'll be fine," Martin said.

"Humor me." Howe left the room, and Emma knew he would go to the telephone down the hall. Talk of installing more phones circulated in the office, but so far the Signal Corps' budget wouldn't allow that. They got by with two in the building—a telephone mounted in the second floor hallway and a desk phone in Mrs. Harper's office downstairs.

Emma went to her cupboard for her hat, gloves, and purse.

Howe met her and Martin outside Room 20. "They tell me there's a car waiting outside. Good night."

Emma and Martin walked down the broad staircase.

When they reached the bottom, one of the marines opened the door. Both armed men went with them, down the walkway to the waiting car.

"Credentials?" one of the marines asked the driver. "Oh, Lieutenant."

John stepped out of the car. "Yes. I'll be taking them home tonight. It may be someone else bringing them back in the morning, though."

Emma climbed into the car once more and leaned back against the leather seat. Before John had pulled out of the residential street where Trafton House lay, she'd drifted into sleep.

"Here we go."

She sat up and blinked at the house before them. "We're home already?"

From behind her came Martin's deep chuckle. "Yes, Sleeping Beauty. Let your knight in shining armor get you inside, and you get to bed."

John came around, and she grasped his hand and stepped down. He walked her up to the door.

"Thank you. I'm sorry—I'm a bit muddled. That was rather rude of me."

"What, falling asleep when you're exhausted? Think nothing of it."

She managed a wobbly smile. "I guess you don't have to call me at eight tonight."

"I'll phone tomorrow evening and see how it went. Perhaps we'll be able to see each other after church Sunday."

"Yes. And if by some miracle we're done early tomorrow..."

"If I'm not required to amuse Mr. Hibbert tomorrow, maybe I'll swing by Trafton House after noon and see if you're still there."

She looked up at him in the fading sunlight. "You're under orders to spend time with Clark?"

He shrugged. "I shouldn't have told you."

"How dreadful."

John laughed. "He's not so horrible. He's just…"

"I know. Tedious."

"Well, yes. They don't want him going about by himself off the base and spilling the nature of his work to anyone."

"I should think not. I'm sorry you've been pegged for that job, though." She held out her hand. "Good night, John. And thank you again."

He held her hand for a long moment, gazing down into her eyes. "Good night, Emma. It was a pleasure."

She went inside and stumbled up the stairs, too tired to figure out whether she'd missed the deadline for a supper plate. Someday she and John would talk, and things would smooth out between them. They had to.

* * * * *

Saturday, June 19, 1915

The next morning, an ensign arrived at Mrs. Draper's at 8:40 to take Emma to Trafton House. When she got there, Martin was just accepting their folders from Lieutenant-Commander Nash.

"Do you want to work up here?" Martin asked.

A half dozen men had begun their morning's work in Room 20. Emma hesitated. She'd found that the room downstairs shut out distractions, but she'd hate for Martin—or John—to misconstrue her actions.

"I can work either place," she said.

"Then let's go downstairs. The fewer distractions, the better, I think."

They carried their papers, reference works, and a pot of tea down to their workroom. Martin took three newly sharpened pencils from his pocket and laid them carefully in a row above his folder.

She smiled and opened hers. "Where did we leave off?"

"We'd tried over a hundred alphabet combinations. I marked where we left off in trying shift alphabets."

"Did we try every possible configuration of rectangles yet?"

"No. Here are the ones we've covered." He shoved a list across the table. "I do hope we're not here again tomorrow working on this."

She studied his work sheet. "All right. I'm going to pick up where we left off last night."

"And I'll start a different grid."

They worked in silence for nearly two hours. Emma's back began to ache, and she sat up and stretched.

"I may have something." Martin bent closer over his paper, his pencil moving rapidly.

"I hope you're right." Just the prospect encouraged Emma to keep trying.

"Yes, here. Columns of six, in this order." He passed his work sheet toward her. "Line them all up then read it in a spiral. Try it. My head is spinning. Do you get the German word for factory?"

Emma frowned over the sheet for half a minute before she caught the pattern he'd glimpsed. "Yes! Absolutely. But what…" She scanned down the columns and tried to find other German words in other rows, without success.

"It reads backward," Martin noted.

"Can you make me a copy?"

"Will do."

A few minutes later they both sat back in their chairs, studying their copies of the message. Emma traced the thread Martin had discovered backward, then forward on the next line, and again backward. "I see '*rand*' in row nine. Could that be—"

"Border." Martin sat up straighter.

"Or is it part of a longer word?"

"No, I think you're right."

Emma raced on in her pattern, mentally translating the message, though some words seemed to be English names inserted in the text. "Invincible factories—can that be right?"

"I think it can."

She jotted down her translation, struggling with both the cipher and the language difference.

Martin said, "Tell me if this makes sense to you: 'I believe we can disorganize and hold up for months, if not indefinitely, the manufacture of munitions and other war supplies on both sides of the border.'"

"It makes so much sense it's terrifying. Look at the part just before 'Invincible.'" She leaned across the table and tapped the spot on his paper with her pencil point. "I think it says, 'Peabody, Gramm, and Invincible factories—action to take place—'" She squinted and held her paper closer. "Two-zero-six?"

Martin slapped the table with his palm. "June twentieth, European style. That's tomorrow, isn't it?"

They stared at each other for a moment. "We've got to tell Commander Howe at once." Emma leaped from her chair.

"Do you think he's here?" Martin asked. "He said he'd come by today."

"If he's not, Nash will be able to reach him."

"Let me make a copy of what we have so far. I'll stay and keep working out the rest." Martin wrote out the first part of the message in his neat printing. All of the cryptographers learned to set down legible capital letters nearly as fast as they could write in cursive.

Emma hurried upstairs to Room 20, where six men worked in silence. Howe and the Saturday supervisor, Lieutenant-Commander Nash, sat behind the desk talking in low tones.

As Emma entered the room, Howe glanced her way and rose. "Something tells me you have news."

"Yes," Emma said, "and it's not good. They're planning some action against at least three factories tomorrow. We don't have the entire message in clear yet, but we thought you should know as soon as possible, so that you can alert whoever necessary to try to stop this."

Howe took the paper and studied it. "How much of the message is this?"

"Less than half. We don't know where these factories are located, and that probably won't be in the plaintext."

"I'll get right on it. I think Invincible is in the Chicago area. Munitions, if I'm not mistaken."

"We'd better wire Chicago," Nash said.

"Yes. As soon as we're sure of the targets." Howe looked at Emma. "All right, get to it. Would it help to have these other men assist you?"

"I think Mr. Glazer will have the complete clear for you very soon. If we stop to explain the method…"

"All right. Go."

She dashed back down the stairs.

Martin still labored over the rest of the message. He nodded to her. "Here, let me call out the new letters and you write them down."

In barely ten minutes, they had put the entire message into plain English. Together they hustled back to Howe's desk.

Emma gave him the fresh copy she'd made. "They're planning explosions in all three factories, but even worse, they plan to hit an armory near one of the plants," she said.

"Can we stop them?" Martin asked. "This could mean hundreds of casualties."

Howe read the message, his brow creased in thought, with Nash reading over his shoulder. "We'll certainly try. We've discovered the locations of all three plants. The Peabody factory is in Ontario, near Windsor."

"That explains the armory then," Martin said. "The saboteurs want to bomb a place where Canada is gathering her soldiers to send to the front in Europe."

"We'd better wire Ottawa," Nash said.

"Yes. I'm afraid time is so precious we should just send it in clear." Howe shrugged in apology. "If the telegrapher made a mistake, or if their night person for whatever reason laid it aside over the weekend, it might be too late."

It was true. In her orientation, Emma had learned of many cases where lives were lost in battle because of mistakes made in encrypting orders. Sending a message of a sensitive nature in plaintext was an affront to the cryptographers, but sometimes expedience overruled secrecy.

"It may be too late anyway." Nash reached for a pen. "Tell me exactly what to put in the message and who to address it to. I'll go to the nearest hotel and send it."

"We'll have several messages to send," Howe said. "You stay here with the men who are still working. They've got other messages that may turn out to be just as important. I'll telephone Captain Waller and tell him what we've got, and then I'll start alerting our people and our friends in Canada. Unless I'm mistaken, we'll have a lot of work to do on this." He looked over at Emma and Martin. "Good work, you two. I'd like to give you a vacation. Unfortunately, I'm afraid we'll need you back here again Monday morning. But for now, get out of here."

* * * * *

When Emma reached the boardinghouse, Freddie met her in the entry hall. "Emma, a man came here and asked if you were in."

Emma's heart raced, and she sank down on a chair near the telephone. "What man?"

"I don't know. Not your lieutenant."

"Did Doris see him?"

"I don't think so. Why?"

"There's a man who knew me in Maine, and Doris saw him Sunday at church. If it were the same man, she would recognize him." And if it wasn't Clark Hibbert, Emma wondered, who could it have been? She thought of the man in the park and shivered.

"Sorry. I don't think she got a look at him. He came just as we were sitting down to supper. I told him you weren't here. Say, you're awfully late, and on Saturday, too."

"Yes, we had some extra work."

"Well, you'd best get your plate. Mrs. Draper won't hold it after eight o'clock."

"Thank you." Emma waited until Freddie had gone upstairs then stood. Her legs trembled, and she leaned against the wall for a moment before lifting the receiver and asking for the emergency number Waller had given her.

CHAPTER EIGHTEEN

Saturday to Tuesday, June 19 to 22, 1915

John boarded the train for Chicago that night at 9:15. Already federal agents in Illinois and the local police department had been alerted to the potential damage. They would contact the factory owners and go to the sites. John hoped they could catch the men commissioned to carry out the bombings this time.

Emma had discovered this plot—she and Martin Glazer. John's pride in her soared. He sent up a prayer of thanks for her and the work she had done. *Let our people be in time, Lord. Let us save lives tonight.*

His only regret was that he hadn't been able to meet with Emma yet. He feared she was still put out with him for not realizing Clark had followed him to church last week. He should have been more careful—should have expected it, given what he knew of Clark Hibbert. His low spirits had made him careless.

In time, he hoped that he and Emma could get beyond the friction that incident had caused. When he came home from Chicago, he would concentrate on setting things right with her. He would make sure she understood that he'd had no intention of leading Clark to her. And he'd also make sure she knew how he felt about her.

John was fairly certain she cared for him, though perhaps not as deeply as he cared for—loved—her. He didn't want her to see him as an enamored neurotic, the image she seemed to have of Clark, and perhaps with good reason. What could he do on his return to restore the good rapport they'd had a few weeks ago? Flowers, of course. He should have ordered some before he took the train. But there wouldn't have been time, between receiving his orders and getting to the depot, even if he'd thought of it.

Independence Day was coming up. Two weeks. The White House had announced that fireworks would be displayed over the Potomac that evening. He would scout out a vantage point and invite Emma to watch the show with him. And maybe sometime he could rent a car and take her for a drive out into the beautiful farming country nearby.

He closed his eyes and leaned back against the train seat. *Lord, You know I love her. If it's Your will, please let her forgive me for my mistake. All my mistakes.*

The fiasco in Charleston still hung over him. Though Emma didn't know all the details, he'd told her that he'd blundered on an important assignment. Could she still respect him, knowing he'd let a saboteur get away? Maybe not. After all the hard work she and the others in Room 20 had put in to crack the cipher, he'd let the birds fly.

He could look back now and see all the things he ought to have done. No use going over it again. Better to sleep if he could, while the train sped through the night. And to be smarter. The best way to expunge his record was to do it right this time.

When John stepped off the train in Chicago the next day, a police officer met him on the platform. "I'm here to take you straight to police headquarters, sir. Our officers have got a couple of men for you to interview."

"Already?"

"Yes, sir. After we got the navy's telegram, our men started asking around, and we found a fellow who'd bought some dynamite from a construction supplier a few days ago. They brought him in—and the one he bought it from."

John strode into the police station feeling he had a chance to redeem himself.

The police chief laid out the investigation for him. "The man who sold the dynamite didn't really break any laws, and he's cooperated with us. I just wish he'd told us earlier and not made us hunt him up. Now the fellow who bought it, he's a different story. He's pretty close-mouthed, but I think if we catch his friends doing the job, he'll talk."

"And where is the dynamite now?" John asked.

The police chief leaned back and folded his hands over his stomach. "Well, sir, that's the question, isn't it?"

"You mean, you don't know?"

"We didn't find it."

"What does the prisoner say about it?"

"Won't say anything. But he bought thirty pounds of explosive. The seller is adamant that we've got the right man, but we didn't find the contraband anywhere in or around his lodgings." The chief swung around and yelled, "Sergeant Browne! Come on over here."

A tall, fair-haired man in uniform left his desk and sauntered over. "Yes, sir?"

"This is Lieutenant Patterson. He'd like to see the prisoner. That is, the fellow who bought the dynamite."

John followed the sergeant to a holding cell at the back of the building. The man inside sat on his cot, staring straight ahead. When John and Browne approached, he looked toward them.

"This here fella's from Washington," Browne said. "You'd best talk to him."

The prisoner looked away. John could tell by the set of the man's jaw that he'd do well to get anything out of him. As he feared, the interview gave him nothing new.

That afternoon John and the chief of police discussed how they could catch more of the conspirators.

"If your men made the arrest as quietly as you claim, whoever has that dynamite may still try to plant it at the factory," John said.

The chief shrugged. "I don't know. We can put some men out there to watch the place tomorrow."

"Not tomorrow. Tonight."

"You think they'll set it up tonight?"

"They might."

The chief frowned and scratched his chin. "How many men do you need?"

John exhaled. He would get the support he needed. "Not too many. I don't want them to spot us. Give me three good men. Undercover men, if you've got them. I'll reconnoiter and show them where I want them. They need to go prepared to sit there all night without showing themselves. If nothing happens, we'll swap them for fresh men in the morning, one at a time."

By nightfall their plans were laid, and John positioned his men, including a federal agent who'd joined them late in the day, sent by the Department of Justice's Bureau of Investigation. John took the station from which he could see what he considered the best spot to set a bomb—the wall outside the boiler room. From his hiding place beneath a willow tree, he watched the shadowy back wall of the factory.

He settled down to wait, knowing he'd get sleepy before long, considering that he'd spent the last night on a train.

The minutes ticked by. He watched the quarter moon inch across the sky.

At midnight John stirred. Had he brought these men out here for nothing? In the back of his mind, a voice said, "Call it off. Send them home." He shook himself and began to pray. *Lord, give us success.*

Sometime later, he pulled out his watch to check it. He barely made out the hands—past one o'clock. As he returned the watch to his pocket, he caught a glimpse of movement in the shadows near the building. His adrenaline surged, and his muscles tightened. *Wait. Don't reveal yourself too soon.*

A dark figure edged along the factory's back wall. The man carried a bulky case.

John's pulse raged. Their target had come. He eased his pistol from its holster beneath his jacket. He waited until the man stooped to shove the case close against the wall. Springing from beneath the willow, John sprinted for the building.

Another shadow dashed in from his left—the police officer he'd placed behind a hedge where he could view the corner of the building.

The man near the wall turned and bolted upright.

"Don't move," John called. "You're under arrest. Put your hands above your head."

Slowly, the man complied.

The policeman moved in, his weapon drawn. Striding in from the other side came the federal agent. John relaxed as the police cuffed the intruder.

John nodded to them. "Be careful with that suitcase."

* * * * *

Tuesday, June 22, 1915

When Emma reached Room 20 on Tuesday morning, Commander Howe was sitting on the corner of his desk. He rose and said, "Ah, Miss Shuster."

Eight other cryptographers already sat at their tables. Emma took a seat near Muriel. She stashed her handbag and gloves on the floor. She'd take them to her cupboard later.

Obviously the commander had news to impart. "I believe all our staff is here now. Several of our group have gone to Washington for training today." Howe cleared his throat. "As you're aware, we had some important ciphers come through here last weekend. Miss Shuster and Mr. Glazer solved theirs with heartening results. Because of their swift and accurate work, police and federal agents stopped two bombing incidents. Property was protected, supplies for Great Britain were saved, and lives were spared."

Emma looked over at Martin in confusion. His smile drooped into a puzzled frown.

He lifted a hand. "Two, Commander? There were three incidents planned, were there not?"

Howe sighed. "It pains me to tell you that the Peabody factory in Ontario was bombed. That plant had contracted to make over one million dollars' worth of uniforms for the British government. Their building was badly damaged, and much of their equipment was ruined. Fortunately, no one was injured."

"Thank God for that," Martin said. "Why couldn't the authorities stop it?"

Howe lifted both hands in resignation. "The bombs were planted during the night. Even though we telegraphed Ottawa as soon as we knew about the planned attack, it took them awhile to sort it out and get someone over to the factory in Walkerville. Their law enforcement officers are spread pretty thin, and they weren't in time."

"That's a shame," Rory said.

"Yes. There have been several sabotage attempts up there recently, especially on their railroad lines, tunnels, and bridges. Seems the Germans have the notion that Japan might send troops over to help England by carrying them across Canada on trains. They want to make that impossible. They've kept the Canadian officials hopping for weeks with their plots to cut transportation and communication lines."

"Sounds like it's even worse in Canada than here," Charles said.

"In some ways, it has been." Howe sat on the edge of his desk again. "I'm happy to report that the second part of the plot in Ontario failed. The saboteurs also had orders to place a bomb at the armory in Windsor, where about three hundred men were training for deployment to Europe. For some reason, and we're not clear on what that was yet, the bomb at the armory failed to detonate."

Larry Crane whistled softly.

Howe nodded. "If that one had exploded, many men would have been killed. As I said, the two factories targeted on this side of the border were saved. Our men arrested several suspects connected with the plans to dynamite a munitions factory in Illinois, and a suitcase full of the stuff was found near a truck factory near Detroit. No arrests there, but at least the plant was protected and no one was hurt. So, Miss

Shuster, Mr. Glazer, and *all* of you, good work. This is what our division is all about."

Emma's fatigue disappeared. Despite her worry last weekend over the saboteurs and the mysterious man who had appeared at the boardinghouse, she felt ready to tackle a new cipher. Let Captain Waller and his men worry about the details outside Trafton House. In here, she made a difference in the lives of many people, though they would never know it.

Howe rose. "All right, if you don't have a project you're continuing from your last shift, come see me." He looked directly at Emma. "Miss Shuster and Miss Ainsley, are you interested in a cipher that looks like a first cousin to one you solved not long ago?"

Muriel looked at her, and Emma could see her excitement. She nodded.

Howe brought over a folder. "I've asked a typist to go upstairs for a copy of your Tourmaline Cipher. This one looks very like it."

Muriel's eyes danced. "Wouldn't it be something if they used the same key word again?"

In less than an hour, the message was revealed. Emma sat for a long minute, going over the plaintext. Her mouth went dry.

"Are we ready to turn it in?" Muriel asked.

"Yes." Swallowing hard, Emma stood and clutched the paper. "If you don't mind, I'd like to speak to Commander Howe privately."

"All right."

Muriel's troubled expression caused her a pang of guilt, but Emma turned away and hurried to the desk. "Sir, we have our clear for you."

"That was quick. Same key word?"

"Yes."

"I'll alert the others so that we catch any more messages the radio-men bring us using Tourmaline."

Emma watched his impassive face as he took the paper and read the short message:

We have a man who knows the shipyard. HM will meet with your representative for instructions at nineteen hundred on June two seven.

"Hmm. Initials. That's straightforward, isn't it? Gives us everything but the place of the meeting." Howe glanced up at her. "I'll send this on to people who can deal with it. Ready for a new task, Miss Shuster?"

"No, sir."

His eyebrows shot up. "No? Need a respite?"

"No, it's not that. It's just..." Emma couldn't pull enough air through her tightening throat. "Sir, I couldn't help but wonder— It's probably nothing, but..."

Howe lowered his voice. "Emma, what is it? Your intuition usually stands you in good stead."

A wave of heat crept up her cheeks toward her hairline. "Sir, the initials trouble me. The man they've recruited—H.M...."

"Yes?"

"This message came out of Maine, didn't it? The cover sheet says Portland."

He glanced at it. "That's right. The other Tourmaline message came from the same area."

Emma felt she would strangle. "Sir, I have a relative with those initials. He lives in Woolwich, not far from Portland."

Howe looked into her eyes steadily. "You have reason to think he may be involved in all this?"

"Not really, but…before I came here, there were a couple of minor things that made me wonder what my cousin was up to."

"The shipyard…" Howe flicked another look at the paper. "That could be the one in Portsmouth, on the Maine-New Hampshire border."

"It could be. There's also Bath Iron Works in Maine."

"You're right. Does he know one of those?"

"He lives very close to Bath. When I left Maine, he was working in a woolen mill. But my aunt told me he'd obtained a new job a month or so ago in Portland. But…" She caught her breath and looked down at the orderly piles of paper on the desk, her stomach tossing. "But his father works for Bath Iron Works."

"Your uncle?"

She nodded. "By marriage. He's an accountant, and he had his own office when I was a child, but for at least ten years, he's worked for BIW, keeping their accounts."

Howe inhaled slowly, frowning. "My suggestion is this: write out the names and addresses of both your cousin and uncle, the name of the mill where your cousin worked, and anything else you can think of that might be pertinent."

"Do you want me to call my aunt and ask where Herman is working now?"

"No, we don't want to make anyone suspicious. I'll request that we have someone up there check into their activities. They can speak discreetly with the employers. Do you know the name of the plant supervisor at the yard in Bath?"

"No. But I'll get you the other information." Emma's lower lip quivered, and she bit it as she turned away.

"Are you all right?" Muriel asked as she resumed her seat at the work table.

"Yes, but I have an assignment from the commander that will take a few minutes. Perhaps you should get something else to work on."

Muriel patted her shoulder as she walked past, and Emma's eyes filled with tears. She pulled a handkerchief from her pocket and blotted her damp lashes.

Lord, what am I putting in motion? Had she started something that would tear her family apart? Had she cast suspicion on innocent people? She tried to clear her throat, but the aching lump wouldn't move.

* * * * *

"How did you know where to place the suitcase?" John stood over the prisoner at the police station in Detroit. He could outstare anyone, and the man blinked first, crumpling down into his wrinkled jacket.

"We had instructions."

"We?"

"Me and the others. The ones what were going to other places."

"How many of you?"

The man shifted.

John leaned over him. "How many?"

"Three others that I know of."

John paced to the other side of the table and turned. "Where did you get the suitcase?"

"From the man at the consulate."

"He handed you a suitcase full of dynamite right there at the German consulate, here in Detroit?"

"That's right."

Unbelievable—or it would be if John hadn't seen other incidents as blatant over the past few months. The man's words accounted for the attempts to destroy two American factories and the one in Ontario.

"How were you paid?"

"He gave us an envelope that day."

"Cash?"

"Yes. We were to get more later, after the job was done."

When the prisoner was returned to his cell, the desk sergeant in the outer room called to John. "Lieutenant, we got a message for you." He held out a small sheet of paper.

Call your roommate.

John smiled. He didn't have a roommate, but the word was code for his superior—Captain Waller. The officer directed him to a public telephone box just inside the station door.

"Good morning, Lieutenant. I understand the factories on this side of the border are still in one piece."

"Yes, sir."

"Not so lucky up North, I'm afraid," Waller said.

"I'm sorry to hear that. But we've got a solid lead on where the orders are coming from, at least for this part of the country. I believe Kobold has a close friend in a convenient position out here. I'll bring you the details when I come."

"I may need them sooner than that."

"Oh? Do you want me to tell you now?"

"No. We don't know who may be listening."

John looked around. "Well, I *am* at a police station, sir."

"Still, there seem to be ears everywhere these days. Want to take a trip to Windsor before you come home?"

"Yes, sir, if you think it's expedient. The man I just questioned indicated that two of the three other men who were issued orders and paid at the same time he was went to Canada. I'll head up there this evening. I'm curious as to how those thugs got across the border carrying explosives."

"All right then. Send me your report in cipher before you board the train. Do you have everything you need?"

"I believe so. If I may ask, sir, is everything going all right with our friend the engineer?"

"I've got a petty officer baby tending him. He's taking him to the picture show tonight, just to keep him busy. Oh, and in case you're wondering, a certain young lady has been shining at her job."

"I'm glad. That doesn't surprise me, though."

"She's had a troubling incident with someone calling for her at her boardinghouse when she wasn't in. We've looked into that, and we're certain it wasn't the engineer."

John's adrenaline surged. Someone other than Clark Hibbert made inquiries about Emma. What was going on? He wished he wasn't hundreds of miles away and going farther. "Do you have someone watching out for her?"

"She and Miss Keating will be escorted home this evening. I'm not sure we'll have the man power to keep it up, especially on weekends."

John had to accept that. Resources were stretched thinner than he liked, but he and Waller were powerless to change it.

A few hours later, he boarded a train bound for Ontario and slid his small bag under his seat. As the train rolled over the rails, John slumped down, letting his mind run free. Emma, working at Trafton House... the German sympathizers planning to kill Americans and destroy property...Emma, followed by thugs...criminals buying explosives... Emma laughing in the sunshine as they watched laborers at work on the massive memorial to Lincoln...saboteurs crossing the border to wreak havoc on the Canadian troops and manufacturers.... How?

"Passport."

John looked up at the conductor standing beside his seat. He took his document from his inner pocket and handed it over. The conductor opened it, looked John in the face, and nodded. "Please open your luggage, sir."

Standard procedure for those crossing into Canada. John leaned down to pull his bag from beneath the seat.

That's it! That's how they did it.

He slid the bag out and opened it, all the time seeing a tableau in his mind. As the conductor checked quickly through his clothing and toiletries, John saw it like a motion picture, so clear, so devastatingly easy.

Two men, headed north. Two suitcases. One man held a ticket for the last stop before the border. The other would go through into Canada. The conductor entered the car to check the passports and luggage of the international travelers. The two men unobtrusively switched seats. When the conductor reached the one going to Canada, he opened the bag beneath his seat. No contraband. The other man sat placidly over the suitcase of explosives. He was getting off the train before the border, so he didn't have to open it. The conductor checked his ticket and moved on down the line. After he left the car, the travelers moved back to their original seats. One man left the train with the innocuous bag. The other entered Ontario carrying thirty pounds of dynamite, and his suitcase had never been checked.

John sucked in a deep breath as he watched the conductor move on down the aisle. So simple. So deadly simple.

CHAPTER NINETEEN

Saturday, June 26, 1915

Emma spent a quiet Saturday resting and writing letters. Even that drained her, as she had to stay on guard and word each sentence carefully.

She hadn't heard from John all week. She sank into a blue morass. When she was most tired, dire thoughts scuttled across her mind. John might be injured in a travel accident, or worse, by a German spy. Had he been caught up in one of the violent plots they'd uncovered? If he cared about her, why hadn't he contacted her?

In the bleakest moments, suspicions crept into her mind. He was in the perfect position to aid the saboteurs and to make sure their plans weren't ruined. She hated herself for entertaining even a flicker of such a disloyal thought.

In the late afternoon, Freddie and Doris coaxed her to walk to a nearby shop with them so Freddie could buy some lip rouge and stationery.

"Let's go to the pictures," Doris said as they left the shop.

"Oh no, thank you." Emma smiled at her friend. "I want to turn in early again tonight, while I have the chance."

"Are you feeling well?" Doris asked.

"Yes, I'm fine. I'll meet you at breakfast, and we'll go to church together."

"You two make a regular thing of it, don't you?" Freddie looked from Emma to Doris and back.

"Yes, we do," Doris said.

Emma patted Freddie's shoulder. "You ought to come with us."

"Oh, I don't know."

"Come on," Doris said. "Didn't you go to church before you came here?"

"Yes, and I got sick of it."

Doris eyed her curiously. "I never get sick of church."

"We have a wonderful pastor," Emma said. "He's not so much an orator, but he's a marvelous teacher."

"Well, I've rather stopped thinking about religion since I came here last year."

"How can you not think about God?" Doris frowned and walked sideways, watching her intently.

Freddie shrugged but had no answer. Instead, she laughed. "Maybe I should go and see if I feel any holier afterward."

Her words troubled Emma, but she decided it was best not to say so. Freddie might change her mind and back out on them.

"How long is the service?" Freddie asked.

"Only an hour," Doris said quickly.

Freddie shot her a suspicious glance. "You won't snare me into some long prayer meeting after, will you?"

"Of course not. Why would I?"

Freddie shrugged. "My aunt used to do it. She'd say, 'Freda, come to the meeting with me. You'll enjoy the speaker.' And it would turn out to be two or three hours of sitting and listening to people pray after the sermon was done."

Doris, undaunted, smiled at Freddie. "I promise you we shall be done by noon, or five after at the very latest."

"All right then. What shall I wear?" The rest of the walk back to the boardinghouse centered on Freddie's outfit for the next day.

On Sunday morning the three walked the half mile along the sleepy streets to the church. All had donned their coolest cotton dresses and set off with their parasols. Emma and Doris carried their Bibles.

The dim church sanctuary was cooler than the air outside, and they settled gratefully in a pew two-thirds of the way back. To Emma's chagrin, almost at once Clark came to stand in the aisle beside Doris.

"Good morning." He looked past Doris and Freddie, at Emma. "May I sit with you ladies today?"

"Oh, well…" Emma looked helplessly toward the door, but no one came to her aid.

"We thought perhaps Lieutenant Patterson would join us," Doris said.

"John won't be back for a few days yet," Clark said.

Emma felt a flush rise in her cheeks. Clark knew when John would be back, and she didn't.

Doris threw her a distressed glance and looked back at Clark. "Oh, you've been in touch with him?"

"No, I…I just…he told me when he left that he'd be gone at least a week. That is, he expected to be…"

Freddie laughed. "Well, Mr. Whoever-You-Are, my friends promised me an all-girl outing today, so you'll have to try again some other time." She nodded firmly and turned to Emma, her eyebrows arched as though to ask, "How did I do?"

Emma almost laughed with her. For once she was glad for Freddie's outspokenness.

Doris stood and said earnestly, "Mr. Hibbert, you can see we've brought a friend with us this morning. It would really be better if you found another seat."

"Oh. Of course."

Emma didn't look his way, but a few seconds later, Freddie hissed, "He's gone. You can thank me anytime."

Emma reached over and squeezed Freddie's hand. "I'm glad you came. For several reasons."

To her surprise, Freddie joined in the singing, and she seemed to pay close attention to the sermon. The minister expounded on the parable of the Prodigal Son, and Emma hoped Freddie wouldn't scoff at the oft-told tale. The pastor presented his lesson with simple compassion, and Emma's eyes filled with tears when he described the father's welcome at the errant son's return.

After the benediction, she saw Freddie swipe at her eyes.

"Are you all right?" Doris asked.

Freddie nodded. "I haven't got into all sorts of trouble like that fellow, but I haven't been a good daughter, either."

Emma sat still on the pew as others moved and chattered about them. "What do you mean, Freddie?"

"I lied to my folks. Told them I've been going to church every Sunday—and that I would never go to a nightclub. But I did."

Doris's eyes grew huge. "You did?"

Freddie sniffed and nodded.

"When?"

"Last month. Remember I told you I went to the pictures with Ted, from work?"

"Yes."

Freddie shook her head. "We went dancing."

Emma wasn't surprised, but Doris looked scandalized. "What was it like?"

"Fun. Or I thought so at the time." Freddie grimaced. "Ted said I didn't dance very well, and he hasn't asked me to go out since." She sighed. "My folks would turn gray if they knew. I was never allowed to dance at home. But I promised them I wouldn't let the city corrupt me."

"Well, there are worse things than dancing," Emma said.

Doris eyed her doubtfully, with arched eyebrows.

"Oh, I did them too."

Doris's face paled.

Emma struggled to remain serene. "Dear Freddie, I'm sure that's normal, especially for young people who go away from home for the first time."

Freddie looked up at her with troubled eyes. "I had a glass of beer. Ted wanted me to drink more, but I wouldn't."

"You showed better judgment than most." Emma patted her gloved hand.

"It tasted awful."

Doris sat like a statue, staring at Freddie.

Clark Hibbert appeared once more at the end of the pew and cleared his throat. "I don't suppose you ladies have reconsidered? I ran into a friend from the navy base, and we're going to the café for lunch."

Doris whipped around and scowled at him. "Persistent, aren't you?"

Clark smiled. "Well, yes. It's one of my strong points."

"Well, buzz off."

Freddie's jaw dropped, and Emma suppressed a laugh.

Clark eyed her askance for a moment, then turned and walked away.

"Doris! Where did you learn such language?" Freddie said severely.

Doris's face crumpled into a penitent scowl. "Ruth at work. She says things like that all the time. I'm sorry."

Emma let her chuckle escape and picked up her Bible. "Come, ladies. I think it's time we strolled home and had our dinner."

"Anywhere but the café," Doris said.

"Yes." Freddie looked about at the diminishing crowd. "Who was that annoying fellow anyway?"

* * * * *

"It's a telephone call, sir. The gentleman says it's urgent."

Kobold scowled at his housekeeper. He hated doing business on Sunday and had told most of his underlings not to call him. That was his day to stay home with his family and keep up his image as the loving husband and father. Having his Sunday dinner interrupted was a double insult.

"I'm sorry, sir," the housekeeper said. "I told him you were with your family, but he insists he must speak to you at once."

He shoved his chair back from the table and threw down his linen napkin. "I won't be long," he told his wife in German.

The telephone was mounted on the wall in the front hall.

"Guten tag."

"Sir, we've got her pegged. Miss Shuster. We were ninety percent sure where she lived, but now it's a hundred. Ritter and I saw her come out of that church again with two other young ladies. They went back to the house together. What do you want us to do?"

Kobold scratched his chin. "Wait until sometime when she's gone again. Get in there and search her things."

"But you said you thought she'd given the machine over to the navy. She wouldn't keep it at the boardinghouse, would she?"

"I don't know what she would do."

After a short pause, the man said, "No, sir. I suppose not."

"You don't know what you might find if you get in there."

"What if I can't get in?"

"Is the house guarded?"

"I don't think so."

"Well then, it should be simple."

"Yes, sir." The man sounded rather doubtful.

"Do it." Kobold hung up the receiver. Would he have to act in person to get rid of that disloyal young woman?

* * * * *

Monday, June 28, 1915

As Emma and Doris walked through the door at Mrs. Draper's on Monday evening, Emma's gaze slid as usual to the hall table.

"Mail." Doris scurried past her to snatch up the cluster of envelopes. "You got one." She held out the prize to Emma then riffled through the rest. "And so did I!"

Emma stared down at her name in precise black script. *John.*

"Who's yours from?" Doris tossed down the unclaimed mail and tore open her envelope. "Mine's from my sister."

Emma smiled. "That's nice. Mine's from Lieutenant Patterson."

Doris squealed and gave her a little squeeze. "I'm glad. You've been down all week."

"We'd better hurry and wash for dinner," Emma said. She dashed to her room and opened John's missive.

> *Dear Emma,*
>
> *My travels have expanded, and I'm going to a new place. I hope to return Friday. Could you possibly give me an hour or two Friday evening? I shan't keep you up late. If I can't make it, I'll do my best to telephone you.*
>
> *John*

She sat down on her bed, suddenly as limp as a discarded stocking. He was safe. He would return in a few days, barring unforeseen problems. He wanted to see her at once.

She read through the brief message again. No endearments this time. No hint of affection other than the standard "dear" in the greeting, and his hopeful tone. It must suffice.

Quickly she poured water into her washbowl and rinsed her hands. She glanced in the small mirror and reached for her hairbrush. She stopped with it in midair. The second drawer of her dresser was open just a crack, with the lacy edge of a petticoat peeking from it.

Cautiously she pulled the drawer open. Her clothing looked slightly mussed, but not terribly so. Could she have done that this morning in her haste? She opened the other drawers one by one. They looked fine. She walked to the desk. A few envelopes and a notebook lay where she'd left them. She opened the closet door. Nothing seemed out of place. And she always locked her door when she left.

A light knock sounded. "Emma?"

She tucked John's note in her pocket. "Yes, Doris. I'm ready."

* * * * *

On Thursday Emma left work long past her usual time and arrived home at seven o'clock. All week, she had attacked her assignments and labored diligently. She'd put in extra hours at Trafton House, in hopes she could have the entire weekend off. Only a catastrophe could stop her from keeping Friday evening free for John.

The other boarders had already finished dinner.

When Emma entered, Doris headed her off in the lower hall. "Emma! I was beginning to worry about you. That man from the church is here—Mr. Hibbert."

Emma sighed and leaned back against the closed door. "I guessed he would find my address sooner or later." She glanced toward the parlor door. "Is he in there?"

"Yes. Louise is entertaining him. I would have shooed him off, but by the time I realized who was calling, she'd already told him you'd probably be home soon."

With no way to avoid another encounter, Emma steeled herself and walked to the parlor doorway. "Good evening, Mr. Hibbert."

Clark broke off his conversation with Louise in mid-sentence and jumped up. "Emma! At last."

"I—had some extra work this evening."

Clark approached her, smiling. "You work too hard. Would you like to go to the pictures? They're showing *The Warrens of Virginia* at the Strand."

"No, thank you, I couldn't go out again tonight."

His smile drooped. "It would take your mind off your work."

"Thank you, but it's been a long and fatiguing day. But perhaps Miss Newton…"

Louise's eyes widened, but she stepped forward with a smile. "I've been wanting to see that picture, Mr. Hibbert. Do you think it's as good as people say?"

"I'm not sure." He shot a distracted glance Louise's way but turned back to Emma. "I'd really like a chance to speak with you. We don't have to go out. Perhaps we could sit here and talk for a short time."

"No, really." Emma pulled her gloves off. "I haven't had dinner, and I—"

"I'd be happy to take you out to eat."

Emma held up both hands. "Mr. Hibbert, please. Allow me to speak."

He opened his mouth but remained silent for a moment.

She seized the opportunity. "I do not wish to go out nor sit here and chat with you this evening. Furthermore, I shall have to report to Captain Waller that you've broken your word to him. He expressly forbade you to bother me, did he not?"

"Well, I—it wasn't my intention to bother you, Emma."

"And would you please stop calling me Emma?"

A tense stillness descended over the parlor. Emma regretted letting her voice take on such a peeved note. Louise stared at her, and Doris's face froze in a stricken mask. Clark's mouth worked for a few seconds and then he swallowed hard.

"Forgive me." Emma put her hands to her temples and swung around. She dashed across the entry and up the stairs. With trembling hands, she unlocked her door and opened it. Flinging herself across her bed, she gave way to tears for the first time since her arrival in Virginia. "Forgive me," she gasped, but this time her plea was to her heavenly Father.

Ten minutes later she had cried herself out and sat up to wipe her face.

A gentle knock came at the door.

"Who is it?"

"Doris."

"Come in."

The door squeaked open, and her friend peeked in at her. "Are you all right, Emma dear?"

She nodded. "I was terribly rude, wasn't I?"

"I didn't think so. Not after he tracked you down and came unannounced to your lodgings. If his commander told him not to, then his actions were unconscionable."

"The trouble is, Mr. Hibbert is a civilian, and he doesn't actually have to obey Captain Waller unless he wants to." Emma wiped her weepy eyelids once more.

Doris stepped into the room. "Well, just in case you felt like eating, I rescued your plate before Mrs. Draper could throw it out." She laid back the linen towel that covered a tray with a glass of milk and a plateful of roast chicken, dressing, peas, and a baked potato.

"I'm ravenous." Emma stood and walked to her. Before taking the plate, she leaned over and kissed Doris's cheek. "Thank you so much. And, if I may ask, what did you do with Mr. Hibbert?"

Doris gave her a wan smile. "Can you believe it? Louise bundled him off to the movies."

"No."

"Yes. When I told Freddie, she said I ought to have gone with them, but I couldn't bear to do that."

Emma sat down at her desk and set the dishes off the tray. "Don't trouble yourself. Louise can handle him, and when he brings her home, I'll have retired."

"I'll make sure he doesn't make a fuss." Doris strode to the door. "Now, if you need anything, come to my room."

"Thank you, but I don't plan to stay up much longer."

Doris smiled and shook her head. "Do you know, I prayed that God would give me a friend here, and He has. I had Freddie and Louise, but they didn't believe as I did, and I always felt there was a gap between us. But with you it's different."

Emma smiled. "Yes, it is. I'm glad to have you too. I'll see you at breakfast."

* * * * *

Friday, July 2, 1915

The next morning, Emma arrived in the dining room before most of the other boarders. Only Freddie sat at the table, shelling her boiled egg. Emma helped herself to an egg, toast, and a glass of milk from the sideboard and sat down next to her.

"I heard about last night's fracas," Freddie said.

"Oh." Emma pulled a face at her. "I never intended to become the topic of rumors."

"When it comes from Doris, I'm sure it's no rumor. I'm sorry that fellow's been bothering you again. But Doris said you gave him a proper set-down."

"Nothing proper about it. I'd simply had enough."

Mrs. Draper came out of the kitchen carrying a coffeepot and a covered pan. "Good morning, ladies! I've got a pan of biscuits fresh out of the oven and hot coffee."

"Oh, Mrs. Draper, you're trying to fatten us all up, aren't you?" Freddie smiled and rose to claim one of the steaming biscuits.

The kitchen door thumped open again, and Lonnie stuck his head into the dining room. "Ma! Did you hear?"

All three women swiveled toward him.

"Really, Lonnie, you needn't be so rude. I'll be back in the kitchen in just a moment."

"But, Ma!" Lonnie walked into the dining room, holding up a newspaper. "It's all over the morning papers. Someone bombed the Capitol building last night."

CHAPTER TWENTY

John stole a precious minute on his way out of Captain Waller's office to call the boardinghouse. A woman answered and promised to fetch Miss Shuster. John pulled out his watch and checked the time to be sure he wouldn't miss his train.

"Hello?" Emma sounded breathless and a bit wary.

"It's me, John. Sorry to bother you so early."

"It's all right. We were all at breakfast and talking about the bomb at the Senate chamber."

"Oh, you've heard, then. It was the Senate reception room actually, but it's an awful mess."

"You've seen it? What happened? The paper said there was an explosion last night."

"Just before midnight. I'm involved in the investigation, Emma. I have to leave town at once."

"But—it happened in Washington."

"Yes, but the police have some witnesses and an idea of who to look for. I'm heading for New York, but I can't tell you any more. I'm sorry—I'll call you as soon as I can, but I'm afraid our engagement for this evening is off, and probably the fireworks on Sunday night as well. I was planning to ask you to go, but—"

"I understand. John—"

"Yes?"

"Be safe."

"I'd appreciate your prayers," he said.

"Always."

John hung up the phone and raced for the platform.

* * * * *

Emma hurried with Doris toward the trolley station as soon as they were free from work. They had no escort, and Emma tried to stay alert and watched the pedestrians as they walked.

"I'm glad you were able to get out at a decent hour tonight," Doris said.

"So am I."

A newsboy stood on the corner shouting, "Explosion at the Capitol, read all about it!"

Emma fished in her purse for a nickel and handed it to him. She tucked the evening paper under her arm.

"At least Congress wasn't in session," she said.

"Come on." Doris seized her hand and pulled her toward the stop, where their trolley car had just pulled up.

On the short ride, Emma and Doris exchanged sections of the newspaper. The notice about the explosion was short and vague. Emma had learned little new at work, though the cryptographers talked about it that day.

While Mrs. Draper's boarders sat at dinner, the telephone in the hallway rang. Freddie ran to answer it and reported that the caller had asked for Miss Shuster.

Emma's pulse quickened as she stepped into the hall. What if Clark was telephoning her? Or the unknown man who hadn't left his name? Her stomach clenched.

"Hello?"

"Emma."

The tension melted as though she'd poured hot tea over an ice cube. "John. I didn't expect to hear from you again so soon."

"I'm in New York, and I expect to be here a few days. There have been some new developments."

"Oh?" Emma's chest tightened. "Anything you can tell me over the telephone?"

"It will be splashed all over the papers tomorrow, so I don't see any harm in telling you. The fellow who set the dynamite off in the Capitol came up here and shot J. P. Morgan this morning."

"What?" Emma clutched the edge of the hall table and sank onto the chair beside it. "The financier? Is he dead?"

"No, he'll likely make a good recovery, but the suspect went out to his house and shot him. Morgan and his servants overpowered the man, and the police have him in custody."

Emma exhaled sharply. "And this same man placed a bomb..."

"Yes, in the Capitol. Dynamite. They think he had more, and they're looking for it now."

"Oh my. John, was he—do you think he's connected to—you know...?"

"The ones we've been trying to stop?"

"Yes."

"There's no way of knowing yet, but you can be sure the police will question him extensively. If they find any connection whatso-ever, I'll take my turn at him too. They've found the house where he lived and are searching it. Emma, if possible, I'll be there Sunday, but if not…"

"I'll be thinking of you."

When she re-entered the dining room, Freddie smirked and elbowed Louise. Doris smiled at her, but her eyebrows rose in silent question.

"Well, well, the dashing lieutenant must be in town again," said Louise.

"Actually, no," Emma said. "He called to express his regrets."

"Oh." Louise hesitated then reached for her water glass.

"Say, Louise," said Freddie, "how did your outing go last evening?"

Louise choked slightly, cleared her throat, and set down the glass. "Fine."

Emma's cheeks warmed. "I owe you a thank-you, Louise. You helped me out of an awkward spot."

"Hibbert's not so bad," Louise said, gazing pointedly at her. "He talks a lot, but he's an intelligent man."

Down the table, Charlotte Hannady, one of the other boarders, arched her eyebrows as though baffled at this turn in the conversation.

"I'm glad you found his company less than cloying," Emma said.

"Actually…" Louise glanced about then shrugged. "We're going out again tomorrow evening."

Freddie's jaw dropped, but Emma managed to remain calm.

"Splendid. I hope you have a pleasant time." Emma placidly finished her dinner while her mind darted thither and back again. Would Clark become a regular visitor at Mrs. Draper's? And would it matter, if he were pursuing Louise Newton?

* * * * *

Saturday, July 3, 1915

Freddie turned her infectious smile on Emma as they finished their dinner Saturday evening. "Since your young man is away and you're not going out this evening, why don't we get up a game of Old Maid?"

"Old Maid?" Doris's voice held an injured tone. "Please, Freddie. Flinch, maybe, but Old Maid?"

Emma let them persuade her to join them. For the first time in weeks, she let herself relax and join in the banter as Doris dealt out the cards. Charlotte Hannady sat down with them, and soon a lively game was under way.

Between hands, Freddie turned to the window and pushed the curtain aside.

"There's a man coming up the walk."

"Is it Mr. Hibbert coming for Louise?" Doris asked.

Before Freddie could answer, someone knocked on the door and she skipped into the entry to open it. Emma had no trouble catching their words.

"Hello. Is Miss Shuster in?"

"Well…maybe she is, and maybe she isn't."

Emma's heart leaped to her throat at the first words from Clark's mouth. She sank onto the settee, knotting her hands together. "Doris, what shall I do?"

"That skunk." Doris rose and walked to the doorway. "Good evening, Mr. Hibbert. Are you here to collect Miss Newton?"

"Oh, Doris, it's you."

"I beg your pardon? I don't recall being on a first-name basis with you, sir."

Clark coughed or cleared his throat, Emma wasn't certain which. Why hadn't she responded to him in that icy tone a year or two ago? But she knew why. It wasn't in her nature to speak harshly or turn away a person who sought her friendship.

Clark's persistence, however, went beyond common courtesy. She winged a swift prayer heavenward. *Dear Father, show me what to say to him.*

With three deliberate steps she reached Doris's side.

"Emma!" Clark beamed when she appeared. "I only wanted a few words with you, and it seems these young ladies are trying to keep me from seeing you."

"That is because they know how vexed I am that you came asking for me when you have an engagement with Miss Newton."

His eager expression faded. "I only want to talk to you for a moment."

"Really? Is that the truth, Mr. Hibbert? That you want nothing more than conversation from me? Because you've sought me out in the most flagrant manner, even though Captain Waller asked you not to. Indeed, I asked you myself not to try to see me without my consent. Yet here you are—again."

He had the grace to flush, but instead of apologizing, he raised his chin. "You know I spoke to your father once, seeking his permission to court you."

"Yes, I know."

He stepped toward her, and Emma drew back her shoulders.

"Come no closer, sir. I did know of your quest, and you also knew of my feelings. I said no. I did not wish to see you socially at that time, and I do not now."

Clark stood still for a long moment, inhaling deeply and studying her. At last he said, "What will change your mind?"

"Nothing. It pains me to say so, but you've been rude and obnoxious, and now you're insulting Louise Newton, who is a very nice person. The idea of your asking me such questions when she is upstairs waiting for you to call for her. I do not wish to see you again. Ever." Emma trembled but managed to stand her ground and keep a glare fixed on her face.

Clark's eyes narrowed. He glanced around at Doris and Freddie then moved one foot forward. "Emma—"

"No. Do not call me Emma. I've never given you permission to do so, and I've requested that you stop, yet you persist. If I didn't know you had made plans with Miss Newton, I'd ask you to leave."

"But—"

Freddie's firm hand clamped down on Clark's shoulder. "Whoa there, bucko. What part of that are you having trouble interpreting? Miss Shuster doesn't want to talk to you. Now, you can wait here quietly while I get Miss Newton, or I can ask Mrs. Draper's son to toss you out. Which is it?"

Clark turned his head slowly and gave Freddie a withering look, but Freddie came from sturdy stock and held his gaze with a glare of her own.

Doris stepped closer to Emma and seized her hand. "Come, dear."

Emma pivoted and retreated into the parlor with Doris, who closed the door behind them. Through the panel, she could hear Freddie say, "All right. Stay put, and I'll fetch Miss Newton."

"Whatever's going on?" Charlotte asked.

"Emma's erstwhile suitor," Doris whispered. "He's rather a boor, but Louise seems to like him."

"Oh, dear." Charlotte eyed Emma cautiously. "Has that Newton girl stolen your young man?"

"No, no." Emma's fears that she would burst into tears fled, and instead she laughed aloud. "I don't mind if she steals this one."

Doris patted Emma's shoulder, and they waited in silence until they heard steps on the stairs and Louise's effusive greeting. A moment later, the front door closed.

Doris pulled Freddie's trick and lifted the edge of the curtain with one finger. "They're going down the walk. You're safe."

Freddie opened the door and came in. "All clear."

"Thank you, my dears." Emma sat down on the edge of the settee and squeezed her eyes shut.

"Are you all right?" Doris asked.

Emma pulled in a deep breath. "Yes, I am. Let's play Flinch."

Freddie grinned. "That's our girl. Come on."

Nearly an hour had passed when another knock at the door caused them all to pause their play and look at each other.

"That can't be Mr. Hibbert," Doris whispered.

Freddie strode to the window. "No, it's Lieutenant Patterson."

Doris dashed into the hallway, and a second later John's deep voice greeted her.

"Emma's in here. I know she'll be ever so pleased to see you." Doris sounded a little breathless as she led the lieutenant into the parlor.

Emma stood. "John. How delightful!"

He clasped her hand. "Thank you. I'm happy to be here. I received new orders shortly after we spoke and was able to get a train home, but there was no time to phone you."

Emma turned to her friends. "I believe you know Miss Keating and Miss Fisher. I'd like to present Miss Hannady."

Charlotte rose and shook his hand. "Pleased to meet you, Lieutenant."

"Perhaps we'll get to view the fireworks together after all," John said. "If you wish, your friends could join us."

"That would be lovely." Though quiet Doris and irrepressible Freddie might hinder them from talking privately, the company of Emma's friends would take away her nerves.

"That's splendid," Freddie said, "but Doris and I have plans for the Fourth."

Doris shot her a "We do?" glance.

"I didn't know," Emma said.

"Yes, we're meeting a couple of fellows I know from work. They're nice lads."

Doris's face registered alarm.

Freddie hurried on, "As a matter of fact, I need to settle the details with Doris. Come on." She seized Doris's hand and practically dragged her toward the hall. "You come too, Charlotte."

Charlotte's eyes widened, but she took the less than subtle hint and followed them to the door. "Have a good evening."

"Nice to see you again, Lieutenant," Freddie called. On their way out, she closed the parlor door.

John smiled sheepishly at Emma. "Something tells me Miss Fisher is a bit of a matchmaker."

"Oh, yes. Freddie is in rare form this evening. Would you like to sit down? I'm sure Mrs. Draper has a kettle on, if you'd like some tea."

"Actually, it's a lovely night. I thought perhaps we could walk a bit."

"I'd love to. Let me just fetch my sweater."

A few minutes later, they strolled down the sidewalk, past the trolley stop, and along the edge of the schoolyard. John found a bench just off the walk, and they sat down in the twilight.

"It's been less muggy this week," Emma said.

"Yes, it feels quite pleasant." John sighed and leaned back against the bench. "Emma, this man they caught—Frank Holt, he's called."

"Is he one of Kobold's men?"

John's brow furrowed and he shook his head. "I don't think so, but we know so little. When they caught him, he said he had three plans."

"What sort of plans?"

"One was the Capitol bombing. He wanted to make the public sit up and take notice."

"Well, we have."

He smiled faintly. "Yes. Somehow he thought that would convince us to stop sending munitions to the Allies."

"So he *is* a German sympathizer."

John nodded. "He has a faint accent, and he's studied languages. In fact, he told the police he is a professor at Cornell University. They're still looking into his background."

"What was his second plan? To kill Mr. Morgan?"

"To persuade him to stop his work for Great Britain."

Emma cocked her head to one side. "He's been helping the Allies get funding for their war effort, hasn't he?"

"Morgan's been their main agent for financing. Holt said he wanted to stop him. I'm not sure he intended to shoot him, but when Morgan's butler didn't want to let him in, he pulled a gun. Mr. Morgan heard them wrestling and ran to aid the servant. Got himself wounded for his trouble, but they subdued Holt. That's the main thing."

"If he'd got away, what would have been his third act?"

John shook his head. "He won't say. At least—" He sat up. "He says the world will know on Wednesday."

Emma stared at him. "He's planned something worse?"

"Maybe."

They eyed each other bleakly. Emma considered what sort of plans the man might have instigated that would go on while he sat in prison.

"He might have accomplices," John said.

"And if he's connected to a network of spies, they may have something large planned for next week."

"That's what I'm afraid of." John rubbed the back of his neck, and Emma noticed a dark shadow beneath his eyes.

"You ought to be home sleeping."

"I wanted to see you. To make sure the whole world hadn't gone mad, and there was still a spot of beauty here in Fairfax." He took her hand.

A pleasant shiver rippled through Emma. "I'm so glad you came home safely."

"So am I. I'd hardly gotten to New York before Waller called me back. The Washington papers received letters from Holt yesterday morning."

"Oh? I hadn't heard about that."

"I don't think they've made it public yet. The letters were signed by someone called Pierce, claiming he set the dynamite off in the Capitol."

"Pierce?"

"An associate of Holt's perhaps...or another alias."

"You're certain Holt is not his real name?"

John shrugged. "I'm not sure of anything, but the investigators can't find out much about him. Indications are that it's a false name." He squeezed her hand. "Let's talk of something less dreary."

"All right, I'm willing."

He smiled down at her. "I appreciate you, Emma. You're practical, and yet you've got a sweet, romantic side that always leaves me feeling uplifted."

As he bent toward her, Emma's heart raced. How long had she waited for this moment? John's lips touched hers, and she laid her hand on his shoulder. He pulled her closer, wrapping his arms around her. A moment later she nestled her head against his uniform jacket and thought what a wonderful, safe place she had found in John's embrace.

A scream cut through the dusk.

John leaped up and ran toward the trolley stop.

CHAPTER TWENTY-ONE

John sprinted toward the woman's scream. As he ran, he saw several figures struggling. A car was drawn up by the sidewalk just beyond the trolley stop. When he drew within a few yards of the scuffle, a feminine figure separated from the others and drew back, shrinking from the grappling men.

"Leave her alone!"

John caught his breath in a gasp. The voice of the shorter man was unmistakably Clark Hibbert's. He reached beneath his tunic as he ran and pulled out the gun he wore in a shoulder holster while traveling under secret orders—the gun he'd almost left in his room when he set out to visit Emma. He halted and raised both hands to steady the weapon. "Put your hands up. Now!"

As the last word came out, a shot cracked. The woman screamed again and faded back against the trolley sign. One of the men fell, and the other ran for the car.

John aimed at the fleeing figure, but he couldn't shoot without endangering the woman and any passersby near the trolley stop.

The car gained momentum almost before the man was inside and sped away, careening around the nearest corner.

John lowered the pistol and ran to the fallen man. "Hibbert! It's me. Do you hear me?"

He rolled Clark's body over. The arms flopped with a dreadful looseness.

The woman, three yards from him, sobbed, and John darted a glance at her. "What happened?"

"I don't know. That man—he jumped out at us. He just— He had a gun." She sobbed again.

Clark moaned, and John leaned close to him. "Clark, can you speak to me? Where are you hit?"

"I—I thought—"

"What is it?" John waited, wondering if he should do something—summon help, put pressure on the wound—anything.

"The machine—he said—for her to go with—" Clark sagged and his head slumped to one side.

John put his fingers to the artery at Clark's throat but felt no pulse. Hurried footsteps on the sidewalk drew his attention in the other direction.

Emma ran toward him. "John! Are you all right? Shall I try to find help?"

"Stay back, Emma."

She drew up a few feet away.

"Emma?" The woman gasped and raised one hand to her throat.

"Louise?" Emma stared at her and then at the man on the ground. "That's not—"

"Yes," John said. "It's Hibbert. He's been shot."

Emma hurried to Clark and went to her knees on the packed earth. She reached for Clark's wrist and sat motionless, while Louise stood with her hand over her mouth, watching and catching choppy breaths.

"I'm afraid he's gone," John said softly.

Louise flung herself onto the bench and wailed ragged, gulping sobs.

Emma laid Clark's hand down gently and rose. She sat down and placed her arms around Louise. "My dear, we're here to help you. Do you know who that other man was?"

"No, no. He came out of nowhere and shoved against Clark then grabbed me. He was pulling me toward the car—" She looked around, her tear-filled eyes wide. "There was a car. Did you see it?"

"Yes," Emma said. "It drove away just before I got here."

"I saw it as well," John said. "The man dove into it, and it took off. There must have been someone else driving."

"I heard a shout," Louise said.

John nodded. "Perhaps the driver called to him to get in when he saw me coming."

"We must get aid for Clark," Louise said.

Emma looked up at John, her lips parted, her eyes seeking hope, but he had none for her.

"Where's the nearest telephone?" he asked.

"Back at Mrs. Draper's, so far as I know," Emma said.

"Right." He looked down the street. "You two go together. Call the police and have them come here. And stay at the boardinghouse. I'll come there later. Don't come out again."

* * * * *

Emma ran the four blocks to the boardinghouse, pulling Louise along by the hand. They burst into the entry, and Emma went straight to the telephone.

"Emma? Louise? What happened?" Freddie stood in the parlor doorway. "Goodness, you look like death, Louise."

Louise let out a wail, and Doris appeared behind Freddie. "What's going on?"

Emma lifted the receiver from the telephone box. "Take Louise upstairs. I need to make a phone call."

Doris put an arm around the weeping woman's shoulders. "Come, dear."

"What number?" asked a voice in Emma's ear.

"Get me the police."

Freddie came to stand beside her, staring with unblinking brown eyes.

A man came on the wire, and Emma quickly gave her name and location. "It's a shooting at the trolley stop. Lieutenant John Patterson, of the navy, is waiting there for your officers. One man was shot, and the one who did it drove off in a car. We have a witness here at this address."

The officer asked more questions. By the time he told Emma she could hang up, Mrs. Draper, Lonnie, and four other boarders crowded the entryway.

"Who was shot?" Mrs. Draper asked. "Not your young man."

"No. He's staying there with—with the victim. I'm afraid it was Clark Hibbert."

"That fellow Louise went out with?" Charlotte asked. "The one who kept bothering you?"

Emma gulped.

Freddie squeezed her hand. "Leave Emma alone, folks. She's had a shock."

"Yes, you'd better lie down," Mrs. Draper said.

"I must wait for a police officer to come and take a statement from Louise and me. And John said he'd come here when he could."

"Then sit down in the parlor. I'll bring you some coffee."

The boarders drifted in and out over the next hour. Emma asked for a notepad and jotted down a few details she wanted to remember—the sound of the shot, the car that sped off.

The second pot of coffee cooled. Finally a police officer came and spoke to her while Freddie went upstairs to get Louise.

Emma told the officer everything she'd seen. "I didn't realize that it was Miss Newton and Mr. Hibbert at first. Not until after. We heard her scream, but I couldn't tell anything by that. John ran down there, and I was frightened out of my mind. I followed along slower, and when the gunshot went off, I stopped and waited. I saw the car leave and John kneeling by the man who'd been shot. Then I went and spoke to him." She stopped and drew in a deep breath. Tears bathed her face. She pulled a handkerchief from her pocket and wiped her eyes.

"This John you mentioned—that would be Lieutenant Patterson?"

"Yes. We'd walked down past the school." She looked up at him, nonplussed. Did she need to explain her relationship to John? "It was such a lovely night."

"Yes, miss. And when did you realize that you knew the people who'd been attacked?"

"When John spoke to me, he said my name, and Louise Newton said, 'Emma.' That's when I knew who she was, and that it must be Mr. Hibbert lying on the ground, because they'd left the house together earlier to go to the picture show."

"You and Miss Newton both live here, I believe?"

"Yes, sir."

A shadow darkened the doorway, and Emma looked up. Louise,

supported by Doris and Freddie, stood on the threshold, her face blotched with red patches.

"There's Miss Newton," Emma said.

"Thank you, Miss Shuster. I'll excuse you now and speak with her."

Emma nodded and rose. Freddie and Doris went with her into the dining room. Mrs. Draper hovered in the kitchen doorway muttering, "Dreadful. Just dreadful."

When at last they heard voices in the hall, signaling the end of the officer's session with Louise, Freddie opened the dining room door. "May I show you out, sir?"

She went out, and Doris reached over and patted Emma's arm. "I'm sorry this happened to you. And poor Louise. She probably needs me now."

"Yes," Emma said. "You might ask her if she wants to call her family. There's something about a tragedy that makes you long to hear your loved ones' voices."

"That's a good idea."

As Doris walked out, Emma determined not to fall to pieces as Louise had done. She'd been strong for Louise. She could continue the role. John would need her. The shock must have rocked him too. He'd been as close to a friend as Clark had here in Virginia, and though he'd tried to help, he'd been unable to stop the gunman from killing Clark. She clenched her teeth and raised her chin.

John found Emma still sitting at the long dining table a half hour later. He strode swiftly around to her chair and knelt beside her. "Emma, my darling, I'm so sorry."

His tender words brought back the regret, the remorse, and the guilt.

"Oh, John, this is my fault." She fell into his arms, unable to hold back her sobbing. Ashamed of her weeping, she cried even harder.

"There, now." He stroked her hair and held her close. "Hush, my love. It's going to be all right."

* * * * *

Sometime later, a timid knock on the dining room door brought John to his feet. Still clasping Emma's hands, he called, "Enter."

Doris pushed the door open and nodded gravely at him. "There's a captain in the parlor, sir. He said you called for him."

"Yes, thank you."

John crouched beside Emma and looked into her reddened eyes. "I asked Captain Waller to come. Can you go into the parlor with me and speak with him?"

Emma sniffed and rose, clinging to his arm for support. "I'm sorry," she whispered.

"You've nothing to be sorry for." He closed his hand over hers and led her past Doris, who gave him a tremulous smile, and into the parlor.

Behind him, Doris said, "I shall retire now, but, Emma, if you need me, dear, please do come to my room. Any time."

"Thank you," Emma said.

Captain Waller rose and took both of Emma's hands. "My dear Miss Shuster, what a shock you've had. I'm so sorry."

"It's good of you to come," she said.

"Won't you sit down for a moment?" The captain led her to the sofa and sat in a wing chair beside it. John took the spot next to Emma and watched her anxiously.

"My dear..." Waller paused and John realized the moment was painful for him as well. Captain Waller had recruited both Emma and Clark to work for him, and now he felt responsible.

"Captain, this is all my fault," Emma said.

"Nonsense."

"No, listen to me. Clark Hibbert came here Thursday evening, and I was rude to him. My friends and I foisted Louise Newton on him, and he took her out. He asked her to step out with him again tonight, but I suspect it was only to give him another chance to speak to me."

"What makes you say that?"

"When he came here this evening for their date, he asked for me. We had another encounter, and I fear I was most uncivil to him."

John would have chuckled if the circumstances were not so tragic. Emma being uncivil, even to the person she most loathed, was nearly unthinkable. He almost wished he could have heard her exchange with Clark.

"And he took Miss Newton out again," Captain Waller said.

"Yes, sir. And then John came. I didn't expect him." Emma looked his way, her eyelids still puffy and her cheeks streaked with dried tears. "I was so happy to see him, I forgot about Louise and Clark."

"That doesn't make what happened your fault." Captain Waller leaned forward and spoke quietly, looking into her eyes. "Emma, you mustn't blame yourself for this. But with all that's happened, I'm concerned about your safety."

"*My* safety?" She looked from him to John. "But Clark is the one who was murdered."

"Yes." The captain sat back, his face grim.

John wasn't sure what to say, so he waited for a cue from Waller.

The captain drew a deep breath. "I've set things in motion to move you to a new location."

"What?" Emma stared at him. "You mean—"

"I mean you're not safe here. For tonight, Lieutenant Patterson and a detail of two marines will escort you to Miss Ainsley's home."

Emma turned to John and looked back to the captain. "Is this necessary?"

"I think it is." Waller nodded to John.

He reached over and took Emma's hand. "Think about this, Emma. Your father was murdered. Your home in Maine was the target of an intruder scared off by your neighbors and the police. Who knows what would have happened if your uncle hadn't brought those insufferable dogs to the house?"

"What? John, surely—"

He squeezed her hand. "My dear, you cannot deny someone broke into the barn where your possessions were stored."

"Yes. We thought—"

"We're quite certain they were after your father's cipher machine, the same thing they wanted the day they killed your father. And a stranger has followed you and Martin Glazer about the park, and an unknown man called for you here one evening when you were out."

She nodded slowly. "And all those incidents are related?"

"How could they not be?"

Captain Waller cleared his throat. "We know someone also followed Clark Hibbert about in Maine and searched his lodgings. Again, the logical conclusion is that they knew he'd worked on the Shuster machine. When they didn't find it in your possession, they tried his rooms."

"But Clark didn't have it. Not after that day…the Monday after the funeral."

"Yes," John said. "The day the burglar returned to your father's office. We'd gone to lunch. Clark brought you the machine shortly after we got back, but they didn't know that."

Emma sank her face into her hands. "I knew they wanted the machine. But how did they learn it was here?"

"Simple," Waller said. "You know Hibbert talks too much. Our man who was watching him in Maine reported that he made it no secret he was coming to Virginia to work for the navy."

"Oh, dear."

"Yes. And when he came down here, they followed him."

"They can't get at the machine, so long as it's in the navy compound," Emma said.

"True, and I'm not sure they know it's there. But they knew you and Hibbert had a connection, and I believe they let him lead them to you."

Emma's brow furrowed. "Do you mean, when he came to the house Thursday evening?"

"Or before that."

John said, "You remember the day Clark followed me to the church."

"Yes, but—oh, John, that was weeks ago."

"It was, but what if one of Kobold's men followed Clark that day?"

Emma caught her breath. "He came again and spoke to me at the church last Sunday, while you were away."

"That's likely when Kobold's man found out where you lived. I suspect one of them had his first sight of you the day you and Martin Glazer were followed. They knew then where you worked, but not where you lived. But they realized that if they waited, Hibbert would provide that information." Waller looked at his watch. "We must get you over to Miss Ainsley's apartment. She's waiting up for you. We'll post a guard outside for the night, and tomorrow we'll take you to new quarters."

"Where will that be?" Emma asked.

"I think it's best that you don't know until we take you there."

"Will I still be able to get to work?"

"We'll have you escorted each day until we stop these thugs. I don't think it's safe for you to take the trolley anymore. They'd see you get off at the stop near Trafton House and follow you back that evening."

"Excuse me, sir," John said. "Do you think it might be wise if Emma took a few days off and just lay low?"

"Hmm. Maybe. But she's doing important work."

"Someone could take her work to her." John arched his eyebrows at Emma.

She nodded. "If you think it's best, I could do that for a short time. Commander Howe could send over some work for me."

"We'll see." Waller rose. "Come now. You need to pack your things. I've a couple of sailors waiting outside to carry them out."

Emma's dismay was evident on her face.

"I had a word with Mrs. Draper earlier," John said. "She knows you'll be safe, and we'll compensate her for her trouble."

"Yes, and likely send her a new boarder soon."

John and Emma stood, and Emma stepped toward Waller. "Captain, you still haven't told me—do you believe Kobold thinks I have the machine here at Mrs. Draper's?"

"No, but they're sure you know where it is. That's why they tried to snatch you tonight."

"To—" Emma's face paled.

John wrapped his arm firmly around her as Waller spoke again.

"That's right. Miss Newton told the police the gunman said something like, 'You're coming with us.' And Mr. Hibbert's last words to Patterson concerned the machine. It's obvious—they mistook Louise Newton for you."

CHAPTER TWENTY-TWO

Monday, July 5, 1915

Emma awoke Monday morning in her new lodgings—an upstairs back bedroom in the home of a navy wife whose husband was out to sea. The small room was pleasantly situated, but the cries of a fretful infant had kept Emma from getting much rest. She took her Bible from the top of the bookcase beside the bed and opened to the first chapter of Isaiah for her daily reading.

As she read, her mind kept bouncing back to Saturday night and Clark. Had she somehow doomed him by rejecting him and watching him go off with Louise? Every time she thought about his death too closely, a load of guilt weighed upon her. She'd treated him uncivilly. Had she let her pride take over when she said mean things to him?

The eighteenth verse caught her attention. *"Come now, and let us reason together, saith the LORD: though your sins be as scarlet, they shall be as white as snow; though they be red like crimson, they shall be as wool."*

She knew that her guilt, whether real or perceived, was forgiven by God. *Thank You, Lord,* she prayed. *Thank You for accepting me, even though I'm worthless.*

She rose and dressed, determined to be a blessing to Nora South-ard, her new landlady. *Lord, show me small ways I can help Nora.*

She fixed tea and oatmeal while Nora tended the baby. They had only a few minutes to get acquainted, as a car arrived while they finished breakfast.

The driver took Emma to Fort Myer, where Commander Howe met her. "The army is loaning us some space here for an indefinite time—until we figure out last weekend's business. You'll be working here with Mr. Glazer today, and unless something breaks in this attempted kidnapping case, you may be joined by other Signal Corps workers later in the week. Our unit is vital to national security, and we need to make sure you're safe." He ushered Emma into an office where Martin Glazer sat at a folding table.

Martin jumped up and met her in the middle of the small room. "My dear Emma! What a time you've had. Are you all right?"

"Yes, Martin. Thank you." She smiled as she removed her hat and gloves. "It's been a trying weekend, but I'm ready to work."

His troubled expression told her his concern ran deep.

When the commander had left them, Martin told her, "It was a bit of a shock when Captain Waller phoned me and told me not to go out yesterday."

"Yes, I stayed in as well," she said. "Muriel Ainsley put me up Saturday night, and the captain's men came yesterday to move me again."

Martin walked with her to the table, still grave. "He said they were moving you out of that boardinghouse. Don't tell me where they've put you."

"I shan't."

He nodded and pulled out a chair for her. "Howe said several of the other cryptographers will work at home today, while the police try to track down the man who— Emma, are you certain you're all right?"

She chuckled, but it ended in a small sob. "Yes, Martin. It was awful, but I'm unscathed—though I don't know why."

"Providence."

"Yes. I believe God does have a job for me to do here. Today. Now." She looked up into his eyes, hoping he would take the hint and sit down to work.

"They didn't tell us the whole story," he said. "Just that you were in danger, a fellow on our side had been killed, and you were being sequestered for your safety."

Emma could see that they would get nothing done until he had heard everything. "Martin—"

"Yes?" He stood very close to her.

"I appreciate your concern. It was a shock when Captain Waller told me he believed the enemy was after me. Knowing an innocent man was killed for my sake, and a woman traumatized..." She shook her head. "Let's sit down."

She took her seat, but Martin crouched beside her, holding on to the back of her chair, much the way John had done after the shooting. "Emma, when I first heard, I thought it was your young man who was killed. Lieutenant Patterson."

She cringed at the thought and laid her hand on his sleeve. "No. He's fine."

"I'm glad. He seems like a very nice fellow."

"Yes. In fact, he ran the thug off. They say if he hadn't been there, the enemy—I can't call them anything else now—might have kidnapped or killed Louise Newton."

"And who is she?"

"She's the young woman who was with—with the victim."

"Please tell me everything. I was flabbergasted when a marine came to my door this morning and said I'd be working here today. When I opened the briefcase he brought, I found a new cipher. Then you walked in."

She smiled. "I'm glad it's you working with me today."

Martin nodded soberly, still gazing at her face. "Emma, please don't think me too much of a rogue, but when I heard—heard a man was killed—well, my first thought was how alone you would be. You lost your father a few months ago, and now—" He looked away at last and stood slowly. "Forgive me. I have no right to think—"

Emma frowned. "To think what, Martin?"

"The first thing that came to me was, 'Emma will need someone.' I was prepared to offer you my services. Even my hand." He swung around and met her gaze. "I'm sorry. I shouldn't be saying these things. But, my dear, the thought of you in danger like that— If you ever need comfort, or protection, or—or anything at all—" He broke off in a bitter chuckle and paced to the far side of the table. "Listen to me. You've got the entire U.S. Navy to protect you."

Emma stared at him in disbelief. "Martin? I had no idea."

"Of course you hadn't. I'm too old for you. I daresay I'm your father's age."

"He was fifty-nine."

"Oh." He shrugged. "I'm forty-eight. Not that it matters."

"But, Martin, I don't understand."

"Don't you?" His gray eyes zeroed in on her with startling clarity.

"I've admired you since the day you walked into Room 20. But you were so young, and…" Again he shook his head. "What can I say? Forgive me and forget I ever spoke. It's inappropriate and…"

"And very sweet," Emma said. "Thank you, Martin."

He nodded, his eyes glistening. "I wouldn't wish young Patterson gone, but if you ever, *ever* need anything…"

"Thank you," she whispered. "I'll remember. Now, shall we ask for a pot of coffee and get to work on the new cipher?"

"Yes." He cleared his throat. "I think that would be best."

* * * * *

"How can this be?" Kobold puffed his cigar rapidly and sent a stream of smoke across the desk toward the two men facing him. "Once again, you have failed."

Gade, the one who served as the chief go-between for him and the men who followed his unofficial orders, squirmed and flushed. Ritter, the man they'd brought down from Maine, wouldn't even meet his gaze. The two of them sat there like naughty schoolboys.

"I don't know how anyone could fail so many times." Kobold shook his head and tapped the ash off his cigar.

"We'll find out where they've moved her." Gade licked his lips and nudged Ritter.

"Yes, sir. We'll nose around until we learn where they've stashed her." Ritter nodded so hard his hair flopped up and down like a mop being shaken by a housewife.

Kobold shook his head. "I'm thinking of giving this job to someone else."

Gade sat up straight. "Don't do that, sir. We can handle it. We'll get her."

Kobold glared at him for several seconds. "You'd better. We've got to get that machine. Get her and take her to the farm. Call me when you have her. Within the week."

* * * * *

A yeoman brought lunch to Emma and Martin, and they continued their work into the afternoon.

At two o'clock Martin stood and stretched. "Wish we could have a game of baseball."

"Yes, my brain's getting a little fuzzy too," Emma said. "We've made progress, though."

"We have. Perhaps we should let someone know what we've found."

After a brisk knock on the door, Commander Howe entered.

"Commander! I was just saying we ought to let you know that we've found last week's key."

"Good!" Howe flashed a quick glance and a smile Emma's way. "I hope that will help you with the new messages. Anything I should tend to right away?"

Martin shook his head. "We solved all six that you gave us from last week's unsolved batch. Most are innocuous. There is one you'll perhaps want to look into, regarding that passport fraud scheme." He handed Howe the message in question.

"I'll take this with me. How are you doing, Miss Shuster?"

"I'm fine, sir. Working has helped me keep my mind off the weekend's tragic events."

"Good. So…anything on the new cipher?" Howe walked over and looked down at her work sheet.

"Not yet, except that it's the same type as last week's. I think it's a matter of time before we find the key."

"So, they changed the key again."

"Yes. For a while, we thought they might stay with gemstones."

"Because of the tourmaline messages."

"Yes." Emma frowned and flipped her pencil back and forth. "We also tried words near it in the dictionary, and on the next page, in case they were using a dictionary cipher, but nothing seemed to fit."

"Then we had a stroke of luck." Martin beamed at the commander. "Miss Shuster pulled Babbage's attack on last week's cipher, and she found that the key word was likely four letters long."

"Only four." Howe pursed his lips. "Not a four-letter gemstone though?"

"No, sir," Emma said. "We tried ruby and onyx. The interesting thing was that as I fiddled around with the columns trying to make ruby fit, I thought I saw something."

"And then she did her magic." Martin wiggled his fingers at Howe, as though casting a spell on him.

Emma laughed. "It's not magic, and it works better with longer words, like tourmaline. That one had end-of-the-alphabet letters near the beginning of the word, and early-in-the-alphabet letters later. It really didn't take me long to find that one. But with a four-letter word… well, there are so many possibilities."

"And?" Howe asked.

"Blue." Emma picked out one of her discarded work sheets and offered it to him. "Last week's key word was blue."

Howe studied it and smiled. "Excellent work, Miss Shuster."

"Thank you. Unfortunately, it didn't work on today's messages. They must have changed their key by prearrangement."

"I understand. We've known the Germans changed their main cipher several weeks ago. They must have suspected that the British had them pegged. But I hoped their people on this side of the Atlantic would keep using the old one for a while. We get oddball ciphers from the smaller cells, but a lot of them follow the general pattern of the Kaiser's main cipher."

Martin flopped down in his chair. "I'm just happy a lot of them use English over here. I suppose some of the men they hire to do their dirty work don't speak German."

"You may be right," Howe said.

"Well," Emma told him, "we tried blue on the messages that came in this morning, but it didn't work."

"So while she finished deciphering last week's stale messages, I put Babbage's method to work on this new one," Martin said. "Our theory is that it's another color, but this one needs seven letters. That's the most common interval for repetitions."

"Seven." Howe's eyes focused on something beyond the room. "Purple? No, that's only six." After a moment he shook his head. "Well, I'll leave you to it. But I brought you some new fodder. Some of the other fellows are already working on these, but I brought you copies, in case you'd had a breakthrough."

"Thank you, sir." One of the new messages caught Emma's eye. "This was a telegram, wasn't it?"

"Yes, coming out of the German embassy."

Martin nodded. "We won't ask how our people got hold of it."

"You don't want to know." Howe hesitated. "Have you heard any news today?"

"No, sir," Emma said.

"Is there something we should know?" Martin asked.

"Just that we'll continue this arrangement again tomorrow. You're safer here on the base."

"Have you heard anything about the police investigation?" Emma asked.

"No. Perhaps Captain Waller has. There was a bit of news in the paper about that fellow, Holt."

"The one who put the bomb in the Senate reception room?" Martin asked.

"Yes. They're speculating he's really a fugitive named Muenter, who disappeared seven years ago after poisoning his wife. He'd taught German at Harvard before that."

"Really?" Emma felt as though the breath had been knocked out of her.

"They've found some of Muenter's relatives who they hope can positively identify him. And he has another wife in Texas now—married her under the assumed name. Oh, and another thing." Howe grimaced. "The police have learned he bought two hundred sticks of dynamite a short time ago."

"How many did he use on the Capitol bombing?" Martin asked.

"Three."

"Three?" Emma stared at him. "Where's the rest of it?"

"They're looking for it."

"But he had nothing to do with Kobold—this German boss who's setting up all these sabotage jobs in the States and Canada?"

"We don't know yet. Holt seems to have acted alone."

Emma sat down again. "I thought some newspapers got letters afterward from someone called Pierce."

"They did, but the authorities think Muenter—or Holt—wrote those himself. At least we know he had nothing to do with Hibbert's shooting Saturday night."

"Yes, he was in custody by then." She let out a long sigh. "I never would have thought there was so much evil in our country."

Howe nodded. "Well, sorry to leave you folks on such a macabre note. That's good work you're doing. If you find the new key word, give me a call. It will help the others, especially since we're getting new messages almost hourly."

"How can we call you?" Emma asked.

"Oh, sorry. There's a telephone at the desk near the front entrance of this building. Tell them you need to telephone me, and the petty officer on duty will place the call for you." He turned toward the door and took three steps then stopped. He turned and looked keenly at Emma. "Scarlet."

She caught her breath. "Seven letters."

Martin dashed to his chair, and they both began writing the word above the cipher message on their work sheets. Howe came back over to the table and stood in silence.

After a few minutes, Martin threw down his pencil. "That's not it."

"Wait." Emma grasped at something just outside her memory. "Crimson."

"Crimson?" Martin's brow furrowed.

"'Though your sins be as scarlet, they shall be as white as snow,'" Emma said softly.

Martin grinned. "Of course. 'Though they be red like crimson, they shall be as wool.'"

"Try it." Howe's voice was tight.

Emma worked frantically, but before she could be sure, Martin crowed like a rooster. "That's it! Praise God!"

Howe paced while they worked on the message. After ten minutes, he left the room but came back with fresh coffee and a plate of chocolate wafers.

"Almost there," Emma told him. Her pencil flew over the grids, transforming the garbled message into clear.

"Uh-oh," Martin said.

Emma looked up and arched her eyebrows at him. "What do you have?"

"A cannery? They want to bomb a cannery?"

"Must be one packing food for the Allies." Howe took the sheet of paper and scowled at it. "What's this at the end?"

"I dunno. Something about machinery."

"No. A machine. Singular. They want to lay hands on the machine."

Emma gasped. "It can't be…"

"Why couldn't it?" Howe asked. "They're still looking for your father's project. Look here. 'Until we find that machine our plans continue to be ruined.'"

Martin stared at Emma. "Something I don't know about?"

CHAPTER TWENTY-THREE

Thursday, July 8, 1915

By midweek, Room 20 had dissolved and reformed in the borrowed office space at Fort Myer. Muriel Ainsley, Charles Tallie, Rory Ingersoll, and Larry Crane joined Emma and Martin daily in their new workroom. The rest of Howe's crew assembled in another room down the hall. Howe had a desk in an alcove in the hallway between them, and Agnes Harper was given two weeks' leave.

Though the quarters were cramped compared to Trafton House, a great deal of work was processed. The key word crimson had stood them in good stead all week, as more messages came in using that pattern.

They followed the daily news about the Muenter case. On Wednesday the papers had published a letter the prisoner had sent to his wife in Texas prior to his arrest. In it he claimed that a ship that left port Saturday, July 3—either the *Saxonia* or the *Philadelphia*—would sink on Wednesday. The captains of the two ships were radioed and told to thoroughly search their vessels. Both captains reported that no explosives were found, and the ships proceeded in safety. When an agent of the New York police commissioner went to the prison to question Muenter as to which ship was in danger, he learned the man had committed suicide minutes before his arrival.

The next day, Commander Howe called the cryptographers together in one of the work rooms. "I've some news on the ship bombings. It seems the two ships Muenter said were apt to sink are safe. But an explosion went off in the hold of a third ship, the *Minnehaha,* on Wednesday afternoon."

"The day Muenter said the world would know of his mysterious third plan," Martin noted.

"Yes. The sailors are fighting the flames on the *Minnehaha,* and the captain turned his ship and headed for Halifax, Nova Scotia. It looks like they'll make it."

"Praise God," Muriel said. "How many men aboard?"

"Over a hundred. The bomb was placed in the forward hold, with miscellaneous freight, rather than in the main cargo hold. A thick bulkhead kept the fire from reaching the main cargo—munitions bound for England."

Rory whistled. "Too bad he didn't send out a cipher message about it. We might have been able to stop it."

"On days like this, I feel useless," Charles said. "The Germans dash off this drivel about stocks and labor unions and finances, and they put it all in cipher. Then they plan to murder our sailors, and they never give a peep about it until it's too late."

"You're saving lives," Howe said. "This man, Muenter, was outside the conspiracies you've uncovered. He may have had help placing the bomb on the *Minnehaha*—otherwise, why didn't he know the name of the ship it was on? But so far we've no evidence that he worked under orders from Germany."

Rory looked around at the others. "Some days I feel heroic, and other days, I just feel scared."

"That's normal, Ingersoll," Howe said. "I wish I could give you some better news. I knew you'd want to keep up with what's happening outside this building, but I hesitated to tell you all that about Muenter for the very reason Rory just mentioned. We don't want you all becoming despondent. Remember, this is war. We may not officially be in it yet, but we are fighting this war. We are among the few Americans who are stopping the plots that the Germans are hatching on our soil. They will kill some of our people. If we stop our work, they'll kill even more."

"The commander's right," Martin said. "We should all get to work. You can pray for those sailors on the *Minnehaha* while you're at it, but pray that we'll crack these messages quicker. And that the important ones won't get by us."

Howe nodded. "That's the spirit. And we've plenty of new messages for you this morning." He distributed folders and came to Emma last. "Miss Shuster, I'd like to see you outside."

Emma's palms broke out in sweat, and her heart raced. What had happened now? The other cryptographers went to their work stations, and she followed Howe into the hallway.

He set a chair for her near his desk in the alcove and waited until the traffic in the hall cleared. "We've been looking into the information you gave us about your cousin, Herman Meyer, and his father."

"Yes, sir." Prickles in her throat made it difficult to speak.

"I'm sorry to tell you that we suspect Herman, at least, of being involved in an espionage network."

Emma closed her eyes for a moment. When she opened them, Howe was studying her face carefully. "What will you do?"

"It may be best if you don't know."

She thought about that. "Yes. They haven't tried to contact me. As I told you, I've had a few letters from my aunt Thea, and a couple of days ago I heard from my cousin Gretchen. She is Herman's sister. But there was nothing in the letter that I would consider suspicious."

"Could you bring it to me tomorrow?"

"Yes, of course." Her lower lip began to tremble and she touched her hand to it.

"I'm very sorry," Howe said.

She pulled in a ragged breath. "How do you know you can trust me?"

He sat back in his chair. "Miss Shuster. Emma. You must know that you—along with Martin, Charles, Muriel, Rory—all of you—have been the subjects of the most rigorous background probes we've ever done. You most of all."

"Because I'm of German descent?"

"Partly. And because of your father's murder and the unusual circumstances surrounding your recruitment. Captain Waller wanted to be certain he was making the right decision before he brought you into Trafton House."

She sat for a long moment, looking down at her hands clenched together in her lap so tightly her fingers were blotchy red and white. "I promise you, I've done nothing to compromise this unit."

"We know that."

"At least—not intentionally." She looked at him, all the anxiety that had simmered in her heart spilling over now. "I've brought trouble to the Signal Corps."

"It's not your fault."

"But because of me, they've dug around until they found where we worked and where some of us lived. They want to stop us, Commander. To kill us."

He shook his head. "Of course they'd like to put us out of business so that we couldn't read their messages. But after all that's happened, we think they've got a misconception about you. And about your father's cipher machine."

"That machine?" She put her hand to her forehead. "What will happen to it now? Clark is dead, and it's not finished."

"I believe it is, or nearly so."

"Really?" She felt a ray of unexpected hope. "Will it help us?"

"Not much. At least not with what we're doing now. If we go to war, it will help our military encipher their messages more securely than has ever been possible before. But you know how it works. It won't help us solve ciphers unless we have the machine the enemy has, with the same settings."

"Yes."

"But they don't know that."

Slowly, Emma lifted her chin. "Is that their misconception?"

Howe nodded. "Captain Waller and I believe that the Germans think this machine is much more powerful than it actually is. In fact, we've begun to wonder if they don't think you are using your father's machine to crack their ciphers."

"That's ridiculous."

"But somehow they've gotten word that you're here, that you're working for us. And over the last few months, we've solved a lot of their messages. To their way of thinking, it's uncanny the way we learn of their plans before they're carried out. They think you have almost supernatural powers, Emma. That or a wondrous machine that enables you to read the most thoroughly encrypted messages."

She huffed out a little sob. "That would be comical, except...Clark died because of that machine, didn't he? Because he led them to me, or so they thought."

"Yes. They saw you with him, we're sure, and they'd been following him, waiting for a chance to get near you without a lot of military personnel hovering about you. When he took Miss Newton out, they thought in the darkness she was you and seized the chance to grab you."

"Do you think they would have killed me?"

"No. I think they'd have tried to make you tell them where the machine is and how it works. Maybe coerce you to steal it or the plans for it and turn them over."

"I wouldn't do that. I'd run straight to you or Captain Waller."

"We know you're one of us, German name notwithstanding. But Kobold...now, he's another story. And he's not done yet."

She stared glumly at him. "You think they'll come after me again. That's why you've moved us all here."

"Yes."

"So, because of me, the entire staff of Trafton House is endangered and inconvenienced."

"Not so much because of you. Because of the enemy's misconception—one, I might add, that we're not overly anxious to correct. As long as they think we've got a magic machine, they're running scared."

"Well, they're changing their cipher keys more often. That's made it harder for us."

"Yes, but you're still solving them. Don't you see? In their eyes, they keep switching to new ciphers, which is a great deal of trouble for them, and you keep cracking them. They don't realize that it's just you—you and Martin and Charles and several other brilliant people with nothing but pencils and reams of paper. We don't want them to know that. We want them to think they can't outwit us, no matter what they do."

"But…" Emma tried to see beyond the obvious, to feel something besides a huge block of ice pressing down on her chest. "Doesn't that mean he thinks I'm his personal enemy now?"

Howe said nothing for a moment then leaned toward her. "Emma, the last thing I want to do is put you in danger. That's why we've surrounded you with marines here on the military base. But can you see the logic to this? If we can tip this man off balance, make him think there's one dainty little woman out there wrecking all his finely crafted plans, wouldn't you think he'd react to that? Maybe be so angry he'd come out of hiding. Maybe make a mistake."

Emma could barely inhale.

"Please don't be alarmed," Howe said. "We'll do everything humanly possible to protect you."

"Of course."

* * * * *

John showed his credentials at the guard post and hurried across the base to Captain Waller's office.

"Not much new for you today, Patterson," the captain said. "Did you stop by the police station in Fairfax this morning?"

"I did, and they've about run out of clues. If only I'd gotten the registration number off that car."

"It was dark, and you had several people's safety to think about."

"Still—"

Waller waved a hand through the air. "I agree, Patterson. I wrote a letter to the Ford Company yesterday, telling them they need to find a way to illuminate registration plates. How a policeman could ever see one hanging from an axle in the dark is a mystery to me."

"Yes, sir." John reached into his jacket and took out a folded sheet of paper. "Miss Newton wasn't much help. They've spoken to her again, but she couldn't add anything to her statement."

Waller shook his head. "Excitable woman. Now, if Emma Shuster had been as close to the thug as Miss Newton was, we'd have had a minute description, down to the fabric his coat was made from."

John smiled tightly. "Maybe so. But it *was* dark."

"You probably want me to tell you where we've moved her."

"Not if you think it's not safe, sir. But I would like to see her today if I may."

"Don't see why not. And just so you know, we're taking care of her. She's escorted back and forth to work, and we keep a guard on the house all night."

"How long can we afford to do that?"

Waller clenched his teeth. "Not long. Unless something breaks, we'll have to make more changes. I'm looking into getting some space here on the base for several of our female cryptographers and typists. But the base commander isn't keen on the idea. Says we're already crowding them by using one building, and it would disrupt their training and routine business even more if we put civilian women here."

"Maybe they could stay in the same building they work in—you know, take cots in and let them sleep there after the men go home."

"We've got men working on ciphers all night. The radio traffic has increased dramatically over the last few months. And since the

Lusitania... Well, I'll give it some thought, but I hope we can catch Kobold and put a stop to this nonsense."

Even if they caught the master spy, another German would take his place. John knew that, but he didn't want to say so. If he did, Captain Waller would have to agree with him, and the truth would lie there staring at them. This wasn't going to end until the Allies finished the war.

John walked over to the building where the cryptographers now worked and again showed his credentials.

Howe saw him coming down the hall and stood.

"Hello, sir. I'd like to see Miss Shuster if I may."

"Of course, Lieutenant. It's nearly time for her to head home anyway. I'm leaving myself soon."

A door opened across the hall, and Emma came out, her face drawn with anxiety. "John. How good to see you."

He smiled. "I hoped to have a moment with you before you left this evening."

"Yes." She hesitated. "I must speak to Commander Howe, though."

"Yes, Miss Shuster?" Howe came around the desk. "How may I help you?"

Emma thrust two sheets of paper into his hands. "Muriel and I have solved that message the radioman took down this afternoon. I fear it's urgent." She glanced at John and clasped her hands together.

Howe frowned at the papers. "Yes. I'll get right on it. And—I'm sorry, Emma." His tone dropped to a gentle regret, and John wondered what Emma had discovered. "You should go home and get some rest." Howe took out his pocket watch. "Your escort should be waiting outside by now."

"Thank you, sir." Emma turned to John. "The marines would probably wait a few minutes if you'd like to talk outside. I'll fetch my things."

A minute later they went out, and Emma spoke to the waiting detail. John fished a couple of Tootsie Rolls from his jacket pocket and gave them to the men. "We won't be long."

He offered Emma his arm, and they strolled around the parade ground, talking quietly.

"I'm not sure if I'll be able to go to church this week," Emma said.

"I hope you can. If not, perhaps I can meet you here Monday evening when you get off work. We could eat out somewhere and see a picture. Then I could bring you back here to meet your escort."

"Do you think so? I'd like that."

John nodded and squeezed her fingers. "I'll see if I can arrange it."

"John, I'm worried."

"I can see that. Is there anything I can do?"

"Pray."

"Of course."

They walked on, and after they'd passed a group of men, she said, "I confess, I'm tired. The woman where I'm staying has a dear little baby, but he's ill. At least, he cries all the time. I feel so bad for her."

"The baby keeps you awake at night?"

"Yes. And when I do sleep, I see bombs and ships sinking and letters in marching rows. I see alphabets before my eyes day and night."

John's heart wrenched. "Will you get the weekend off?"

"I hope so." She stopped walking and looked up at him. "I probably shouldn't tell you, but I trust you. That last message—the one I gave Commander Howe?"

"Yes?"

"They're going to bomb the shipyard where my uncle works. I'm sick at heart, wondering if Uncle Gregory or Herman is involved."

"I'm sorry." He could see the grief in her eyes. Waller had kept him up to date on the investigation of her family, and he wondered if he'd be taking the train north tonight. They started walking again, slowly. "If I can't see you Sunday or Monday, I'll get a message to you through the captain."

"Thank you. It's easier when I know you're all right."

They had walked back around to where her escort waited, and John led her to the car. He hated to leave her, not knowing when they would meet again.

One of the marines opened the car door and stood waiting.

"Good night, John," Emma said softly.

* * * * *

That evening Emma returned to Nora's small, unassuming house and wearily climbed the steps with a marine at her side. The baby's cries wafted out to them in the twilight. She had to knock twice before Nora opened the door with the wriggling baby in her arms.

"I'm sorry. I didn't hear you." She looked past Emma toward the two men taking up their posts. "I hope you haven't been waiting long."

"No, not at all." Emma stepped inside and hung her hat and wrap on the hooks in the tiny entry. It must be a relief to Nora when she left each morning and took her guards with her. What did the neighbors say? Had Captain Waller given her a script for answering nosy questions?

"I have supper ready," Nora said over the baby's wailing.

"That's very kind of you."

Nora jostled her little one up and down as they ate.

"May I hold Bobby for you?" Emma asked after a few minutes.

"Thank you. He's been so fussy the past few days—I think he's a little colicky."

Emma reached for the baby. His cries increased as she took him. "There, there." She bounced him gently on her lap. "Have you taken him to the doctor?"

"Not yet. But I will if he's not better soon." Nora smiled apologetically. "He's not usually so fussy. I'm sorry he's cried so much since you've come."

"It's not his fault—or yours." Emma laid her cheek against the baby's downy head. "He feels a little warm." She glanced anxiously at Nora. She didn't want to alarm the mother, and she wasn't an expert on infant care.

"Yes, I thought he might have a low fever." Nora sighed. "If you run to the doctor too often, they think you're an alarmist, and besides, it costs money. I suppose I'd better take him in the morning." She came over and reached for Bobby. "I'll lay him down while we finish. We can't hear ourselves think with him crying."

The baby's wailing increased later. Before midnight, Bobby's muffled sobbing turned to screams, and Emma heard Nora moving about in the next room. She rose, put on her dressing gown, and went to tap on their door.

"Nora, is there anything I can do?"

The door opened and she drew back as Bobby's crying assaulted her ears.

Tears streamed down Nora's face. "I don't know what to do."

"Let me go out and call the doctor."

"The nearest telephone is three blocks away, at the drugstore. I don't know if they're still open now. It's after eleven."

"I'll get dressed and ask the guards to help us. If that one's not open, they'll know how we can get hold of someone."

Five minutes later Emma opened the front door, dressed and armed with the doctor's telephone number on a slip of paper. One of the guards came to the bottom of the steps.

"Ma'am?"

"We need the doctor for the baby. There's a telephone at the drugstore."

After consulting the other Marine the guard said, "I'll take you, ma'am."

The second guard took up his post by the door.

"I'm Ashford," the first man said as he took her to their car. "If you can't raise the doctor, I'll drive you and Mrs. Southard to the hospital."

The cool evening air refreshed Emma, though her fatigue ran deep. Nora's drugstore was closed, but Ashford found a public telephone box outside the Arlington post office.

A long wait followed, while the operator rang the doctor's house and the doctor's wife fetched her husband. He agreed to prescribe medicine for Bobby Southard and to call the pharmacist and tell him it was an emergency.

"Go back and knock on the door," the doctor said. "He'll open up for you. And tell Mrs. Southard to bring the baby to my office in the morning."

Ashford drove back and pulled up before the pharmacy. He got out of the car with Emma and pounded on the door.

The druggist unlocked it, grumbling. He yawned and ran a hand through his tousled hair. "It will just be a minute." He went behind his counter and opened a cupboard.

Emma unbuttoned her purse and fingered the money she'd brought. They'd already been gone nearly an hour.

"I'll have to go out back and open a new case," the druggist said.

After another five minutes, he handed her a small bag containing the bottle of medicine.

Emma paid him, and she headed out the door with Ashford. He helped her into the car and then rounded the fender to crank the engine as the lights went out inside the drugstore.

A dark figure burst from the shadows.

Emma gasped and jumped toward the driver's seat, but another man reached into the car from that side and grabbed her by the arm. Before she could scream, he clamped his other arm around her neck and covered her mouth with his hand. She twisted and pulled against him to no avail.

The first man came to the passenger side of the car. "Come on. You're riding with us."

Emma continued to struggle. As soon as the man's hold on her mouth loosened, she tried to scream.

He quickly slapped his hand back into place and squeezed her neck with his forearm. "Shut up. You can come quietly, or you can come unconscious, but you're coming with us. Which is it?"

Emma could barely breathe. She sagged in defeat, and the two men lifted her out of the car.

"Stand up."

As she stood trembling, one of the men bound her hands.

"The boss said to make sure we've got the right one this time," the man behind her said.

"Let's get her to our car first. And no yelling, lady." The one who'd tied her hands stooped and lifted her bodily. As he carried her a few yards, the moonlight gave her a glimpse of Ashford's body lying sprawled in front of their car. The drugstore remained dark.

The thug dropped her into the compartment behind the front seat of another car. His partner struck a match and leaned down to hold it near her face. Emma turned away from its heat.

"It's her. Come on. Cops will be all over this place in a second."

The men climbed into the car. The engine was already throbbing, and it roared and churned as they pulled out on the street.

Emma stirred. Could she raise her head enough to look out and get an idea of where they took her?

"Keep your head down or else." The man who'd lit the match bent over the back of his seat and glared down at her. Moonlight shimmered off a gun barrel.

Emma kept her head down and her lips shut.

CHAPTER TWENTY-FOUR

Friday, July 9, 1915

Frantic pounding on his door awoke John. He sat up and swung his feet over the side of the bed in one movement.

"Yeah. What is it?"

"Your captain. On the phone."

John dashed into the hall past one of the other roomers and down the stairs in his underwear. The dozen men who lived in the house wouldn't find that shocking.

"Patterson, it's Emma. They've kidnapped her."

John clapped a hand to his head. "She had marines guarding her."

"I know, I know. Meet me at this address. It's where they grabbed her." Waller rattled off the number and street. "It's a drugstore. Take the Arlington line."

"What was she doing there?"

"I'll explain when we get there. If we weren't in such chaos, I'd send a car for you."

"The trolley will be faster. I'll be there."

* * * * *

The kidnappers drove on through quiet streets. Curled up in the cramped space, Emma began to feel nauseous. Her throat hurt from her captor's rough handling. She stretched her arms, fastened together at the wrists, over her head. The men didn't seem to notice.

At least her bonds weren't tight enough to numb her hands. She looked up, but the one called Ritter must have tired of watching her and turned forward. She wriggled to get her hip off an uncomfortable lump on the floor. From their sparse conversation, she'd learned only the one name.

"How far to the house?" Ritter asked the driver. She couldn't make out his reply.

They wouldn't kill her, she assured herself. Back in front of the drugstore, they'd mentioned "the boss."

If she died before they delivered her to "the boss," they'd suffer for it. So for the time being, she was probably safe. She closed her eyes and prayed fervently for Ashford, for Nora and Bobby, and for her own life when this journey ended.

After at least a half hour, the car made a turn and rolled slowly over a bumpy lane. Ritter peered at her over the back of the seat. "Wake up, lady. We're here."

Emma sat up as the car stopped in front of a looming, dark house—two and a half stories with windows boarded over. Leaves rustled overhead in the tall trees. She couldn't see any artificial lights or any other houses nearby.

"Maybe we shoulda blindfolded her," the driver said.

"Naw. Let's get her inside."

They pulled her out and herded her into the damp, old house.

One of them—Ritter, she thought—lit a kerosene lamp in the entry.

It was empty of furniture, and it smelled musty. The house must have been beautiful once. A staircase with a curved banister rose to the next story, and four doorways led out of the hall.

"I'll put the car away," the driver said. "Get her upstairs."

"When do we send the telegram, Jud?"

"Shut up, will ya? When the telegraph office opens in the morning. Right now we just need to keep her comfortable until the boss can see her. You know that."

Ritter nodded. "All right, lady. Up you go." He nodded toward the staircase.

Emma considered her options. If she screamed, no one but these two would hear her, and they were armed. With her hands still bound, she found it awkward to mount the steps. Slowly they made their way upward.

When she reached the landing, he prodded her back. "Keep going. That door right over there."

She walked to an open doorway and stood in the threshold. The room beyond was pitch black.

"Go in."

She took a faltering step inside, then another, and stopped. Behind her, a safety match scratched, and the smell of sulfur irritated her nose. She saw an iron bedstead with a sagging mattress on it before she swung around.

Ritter was lighting another lantern. Was now her chance to escape? She could shove him and run past him to the stairs—

Below, she heard the front door bang shut and heavy footsteps approaching.

The light flared up and steadied as Ritter adjusted the lamp. "All right, you can lie down. You might as well sleep. It can't be more than one in the morning."

"I—I don't think I could."

"Well, get over there anyway. I have to tie you to the bed."

She shuddered. "Is that necessary?"

"It's necessary, all right." Jud stood in the doorway with a pistol in his hand, scowling at her. Compared to the swarthy, muscular man, Ritter looked almost friendly.

"What do you want from me?" She tried to keep her teeth from chattering.

"It ain't us, dolly. It's the boss. He'll tell you when he gets here. Now, get over there, or we'll leave you right here on the floor. Which is it?"

Emma swallowed down her revulsion. A musty and perhaps vermin-filled mattress or the hard planks of the floor? "Here," she said.

"All right, lady, sit down then." Ritter pulled a couple of yards of light rope from his coat pocket. "Feet together."

When her ankles were snuggly tied and the rope pulled through the one that held her wrists and knotted a couple more times, Ritter stood back. "All right. Don't try anything. One of us will be right outside the door."

Jud squinted critically at the knots. "You shoulda tied her hands behind her." He shoved his gun into his belt and stepped toward her.

"No, please," Emma said. "I won't escape."

"Huh." Jud smiled. "How do we know you're not lying?"

Yes, why had she said that? Emma closed her eyes for a second and sent up another piece of a prayer. "I give my word."

Jud stood looking down at her a moment longer. "Well, if you think I'm going to untie you because you're so honorable, forget it."

"I don't."

"Good." He nodded toward the side of the room. "That window's nailed shut and boarded over, so if you get some not-so-noble ideas, just can 'em."

"I understand."

He nodded curtly and turned away. "Come on."

Ritter headed out the door. Jud stopped and picked up the lamp.

"Can't you leave that?" Emma asked.

"Oh, sure. You might not try to escape, but would you knock this over and burn the house down on us?" Jud laughed and went out.

The door closed, and Emma sat in utter darkness. For a long time, she didn't move.

Lord, was I stupid to make that promise? Please... She shook her head. *I don't know what to ask for.* She remembered her father's time in the Spanish-American War. He'd served well. She hoped she wouldn't disgrace him. If she met Kobold face to face, would she have the courage to stand up to him? *Whatever You have in mind for me, Lord, let me bring glory to You.*

She rocked until she plopped over onto her side with a thud and lay unmoving, waiting for something to happen.

* * * * *

The marine guard sat on the curb in front of the drugstore, with his head in his hands. A marine sergeant and one of Waller's men watched him while John joined Waller inside the store.

Waller's face was grim. "The guard out there, Hardy, says Emma came out of the house around eleven-thirty and said she needed to fetch a doctor for the baby. The second guard, Ashford, said he'd take her to the drugstore to make the call, and Hardy stayed there."

"They were both supposed to guard her." John clenched his teeth.

"Yes. Hardy says their logic was that someone might try to break into the house while they were gone, so one of them should stay. When Emma and Ashford didn't come back in an hour, he started to worry."

"I should think so."

Waller grimaced. "They had no way to communicate, with each other or with us. Finally Hardy knocked on the door. Mrs. Southard was worried too. They didn't have a car, but Hardy decided he'd better go to the drugstore where they'd planned to make the call from and see if they'd gotten the medicine."

John nodded. "They might have had car trouble on the way."

"He said he ran most of the way. It's less than a mile. The car was sitting in front of the drugstore—and Ashford lay near it, unconscious. The druggist was angry when Hardy woke him up, but as soon as he saw the marine lying there on the ground, he let Hardy go in and call my aide. So here we are."

"What does the druggist say?" John looked toward the counter at the back of the shop. The druggist appeared to be wearily recounting his tale to a policeman.

"He says the doctor telephoned and woke him up. By the time he'd gotten dressed, Emma was there. The marine—that is, Ashford—came in with her. He got the remedy and gave it to Emma. She paid for it, and they left. He went back to bed. Says he didn't hear another sound except the usual nighttime traffic noises until Hardy came hammering on his door about one thirty. Insists he didn't see anything suspicious."

John exhaled heavily. "What do we do?"

"The police will question the neighbors, but this is a commercial area, not residential. Still, some people live here, like the druggist. He has an apartment upstairs. There are a few others nearby. Some insomniac may have heard something." Waller shoved his hands in his pockets. "We should have put more men guarding her, but I was getting enough grousing from higher up. Congress insists we watch our budget."

John thought back to the attack last week, when Clark had been gunned down in Fairfax. "These fellows have shown they'll do anything to get Emma. Kobold has to be behind it."

"Of course." Waller glanced at his watch. "Maybe we should head over to Fort Myer. We can use Commander Howe's station as HQ on this case. His cryptographers solved a message out of the German embassy Monday that mentioned getting 'the machine.' He sent me a copy, with his opinion that they were referring to the Shuster machine. We need to find out if anything new has come in tonight."

John eyed him incredulously. "You think they'd put it in a telegram we'd have access to?"

"Stranger things have happened. And it's possible they'd think that, since they have Emma now, we wouldn't be able to crack it." Waller nodded and slapped him on the shoulder. "Let's go. I'll give the police the telephone number and I'll call Howe in."

* * * * *

"Don't see why we can't make coffee," Ritter muttered. "If we'd brought some, we could have made it in the fireplace yonder."

Emma sat on a stool at the rickety table, gnawing a hard wheat roll while Ritter paced and Jud labored over the message he was writing.

She guessed he was preparing the telegram he would send to the boss when the telegraph station opened at seven.

At least they'd let her out of the dark room this morning. After escorting her to the necessary in the shed behind the house, they'd let her sit down for "breakfast." That, it seemed, consisted of some stale rolls and apples. There was no stove in what she guessed was the old farmhouse's kitchen, so the men hadn't brought food that needed cooking.

"Shut up," Jud said absently. He seemed to be counting. Now and then he made a slash mark on the paper with his pencil.

Emma watched him from beneath her lashes. She had an inkling he was putting his message to "the boss" in cipher and counting off the letters in groups of five for the telegraph operator to send.

At last he shoved back his stool and stood folding the paper. "All right, you stay here while I go send the telegram."

"Can't I send it?"

"No."

"What if they read our message?"

"Who?"

"The government people. You know, the Signal Corps."

"Idiot. We've got her." Jud jerked his head toward Emma. "Without her, they can't use the machine."

"Oh, right."

Emma almost laughed. So that was it. Martin's hints of her magic were close to what the enemy thought. She was the mastermind behind all the solved ciphers.

"Come on," Jud said. "We'd better tie her up again before I leave. Can't have you losing her while I'm gone."

"She said she wouldn't escape," Ritter said.

"That was last night. This is now. Come on. I'm not leaving until I see her tied to the bedstead." He glared at Emma.

She stood, clutching her half-eaten roll. "I'm not finished."

Jud slapped her hand, and the roll skittered across the floor. "Move!"

She flinched and turned toward the entry. Both men followed her up the staircase. As they entered the bedchamber, she eyed the bed once more. In the dim light, it looked more disreputable than ever. She sat down resolutely on the floor.

"Over there." Jud kicked her thigh.

Emma sucked in a breath and scooted toward the bed. She sat with her back against the iron footboard.

Ritter knelt and tied her to it.

"Tie her hands, too," Jud said.

Ritter sighed and wrapped strands of rope around her wrists.

At last they left her again in seclusion. A few rays of light made it through cracks between the boards on the windows, but Emma could barely see. She closed her eyes and resumed her prayers.

* * * * *

John delivered Captain Waller's written order to the cook at Fort Myer and fidgeted while the cook's subordinates filled a box with muffins, biscuits, and fruit. John carried it to the building used by the Navy Signal Corps, arriving just as Commander Howe did.

"Morning, Patterson. How long ago did they snatch her?" Howe asked as they walked down the hall to his desk in the alcove.

"Sometime between midnight and one thirty." John looked ahead and saw Captain Waller pacing near the desk, where the night supervisor sat looking ill at ease.

"Howe." Waller strode toward them.

"Good morning, sir. I'm devastated at this news."

Waller nodded bleakly. "We did everything in our power to protect her."

"What do you want me to do?" Howe asked.

"Stand by with your best cryptographers, ready to take on anything new, and let us camp here as an information post. My office in Washington is too far away. I want to be closer to where they took her."

"Please make yourself at home, Captain."

John set the box of fruit and breads on the desk. "I'll see about a large urn of coffee."

"I'll do it," said the night officer.

Howe opened a file drawer and pulled out several folders. "These are the messages this department received over the past few days. There's been nothing since Monday that I would hazard touched remotely on the topic of the cipher machine or Miss Shuster."

Waller took the folders and opened the top one. "They know we intercept a lot of their communications. Kobold gave the orders for this one verbally, I'm guessing."

Howe called the day shift cryptographers and asked them to come in early. They trickled in yawning as they went to their workrooms.

"I must tell them about Miss Shuster." Howe gritted his teeth and left them.

A yeoman approached with a large coffeepot.

"Coffee's here, sir," John told Captain Waller and nodded at the yeoman.

"Good. Give me a quart or two." Waller sank into Howe's chair.

An hour later, John walked slowly up and down the hall. Howe had commandeered more chairs for them, but he couldn't sit still. Waller had called the police station twice and the marine captain once, but there was no news. The cryptographers hunched over their ciphers and worked in grim silence. John was ready to go back to the drugstore and look for clues himself.

A policeman walked in and went straight to Waller. "Captain, we've found one possible witness."

Waller jumped up. "Tell me."

"A woman living on the cross street heard an engine about midnight. She looked out her window—second floor—and saw an automobile careen around the corner. It drove off, and then all was quiet again. That's it, I'm afraid."

"What direction?"

"West."

Waller stood staring off into space. John watched him. A direction was better than nothing, of course, but it wasn't much.

Waller met his gaze. "Get us a map of Arlington and a smaller scale one."

John was about to go on the quest when a uniformed man ran in the door and dashed to Commander Howe. "Sir, this just came in—going to the German Embassy. You said to bring any traffic in or out to you pronto—"

"Thanks, Aaron." Howe slapped him on the back, turned, and shouted, "Typist!"

Doris Keating came from another room. "Yes, sir?"

"Quick! Eight copies, but do one as fast as you can and give it to me. Then make the others. Accuracy, as always."

"Yes, sir."

Five minutes later, another young woman bustled down the hall and put a sheet of paper in Howe's hands. He strode into the nearest workroom. "Glazer! Take this and see what you can make of it. We've more copies coming for the rest of you."

Martin hurried to him and took the paper, and Howe came back into the hall.

"They'll still get that message at the embassy, right?" John asked.

Howe nodded. "We listen, we write it down, but we can't stop it."

They waited in tense silence. Howe strode periodically to the doorway. Soon Doris brought him more copies of the message, which he handed to Martin's colleagues.

"It could be nothing," Waller said, running his hand through his hair.

Silence ruled the building for twenty minutes. John fixed himself a cup of coffee and prayed for Emma.

Howe walked to the workroom door for the hundredth time and leaned against the jamb.

"Eureka!"

Howe straightened. "What is it, Glazer?"

"It's in the Crimson Cipher, sir, double alphabet—"

"I don't care," Howe snapped. "What does it *say*, man?"

"'We've got her. Come to Nutall Farm.'"

* * * * *

Jud shoved Emma into the kitchen and she stumbled against a chair.

"Miss Shuster. At last we meet."

Emma gritted her teeth and looked the man in the eyes. Fiftyish, glasses, thinning hair, and spreading belly. Not at all the adversary she'd imagined. Why was she afraid of him? If this was the revered Kobold, he looked bland and dull—like a successful businessman who liked rich food—until she saw the hard glint in his eyes.

He was looking from her to something in his hand and back again, to her face. "Yes. You've succeeded this time."

He'd spoken to the men standing just behind her—Ritter and Jud. He laid the object on the table. A photograph.

Her stomach tightened. The picture of her with her father at Old Orchard Beach. Had Herman stolen it and put it into the enemy's hands?

"Where's the code machine?"

She hiked her chin and returned his gaze in what she hoped was a cool manner. "I don't know. They lock it up."

His expression flowed into a hateful glare. He nodded curtly. One of the other two men seized her arm and yanked it painfully behind her back.

She gasped and clenched her teeth.

Kobold walked over and stood only inches from her. "Your father died because of that machine. So did the boy genius who built it. Why do you think you can keep it from me?" He slapped her hard.

Emma pulled away, but the man behind her only twisted her arm tighter. She sucked in a breath, knowing how foolish she'd been. These two were not harmless bumblers. Was it Ritter or Jud who tortured her now? They were killers. All three of them had killed before and would kill her if they thought it expedient.

"Where is it?" Kobold asked again.

"I don't have it."

His eyes narrowed. "I realize that. But you use it every day."

"No, I—" His hand drew back, and she caught her breath, bracing for another blow. Kobold thought she personally made use of her father's invention to solve his ciphers, just as the men had hinted. "What will you do with it?" she asked.

"None of your business. Just tell me where it is."

She swallowed hard. If they knew she didn't use it at all, that she in fact had no access to the machine and that it had never been used to decipher their messages, would they still want it? And would they still have a reason to keep her alive? "I don't keep it at my lodgings."

"We know that. So where is it?"

"I'll bet it's at that house in Fairfax, Poppy," Jud said. "The one where they all worked up until last week."

Emma tried to keep her face impassive, but she felt a small victory. She knew for certain now that this man was the "Poppy" who paid the saboteurs.

Kobold glared at Jud. "If you two hadn't bungled the job last week, they'd still be working there, and we could get at it."

"Maybe it's still in there," Ritter said.

"Yeah, they still have marines guarding the place." Jud sounded happy at the thought. "We could take out the guards tonight and search the place before daylight."

Kobold swore. "You think they'd leave it there, where she couldn't use it? She has to be where the machine is. That's how they knew about the cannery bomb and the factory in Chicago. This young woman is the one who is destroying our plans." He lifted his arm again.

Emma squeezed her eyes shut and turned her face away.

CHAPTER TWENTY-FIVE

Friday, July 9, 1915

"Get a telephone directory," Howe suggested.

"Call the library," Martin said.

Waller frowned. "Where was this telegram sent from?"

John gulped and stepped forward. "Sir, I know where Nutall Farm is."

Everyone stared at him.

"It's out near Vienna. An old, abandoned farm."

Howe looked up from the paper in his hand. "Yes, it was sent from Vienna."

Waller looked at Howe. "Have the sergeant call the marine detail. Patterson, can you take us there?"

"Yes, sir."

"Let's move!"

On the way, John sat in the back, behind Waller, and kept up a steady flow of prayer. After they'd gone several miles, he leaned forward and told the driver, "Turn right up ahead."

Waller blinked at him. "Why do you know where this is, Patterson?"

"My family has a farm. I like to look at farmland, sir. I was driving around over Vienna way once, and I saw an old, weathered sign. Nutall Farm." John shrugged. "We had some walnut trees back in Pennsylvania. I drove up to the house, but it was empty."

"How much farther?"

"Quite a ways. Maybe ten miles."

"I should have set a detail in motion as soon as we got that message."

"You couldn't have known, sir. It might have been anything."

They drove on for another five minutes, and John said, "Sir, what if she tells them she doesn't have the machine and that it would be useless to them anyway?"

Waller huffed out a deep breath. "I doubt they'd believe her. And even if they did, how is the truth better? Emma does crack their ciphers, day after day. Whether she uses the machine to do it or just her own skill, Kobold wants it stopped. The way to do that is to be rid of Emma."

John clenched his jaws and resumed his silent prayer. Gray clouds darkened the sky. When they drew near the lane to Nutall Farm, he tapped Waller on the shoulder. "It's just ahead, sir. Around that curve."

Waller had his driver pull over, and the truck of marines behind them stopped as well. Waller huddled with the marine sergeant for a minute. The sergeant turned and instructed his men to surround the farmhouse, staying behind cover if possible.

"I'm going in with them," John said.

"You can't," Waller said. "You're not prepared."

"I've had much the same training they've had, and I'm armed."

"You'll get in the way. Besides, they plan to use that new tear gas. You don't have the equipment."

"You can't keep me out, sir. Not with Emma's life at stake."

Waller held his gaze for a moment then looked away. "I'm going to be in so much trouble." He clapped John's shoulder then asked the sergeant, "Do you have an extra gas mask?"

"Yes, sir."

"Take Patterson with you. Give him orders the same as you do your own men."

With the sergeant, John flitted up the lane, staying to the side and using the overgrown brush and occasional trees for concealment. The windows appeared to be boarded up, but he wouldn't count on there not being a watchman somewhere. Two cars—a Model T and a Buick roadster—stood on the gravel drive before the front entrance.

"If there's only one entrance open, that will make our job easier," the sergeant said as they peered from behind a dogwood trunk.

When they reached the left front corner of the building, a private joined them from the rear of the house.

"Sir, there appears to be a back door that's been opened up, and the boards have been torn off a window back there. Other than that, all the windows are covered. You want us to try to get a look inside?"

"No, they'd see you."

"What then?"

The sergeant frowned. "Use the gas. I'll have four men at the front door. You keep the rest in the back with you."

John started to speak up but stopped. He hated to think of their throwing the canisters in there when Emma was inside, but the gas wouldn't do permanent damage.

"Sergeant, I'd like to go around back with them."

He nodded. "As you wish, Lieutenant."

John hurried around the house, trying not to make any noise.

Weed seeds clung to his uniform. Just as he reached the trodden grass behind the back door, one of the marines raised his gun and broke a window with the butt, tossing in a canister. John ducked low, as did the marines, and hurriedly buckled on the awkward gas mask.

Shouts and a few gunshots erupted from inside the house. A moment later they heard coughing and running footsteps. The back door burst open and two men ran out. One tripped and rolled into the grass, howling. The other halted when he saw the marines and flung up his hands.

John started to rise, but the sergeant reached out a hand to stop him. A plump, middle-aged man in a suit ran out the door, holding a handkerchief to his face. One of the marines tackled him.

"All right," the sergeant said when the two had been subdued. "Now, Lieutenant."

With two marines, John followed the sergeant inside with his pistol drawn. He peered about the dim room. It appeared to be empty. The marines thundered through a doorway, and he followed. The men spread out. Joined by two more, who came in the front entrance, they searched the gas-filled rooms.

One of the men came from a side room and called to the sergeant, "Nothing here, sir."

John turned to the stairway in the front entry and quickly climbed to the landing. He tried the first door he came to. It swung open, revealing a darkened room. He squinted, trying to see into the shadowy corners.

Nothing.

He dashed back into the hall. Two marines bounded up the stairs. John turned to the next closed door. It was locked. He shoved against it with his shoulder.

"Come here," he yelled to the marines.

They came to his side. One of them tried the door then put his ear to the panel.

"I hear something." John and the other man stood still. "Coughing," the marine said. He stood back, raised his booted foot, and kicked. The door crashed open.

John ran past the soldier into the room. "Emma?"

"John?" Her feeble cry was followed by a choking sound.

He felt his way across the dark room.

"I'm here," she gasped, and he realized she was on the floor.

Someone lit a match.

She sat with her back to an iron bed frame, tied to its footboard. John knelt beside her and yanked off his gas mask. "Put this on, darling."

While he fastened it for her, another man came carrying an electric torch. One of the marines cut through her bonds.

John gathered her in his arms. "Hold on, dearest." His throat burned, and his eyes watered, but he kept his footing as he carried her down the stairs and out the open front door.

Captain Waller reached out to help him, and he climbed down the steps and laid Emma gently on the grass. John turned aside to cough. One of the marines brought him a canteen, and he took a long, soothing drink. He went back to kneel beside Emma.

The captain had removed her gas mask. Her eyes were puffy and bloodshot, and her cheeks streaked with tears. Blood had dried on her lower lip and chin, and her mouth and one cheek looked swollen and bruised.

John held the canteen for her. She took a big swallow and whispered, "Thank you."

Waller touched her cheek gently. "I can see that they hit you. Where else are you hurt, dear?"

Emma cradled her arm and winced. "My arm. I think it's broken." She licked her lips. "And they kicked me."

"She needs a doctor," John said, dashing away his own tears.

Waller laid a comforting hand on his shoulder. "There's a medic in the marine squadron. Let's have him look at her."

The medic came over, and John stood. The marine sergeant was supervising as his men took the three prisoners to their truck.

John hurried over. "Sergeant!"

"Yes, Lieutenant?"

"Just a moment." He stared at the prisoner in the suit. John had seen his photo before. He'd studied it, along with those of several other diplomats. Otto van Wersten, undersecretary to the German ambassador—the man they knew as Kobold.

The desire to hit the man almost overwhelmed him. John stepped back. Van Wersten was a defenseless old man in handcuffs, with tears flooding from his eyes. Hitting him would bring no satisfaction.

John turned on his heel and ran back to where the medic knelt beside Emma. "Is she all right?"

"I'm not sure. She may have internal injuries. Her pulse and respiration are steady. We'll take her right to the hospital."

A lock of Emma's hair fell in a dark swoop over her pale face. John reached to brush it back. She grimaced. Blood still oozed from the cut on her lip.

John sat down in the grass and stroked her hand as rain began to patter down around them. "Sweetheart, how could they do this to you?"

* * * * *

John slumped back and leaned his head against the wall in the hospital waiting room, praying. Always praying.

Captain Waller had called Commander Howe and apprised him of the situation. Then he'd taken the marine sergeant and the other men who'd come with them to the hospital to a canteen in the basement for coffee. Emma was being treated, and no one had come out to update him in more than an hour.

Hurried footsteps clattered in the hallway and stopped abruptly at the waiting room door.

John opened one eye.

"Patterson!"

John sat up. Martin Glazer looked about the room as though he were lost then focused on him once more. John shoved himself off the chair and walked across the room.

"Glazer."

"Where is she? Is she all right?"

"They've got her in surgery." Martin swayed, and John grabbed his elbow. "Sit down." He guided Martin to a sofa and pushed him gently onto the cushions.

Martin ran his hand through his gray-streaked hair. "How bad is she?"

John sat down in his chair again and studied Martin. "They think she'll recover well."

"She was shot?"

"No. No, but she was roughed up a bit. Dislocated shoulder, broken radius, a few cuts, and some deep bruises."

Martin sighed and closed his eyes. "The poor girl."

John watched him with new awareness. "She'll likely be here a couple of days, until they're sure she's mending well. Are you all right, sir?"

"Yes. Yes, I'm fine now."

"Captain Waller's here," John said. "He's bringing a pot of coffee up."

"Good. Howe is on his way. I should have waited for him to bring his car around, but as soon as I knew where she was, I ran for the trolley. I beat the old boy here, didn't I?"

"Yes, sir."

For a long minute, they sat in silence but for the rain thrumming on the windowpanes. At last Martin said, "You're a lucky man, Patterson."

"Thank you. I agree."

Martin rose and walked to the window, where he stood looking out into the downpour. "You should marry her. Soon. Don't wait until we declare war and you're heading off for the front."

John got up and walked over to stand beside him. He wondered what Martin saw out there in the rain. "I think that's sound advice, sir."

＊ ＊ ＊ ＊ ＊

An hour later, the cryptographers had gathered, and the marines lingered. They'd gone through three pots of coffee. When the surgeon appeared in the doorway to the waiting room, they all jumped up and stood waiting to hear the doctor's news. John's pulse beat wildly.

"Who's here for Miss Shuster?"

Captain Waller stepped forward. "We all are. What can you tell us?"

"She's doing well. Resting. We've set her arm and put her shoulder back in place. It's my opinion that her internal injuries are slight, but we'd like to observe her for a day or two. Are any of you relatives?" The surgeon looked toward Muriel and Doris.

"No, but I'm standing in for her family," Waller said.

"Then you may see her for ten minutes."

Waller hesitated then turned to John. "You should go in, Patterson."

John felt as though he should defer to Waller, but he didn't want to. "Thank you, sir." He walked toward the doorway, feeling all their eyes upon him. He followed the surgeon down the hall, through a set of doors, down another hall, and through more doors. At last they came into a large, open ward.

"Over here." The surgeon led John to a curtained area and pushed the drape aside.

Within, Emma lay on a bed, her face as white as the linens that framed it, except for a darkening bruise on her cheek. Her left arm was bound in bandages and a sling. Her eyes were closed, her breathing quick and shallow. Was she really all right? John looked around, but the surgeon had left him. He entered the small enclosure and sat on the stool beside the bed.

She looked so delicate, as though she'd melt away at any moment. He watched the sheet rise and fall with each breath.

Thank You, Lord.

Her left hand lay limp on the folded edge of the sheet. He reached out hesitantly and touched it. Emma's lashes fluttered, and she opened her eyes.

"John."

He barely heard her whisper, but it warmed his core more than quarts of hot coffee could do. He squeezed her hand gently and sobbed.

"Darling, you mustn't. I'm fine."

He nodded and sniffed.

"Bobby?" she asked.

"Who?"

"Nora Southard's baby. I was getting medicine for him."

"His mother's upstairs with him. He's sick, but he'll get better." He sat there for the remaining nine minutes, holding her hand and gazing at her.

"Your time is up, sir," a nurse said softly.

John rose and laid Emma's hand down, giving it a final pat. "I'll come back when they let me."

She smiled.

"Rest." He went out of the curtained area, and the nurse pointed the way to the corridor. When he stepped outside the ward, he found Martin leaning against the wall, his face drawn and gray.

"I'm sorry," John said. "I should have let you go in."

Martin shook his head. "No. I just— Is she really all right?"

"I think so, or will be."

He nodded and clapped John on the shoulder. "I believe I'll head home now."

* * * * *

Monday, July 12, 1915

Three days later, Emma was back in her old room at Mrs. Draper's. Her lip was still tender, and her arm throbbed, but she was home.

Freddie, Louise, and Charlotte stood around the bed, and Doris sat on the end near the footboard.

"You can't really mean to go back to work tomorrow," Freddie said.

Emma smiled. "Why not? I'll have to wear the sling is all."

"Isn't your arm sore?" Doris looked as though she'd cry at any moment.

"Yes, but it's my left arm."

"You've got a stronger constitution than I have," Charlotte said, shaking her head.

"Yes, you may as well get an extra day or two off out of this." Freddie smiled impishly. "That captain was so upset, he'd give you a month off if you wanted it."

Emma looked up at them all and noticed Louise wiping a tear from her cheek. "Dear Louise, are you all right?"

"Yes, I'll be fine. I'm thinking of going north for Mr. Hibbert's funeral, though."

Tears sprang into Emma's eyes. Louise had known Clark only a couple of days, yet she cared enough to make a long journey in his honor.

"Not feeling guilty, are you?" Freddie asked.

"Freddie!" Doris eyed her sternly.

"I think you should do whatever your heart tells you is right," Emma said. "It's true I didn't care for Clark, but I never wished him to come to harm."

Heavy steps in the hall preceded Mrs. Draper's appearance in the doorway. "Miss Shuster," she puffed.

"Yes?"

"Lieutenant Patterson phoned to ask if you'll feel up to seeing him this evening."

"I certainly will."

Doris stood and smoothed the quilt. "Yes, because we're all going to leave now, so you can nap."

"I'll tell him." Mrs. Draper turned toward the stairs.

Freddie paused in the doorway. "I'll come back to help you dress before supper."

"Me too," Doris said. "We'll cover that nasty purple bruise with powder." She blew Emma a kiss, and the boarders left the room.

* * * * *

At seven o'clock on the nose, John entered the parlor.

Emma sat on the sofa with her left arm cushioned on a needlepoint pillow. She started to rise, but he held out one hand.

"Don't get up." He sat down beside her and settled his arm gently about her shoulders. "Are you certain you ought to be down here? You look marvelous, but you must be in pain."

"It's not so bad. Now, tell me everything."

"Everything?"

"Yes. I was afraid they'd send you off to Maine. Wasn't last night the time they planned to target the shipyard?"

"Yes, it was." John hesitated. "Three arrests made. Really, my dear, I intended to let Captain Waller tell you all that tomorrow. I believe he plans to call on you."

"Please tell me. My cousin—"

John bowed his head. "Yes, Herman was arrested. He carried the dynamite."

She let out a deep sigh. "It's as I feared." She looked up into his face again. "Do they know— John, did he have anything to do with Father's death?"

"I don't think so, but they haven't finished their investigation. Right now our men feel that your uncle Gregory was not involved in the shipyard incident."

"I'm glad to hear that."

"Yes. But one of the men captured at Nutall Farm—the man named Ritter—has been linked to the Maine business. I believe the authorities will try to pressure the others into telling them who killed your father."

"What about Kobold?"

"In prison, and likely to be deported soon."

"Deported? John, he ordered all those bombings. He hired people to kill."

"Yes. But he was here as a diplomat."

"Diplomats can get away with murder? Crimes against our country?"

"It's tricky, but the Justice Department will try to get his immunity waived. I don't know what will happen. They're trying to get permission to search his home, but it hasn't been resolved yet. There have been a lot of insults flung back and forth between our ambassadors, too. Ritter and the other man—Judson Gade—will be tried for their crimes. I expect they'll both serve long sentences."

John leaned down and kissed her temple. "Emma, dearest, I can't tell you how grateful I am that you're here and you're getting better. I love you."

A warm euphoria washed over Emma. "I love you too, John."

He ran a finger, feather-light, over her cheekbone. "Darling, will you marry me?"

"Yes."

She turned into his embrace, and he kissed her tenderly. Emma ignored the pain from her healing lip.

They sat for several minutes holding each other close.

"I'd best be on the lookout for a place for us to live," John said. "No ladies allowed at my current lodgings."

She smiled. "I wonder if I can get that parlor set away from Aunt Thea."

"We could just get a new one."

"Shocking expense."

"It might cost as much to ship it down here." He started to kiss her again then sprang back. "Does your lip hurt?"

"Not much."

He kissed her gently then held her close against his shoulder. After a moment, he straightened and patted his pockets. "I nearly forgot." He took out a small box and offered it to her.

"A present?"

"If you like it."

She opened the box and looked down at a gold ring set with a small diamond. "Oh, John. It's beautiful."

He smiled and took her hand. "My mother asked if I could bring you home soon."

"They know about me?"

"Of course. Who else could I babble to while you were in the hospital?"

"I would like to see the farm."

"Good. When can you go?"

"I expect the question is, when can *you* go?"

"I have a week of leave coming."

"Won't they want you for Thanksgiving or Christmas?"

"They will, but...Emma, we don't know how much time we have."

The war, she thought, and gave a quick nod. "You're right. Fix it with Captain Waller, and we'll go as soon as possible. There'll never be a good time, so we should do it now."

He took the ring from the box and slid it onto her finger, then pulled her into his arms once more.

ABOUT THE AUTHOR

 Award-winning author Susan Page Davis has published thirty novels in the historical romance, suspense, mystery, and romance genres. A Maine native, she now lives in Kentucky with her husband, Jim, who is an editor. They have six children and six grandchildren.

www.susanpagedavis.com

CRACK THE CIPHER
AND WIN A FREE BOOK.

Readers are invited to solve the cipher message below and submit their plaintext answers and mailing addresses to author Susan Page Davis at: susan@susanpagedavis.com or Susan Page Davis, PO Box 40, Dexter, KY 42036.

Twenty-five winners will be randomly drawn from the correct entries received by November 1, 2010. No purchase necessary to win. Each winner will receive another Summerside Press novel. This drawing is open to residents of the U.S.A. and Canada only. Void where prohibited by law. Odds of winning depend on the number of entries received. Happy solving!

"PCMR ZKK PCM TDRS'A UDAM XMR JZXM DR, EIP

PCMB JVIKF RVP WMZF PCM DRAJWDGPDVR VW

XZTM TRVUR DPA DRPMWGWMPZPDVR PV PCM

TDRS." ZA DR PCM FZBA VO FZRDMK, WMZFDRS

AMJWMP XMAAZSMA DA ZR DRPWDSIDRS

GWVEKMX. JVRSWZPIKZPDVRA VR BVIW AIJJMAA

DR FMJDGCMWDRS PCDA. D CVGM BVI CZLM

MRNVBMF WMZFDRS PCM JWDXAVR JDGCMW.

summerside
PRESS™

Soul-stirring romance...
set against a historical backdrop readers will love!

Summerside Press™ is pleased to announce the launch of our
fresh line of historical romance fiction—set amid the action-packed
eras of the twentieth century. Watch for a total of six new
Summerside Press™ historical romance titles to release in 2010.

Now Available in Stores

Sons of Thunder
BY SUSAN MAY WARREN

ISBN 978-1-935416-67-8

Stars in the Night
BY CARA PUTMAN

ISBN 978-1-60936-011-5

Songbird Under a German Moon
BY TRICIA GOYER

ISBN 978-1-935416-68-5

Coming Soon

Exciting New Historical Romance Stories by These Great Authors—
Patricia Rushford...Lisa Harris...Melanie Dobson...and MORE!

BODIE & BROCK
THOENE

*Explore the romance, passion, and danger
experienced by those who lived through
Adolf Hitler's rise to power and the Second World War.*

NOW AVAILABLE

THE GATHERING STORM

A desperate escape.
A love ignited.
An ancient secret revealed.

As Nazi forces tighten the noose, Loralei Kepler's harrowing flight from Germany leads her toward a mysterious figure who closely guards an age-old secret.

COMING SOON

AGAINST
THE WIND

A perilous journey.
A race against time.
A dawning hope.

Famous violinist Elisa Lindheim Murphy faces the greatest trial of her life on seas made treacherous by Nazi U-boats as she and Jewish refugee children seek asylum.

THEIR
FINEST HOUR

A fiery struggle.
A fervent pledge.
A heroic last stand.

While the clashes in the skies over Britain increase in ferocity, American flying ace David Meyer also battles for the heart of the feisty Annie Galway.